LIARS
AND SAINTS

LIARS
AND SAINTS

MAILE MELOY

JOHN MURRAY

First published in the United States of America in 2003 by Scribner

First published in Great Britain in 2004 by John Murray (Publishers)
A division of Hodder Headline

1 3 5 7 9 10 8 6 4 2

A CIP catalogue record for this title is available from the British Library

ISBN 0-7195-6644 4

Printed and bound in Great Britain by Clays Ltd, St Ives plc

John Murray (Publishers)
338 Euston Road
London
NW1 3BH

LIARS
AND SAINTS

PART I

The world was all before them, where to choose
Their place of rest, and Providence their guide:
They hand in hand with wandering steps and slow
Through Eden took their solitary way.
                    —JOHN MILTON, *Paradise Lost,* BOOK 12

Don't sit under the apple tree with anyone else but me.
                    —LEW BROWN, THEODORE TOBIAS,
                              AND SAM STEPT, 1942

1

THEY WERE MARRIED during the war, in Santa Barbara, after Mass one morning in the old Mission church. Teddy was solemn; he took the Mass very seriously. Yvette, in a veiled hat and an ivory dress that wasn't a gown, was distracted by the idea that she was in California, without her father there to give her away, and she was about to change her life and her name. "I, Yvette Grenier, take you, Theodore Santerre . . ." It all sounded formal and strange, as if someone else were saying the words, until she realized with surprise that it was her.

It was a quick wedding so Teddy could ship out, but they went two days later to a dance at the beach club, where she met Teddy's commanding officer at the bar.

"You can't leave this girl so soon," the officer said, looking at Yvette. She was wearing the ivory dress she was married in, because it had taken a long time to make it, and she wasn't going to wear it just once. It suited her, she knew—it set off her slimness and the way her dark hair curled under at her shoulders—and she blushed at how the officer looked at her.

Teddy said, "Sir?"

The officer laughed, and shook Teddy's hand again, and said congratulations on the wedding, and then Teddy was able to smile.

They both thought the CO was only joking, but he wasn't. He assigned Teddy to a squadron training at home, so he could stay a few months with Yvette. The Marine Corps put the new couple up at the Biltmore with the rest of the officers—the guests had all fled inland, afraid of bombing—and they went to cocktails and tea dances, and were together every night. By the time Teddy left to fight the Japanese, Yvette was pregnant with Margot.

She didn't tell her family about the baby right away. They were back in Canada, too expensive to call, and she didn't want to hear what they would say. Her father and brothers had said she was crazy to marry that flyboy—he was an American, even if he had a Canadian name, and he didn't speak French. They would be poor as sin on his military pay, and then Teddy would just get himself killed and leave her stranded in California with nothing—or worse, with a baby. Yvette thought they were being unfair. She couldn't please her father unless she stayed at home forever, and she couldn't do that.

With Teddy out in the Pacific, fighting in the war, she tried to read Hitler's hateful little book, to make sense of it. But the book made her angry, and she didn't see how the Japanese fit in, so she put it away. She was happiest when Teddy came home on leave, and they could go dancing and then stay up all night, in bed in the little rented apartment she'd moved to from the Biltmore. Teddy joked that sex made her talkative, instead of sleepy like normal people, but he would listen anyway, watching her and smiling in the dark. Sometimes he would kiss her in midsentence, as she told him everything she'd stored up while he was away.

And then the war was finally over, and Teddy was home for good. Little Margot was two, and the new baby, Clarissa, was almost one. Teddy took a job selling airplane parts for North American, and built a house in Hermosa Beach with a veteran's loan. When he couldn't stand the baby's crying, he pushed the bassinet out to the service porch and steered Yvette back to bed.

With a place of their own, they could invite people to it, and Yvette learned to cook for a houseful: John Wayne eggs and Bloody Marys for brunch. She made herself new dresses, and they had dancing right in the house. Cocktails started at five and the dancing went on till two or three in the morning, when Yvette would find herself singing "Those Wedding Bells Are Breaking Up That Old Gang of Mine."

Teddy didn't like to let her out of his sight, at the parties, but that was just because they'd spent so much time apart. Yvette was happy. Teddy stayed in the Reserves so he could fly once a month, and he loved those weekends in the planes. And the extra money was useful, with the girls growing out of their clothes as fast as Yvette could sew them.

Then Teddy was called to Korea, and they realized what a mistake the Reserves had been. At first Yvette thought it couldn't be true, that it must be a clerical error. Teddy had a family—Margot was seven and Clarissa was six. Clarissa's face was a little mirror of his, and she watched him in the house, staring him down. When Teddy caught her at it, he laughed, and she laughed, too. Yvette couldn't believe the Marines would ask him to leave again. But it wasn't an error, and she took the girls to see him off on the train.

At the station, two of the young Marines were joking for the crowd, making sobbing faces out the train windows, saying, "No, don't take us, we don't want to go."

Clarissa started to cry. "Why are they taking them?" she demanded. "They don't want to go!"

Yvette said the men were joking and they *did* want to go, but Clarissa didn't understand. She threw herself on the floor of the Plymouth, wailing, and cried all the way home. Yvette was surprised at the passion of Clarissa's grief. She thought her daughter might make herself ill, screaming so hard on the floor of the car. She didn't have time to cry herself, she was so busy tending to Clarissa.

Being at home alone with two children was harder than being first married, when the other wives had all been waiting for their husbands, too. It was busier, but it was also lonelier. Yvette couldn't entertain alone, and she wasn't invited out. A woman alone was a liability, a wild card. She didn't know any women whose husbands were in Korea; they were all younger than she. When her only single friend, Rita, got married, Yvette couldn't go to the wedding, because it was in a Protestant church. Rita was hurt by Yvette's absence, and then she was another busy wife, and Yvette didn't see her anymore.

One day, while Teddy was still in Korea, Yvette took Margot and Clarissa to the beach. While the girls were playing in the water, a man came and sat beside her. She was ready to ask him to leave, but he was polite, and they talked about the girls, and she was hungry for talk. He said he was a photographer, and offered to take their picture for her husband; he said it was the least he could do for a man who was at war. So he came to the house, with a big flash umbrella and a camera on a tripod, and set up his equipment in the living room. Yvette made him a highball, and because the bottle of ginger ale was open, she made herself one, too. On an empty stomach it went right to her head. It was three in the afternoon on a Saturday, and she'd dressed the girls up for the picture, but the photographer wasn't in any hurry. He was clean-cut with clear green eyes and looked like he could have been a soldier himself, in khaki trousers and a pressed shirt. They talked about the situation in Korea, and he told an off-color joke about war brides. He asked for another drink and she made him one, but Clarissa stalked in and said she wasn't wearing nice clothes another minute, so the photographer arranged them on the sofa and started to fiddle with his flash.

Clarissa sat on the ottoman, and Margot stood behind, with her hands on her sister's shoulders. Clarissa hated to be touched by Margot, and her hair was coming out of its curls. Yvette pulled the hem of Clarissa's skirt to cover her knees. Margot smiled serenely at the camera, and nothing about her was out of place. Yvette felt like her own smile might look tipsy, so she pressed her hand against her lips to try to straighten her mouth without smearing her lipstick. Then they all smiled and got a big flash in the eyes.

The photographer took a few more pictures and said he thought he had it, but made no move to leave. He took up his drink, and Yvette let the girls go outside. She asked if he wouldn't take payment, though there was so little money, but he refused.

"A man with such a beautiful wife will want a remembrance of her," he said.

Yvette said nothing.

"Such pretty little girls, too," he said.

Yvette agreed that the children were sweet. Then the photographer grew serious.

"You are," he said, "the most beautiful woman I've ever seen."

She laughed, and tried to shake the way the whiskey was keeping a smile on her face so she could frown and send him on his way.

"I work with models," he said, still serious. "I know beautiful women. But your beauty is a radiance, it comes from within."

She wanted to tell him the radiance was from the whiskey, but she was afraid she might seem flirtatious. She thought of her father, who hadn't allowed her mother to go shopping without taking Yvette with her, in case she might be meeting men somewhere. But there had been no wars for her father, just the Depression, and the family under a tighter rein in a smaller house. And here was Teddy gone again, and this strange man who wouldn't leave.

Yvette stood from her chair to show the photographer he should leave, and then he had an arm around her waist and his lips pressed against hers. He kissed her so hard that when she twisted free, his teeth cut her lip. She sent him away then, with his camera and his flash, and did what she'd never done as a hostess: closed the door on him before he was halfway down the walk. Then she opened it again to check for the girls, and saw the photographer, flushed and angry, get into his car and drive away.

She didn't know how to tell Teddy what had happened. She tried to put it in writing but it came out wrong, and she tore the letters to pieces and started again.

The photographer came back with his prints when Yvette was alone in the house, and she opened the door just a few inches. He acted like nothing had happened, but she was cool with him. She made him turn the envelope sideways to get it through the door. It seemed better to keep the pictures than to have them out in the world. All week she had blushed when she thought of them.

"I'll get you a check," she said, when he let go of his end of the envelope.

"I don't—" he said.

She closed and locked the door, found her purse and fumbled it open, feeling her heart in her chest. Teddy's name was printed on the checks with hers. She had no idea how much to give the man. Ten dollars? She wrote the check for fifteen.

"I don't want a check," he said, when she opened the door again. He was standing in the same posture as before, a hand on the door frame to support himself. She thought he was trying to be casual, but his voice was angry, and he wouldn't look at the check she offered. "I wanted to do something nice for you, that's all," he said. "I just wanted to do something for you."

"Thank you," she said.

"I'm not a bad man," he said. "I thought we could have made each other's lives a little better, that's all. That doesn't happen very often, you know."

"I'm married," she said, and she started to close the door, but he put a hand flat against it from the outside.

"I want you to tell me something," he said. "Is it really because you're married, or is it me?"

She closed the door against the pressure of his hand, and locked it, and hung the chain. Her heart slowed as she leaned against the door. The fold of the envelope, when she opened it, was damp with the imprint of her fingers. They were good, big prints on heavy paper. The girls looked like themselves: Clarissa a mess and Margot a perfect little nun. Yvette had a wild smile on her face, her eyes too wide, but you might not notice if you didn't know she'd had a drink in the afternoon.

She didn't send the photographs to Teddy. She talked to him on the telephone when he was able to call, but she didn't tell him anything because the girls were in the room. There was no one else to tell. She had never made up with her family over their disapproval of Teddy. Her older sister, Adele, was unhappily married, and in Canada, too, and no help.

Weeks went by, and every night she lay thinking about the photographer's kiss and the blood on her lip in the mirror, and it occurred to her to go to confession. She hadn't been to Mass since Teddy left; it was too much trouble to get Clarissa into

Sunday clothes. Now she thought if she could just say what had happened, she might feel better, so she went alone to a church in the city, where neither Teddy nor she would know the priest.

The smell was overwhelming, of candles and flowers and polished wood. It was the smell of every Sunday of her childhood, the old ladies speaking French to her, the priest speaking Latin, the sins she could think of: *I talked back to my mother. I fought with my sister. I didn't clean my side of the room when I came home from school.*

She said a little prayer outside the confessional, and then she went in, all the trumped-up sins of her childhood following her, and the little window slid open.

"Bless me, Father, for I have sinned," she said. "It has been six months since my last confession." Six months was how long Teddy had been on this tour.

"What have you done, my child?" the voice said.

"I . . ." She realized she didn't know what she was going to say. It had to be a confession, not an accusation of the photographer. "I tempted a man," she said.

"In what way?"

"My husband is in Korea. A man came to take a photograph of my family, to send to my husband."

"And?" the priest asked, when she didn't go on.

"I had a drink with him in my house, with my children there in the middle of the afternoon, and then he kissed me."

"In front of your children?"

"The children were outside."

"Did he only kiss you?"

"He had his arms around me. I struggled, and he cut my lip with his teeth." It was beginning to sound like an accusation. "But I tempted him, Father," she said. "I flirted with him. I shouldn't have let him come."

"What did you do after he kissed you?"

"I sent him away."

"Right away?"

"Right away," she said.

"Have you told your husband?"

"I've tried to write a letter, but it sounds wrong, and I'm afraid my husband will misunderstand."

"Is your husband a jealous man?"

"I've never tested him." She thought of her father pulling her onto his lap, asking about her shopping trips with her mother. She always knew what her mother had bought, and had been in the departments before—Kitchens and Linens and Hats—so she could describe them to him, when she had really spent the whole day reading in the bookstore on the mezzanine.

"You're afraid you might test him now," the priest said.

"He's fighting for our country. And I've allowed a man to kiss me."

"But you struggled," the priest said. "You did what you could."

"Yes," she said, grateful. The weight of the last weeks lifted from her heart. It sounded like he would take her side.

"You were lucky the man didn't do more," he said.

"I know," she said happily, full of relief.

"You must tell your husband," the priest said, and the weight dropped on her heart again. "The sin of omission is as vile between husband and wife as it is between priest and confessor."

"Yes, Father." Her moment of hope had been foolish, selfish.

"Maybe it's not wise to have men in your house," he said.

"Yes."

"Say ten Hail Marys and ten Our Fathers, and say a prayer for me," he said.

She knelt in a front pew to do her penance. When she heard the priest come out of the confessional, she interrupted the Our

Fathers to look at him over her shoulder. He was a tall man with a great girth, in Dominican robes, with black hair turning gray. She saw him look over the pews until his eyes stopped on her, and then he looked away. She finished her penance and said her prayer for him, and went out into the clear blue day, feeling more of a burden than she had felt going in, because now she knew without question that she had to tell Teddy what she had done.

Teddy was home on leave before she had time to write a letter that sounded right, and she put off telling him; she didn't want to ruin the lovely way it felt to have him home. It was just before Christmas, and they had a party and all the couples came. Yvette wore orange sequined balls for earrings and a new white cocktail dress, and Teddy made martinis with onions, and everyone danced. The girls stayed up for Midnight Mass for the first time, and it was so beautiful, with the lights and the choir. New Year's Eve they went to the officers' party, where there was a full big band, and they didn't get home until three-thirty in the morning, even though Teddy had to leave at six to go back to Korea. She had been pretending he wasn't going to go, but as she took off her shoes and her dress, she knew he *was* leaving and she had to tell him. She checked herself in her slip to see if she looked too drunk, and then she went out to the bedroom.

"I have something for you, before you go," she said. She got the envelope from the night table and pulled out the prints to lay them on the bed.

Teddy sat down to look. He said, "Look at you. You're so pretty."

She thought for a second that she could leave the story out; he wasn't angry and he thought she was pretty. But she went on. "There was a photographer," she said. "I met him at the beach, when the girls were swimming, and he offered to take a picture for you, since you were away."

Teddy's jaw tightened and he looked up at her and waited.

Yvette had to keep talking or she would never say it. "He came over and took the picture, and then he wouldn't leave, and he tried to kiss me."

There was a pause.

"*Did* he kiss you?" Teddy asked.

"I made him stop."

"What kind of kiss?"

"I don't know," she said. "He grabbed me, and kissed me, and then I got away."

"So he touched you, too?" Teddy's eyes were hard and intent.

"Just to grab me."

"Where did he touch you?" Teddy asked, in a voice that was like a threat.

"I don't know!" she said. "Around the waist."

Teddy looked back at the picture and studied it. Then he looked up at her again. "Were you drunk?" he asked.

She paused, trying to answer.

"You were drunk," Teddy said, and his voice was sharp and military, but low enough not to wake the children.

"I'd had a drink. I made him a drink, and I had one. But I didn't kiss him back, I didn't want him to kiss me. I made him leave then. I sent him away."

Teddy stacked the photographs deliberately. "How did you get these prints?" he asked, tapping their edges straight against the envelope on the bed.

"He brought them to the house. I didn't let him in."

"But you accepted the photographs."

"I didn't want *him* to have them." Her voice sounded desperate and she tried to control it. "They were for you."

"Did you pay him?"

"He wouldn't let me."

Teddy slid the prints into the envelope and looked at it on his knees.

Yvette had her mother's rule with the girls, that they couldn't go to bed angry with each other. If they fought, they had to make up before they went to sleep. Teddy washed up and went to bed without speaking. He had never been short with her before, and now he looked so unforgiving.

"Teddy," she said as she got in bed and turned out the light. "You're leaving soon. Don't be angry. I only love you. I never want to see that man again."

Teddy rolled over and propped himself on his elbow, and her vision adjusted to the dark so she could see his serious eyes on her. He made love to her then but he was angry, she could feel it in his body, and he finished with a hard-looking glare over the top of her head. By then the sun had started to come up. He packed the envelope in his duffel, and before the room was fully light, he was gone.

That tour was difficult for her; she wrote Teddy many letters, and received none. He called to give brief reports, but he didn't ask questions and the calls were short. The fighting was getting harder, and Teddy's fleet was losing planes. He was flying a C-2, which wasn't designed to dive-bomb, but they learned to make it dive-bomb, to support the men fighting on the ground. Over and over he would go in and drop his load in the dark mountains where the fire came at the troops below.

When he came back, his ears were damaged from the diving, and his balance was off. Sometimes he had to catch Yvette's arm suddenly, stepping over a curb or a threshold, to keep from falling over. He'd killed men from very low, and seeing the people he was killing changed him, too. He didn't talk about it as if it had changed him, but Yvette could tell it had. Korea wasn't the same as the last war. The fighting was harder than it had been in the Pacific, for him, and if he felt sure about the reasons for fighting, he wasn't backed up by so many other people feeling sure.

They didn't talk about the photographer, but the fact of him had gotten into their marriage, and she didn't know how to get it out. She thought the priest had been wrong, to say she should tell Teddy. Her mother had been right, to let her father think they had been shopping together in Kitchens and Linens and Hats. That was where her mother had been, shopping alone, so what harm was there? She mounted the clippings about Teddy in the photo albums, and she took pictures of the children to replace the photographer's prints in her mind. She didn't know where Teddy kept the envelope, or if he kept it, but she knew he had become a different man, not as hard as he was that night, but with more of the Marine Corps in his everyday voice and more suspicion in his eyes. He left the Reserves and took his job at North American again, and they settled into a life together that felt like a truce.

2

IN THE SUMMER of 1945, in the middle of the Pacific, the war took on a strange stillness. Teddy flew out every day on patrol, looking for submarines that weren't there, and returned to the carrier to file his reports, maintain his equipment, and think. The rumors said they were preparing for a land invasion of Japan. Pilots were never fully briefed, in case of capture, but Teddy could make guesses based on the training exercises, and the invasion rumors sounded right. He played gin rummy in the wardroom lounge with a pilot named Rand, who said the Japanese would fight to the death and never surrender, and kill themselves rather than be captured. Teddy wondered if he would do that, but guessed he would be shot out of the air before he had to decide.

Their carrier was a small CVE, a jeep carrier, with a runway so short they used a hydraulic catapult to shoot the planes off the flight deck, as if firing them from a cannon. The pilots couldn't hold the controls, because they might pull them when the G-force hit, so they locked their elbows to their sides, with an open left hand over the throttle and an open right on the stick, and pressed their heads back. Then the explosive charge made the plane into a bullet, and the acceleration nailed their stomachs to the backs of their seats, and they took hold of the controls. But there was always a moment before the impact, a moment of absolute stillness and blue sky above, when the shock was imminent. The catapult crew was set up and ready below, and that long second was perfectly still. It was how Teddy imagined death: the waiting moment, the blue sky, something surprising and expected about to come.

What troubled him most about the possibility of death was that it would leave his wife alone. Yvette had an over-the-shoulder smile like a pinup girl, and when the smile caught him right, it made it hard for Teddy to breathe. She had a chipped tooth on the right, a tiny chip you only noticed up close, and Teddy loved it. Even more, he loved the smile that forgot the chip was there. He wanted to kiss her teeth when he thought of it. She was down from Canada like he was, and came from Catholics like he did, and he felt he knew her in his blood, and had always known her. It hurt him to be away.

For three months in Santa Barbara, man and wife, they had been happy. There was always music playing somewhere, and Yvette had danced him off his feet—if Teddy hadn't kept dancing, she would have danced someone else off his feet. She had a look of pure happiness when she was dancing: her over-the-shoulder smile coming under his arm as she turned. The thought of her turning, and the smile appearing, ran through Teddy's mind on the long days of waiting. It made him hate the stretch of Pacific between them.

There was so little to do on the carrier, and so much time, that his brain turned on the topic of Yvette like gears that couldn't connect, had nothing to take their energy, and so spun on and on. His commanding officer had been right to keep him home, but even three months wasn't long enough for a girl like Yvette to feel married. She was so used to being adored—her father and brothers and uncles all in love with her—that the thought of her alone in California was a terrible thing.

Teddy began, that summer in the Pacific—although he didn't want to—to imagine scenes in which Yvette entertained men they knew. Sometimes it was in the house, sometimes in their own bedroom, sometimes in a car in the dark. There was the old grocer, and the mechanic with the bum leg, and sometimes there was Rand, who was on the carrier with Teddy, not home with Yvette at all. It embarrassed Teddy to think about his friend and then later to see him on deck, so he left Rand out. He became more focused. It had to be someone at home. It began with a drink, always. His friend Martin who was 4-F would stop by to check on Yvette and the children. Yvette would pour Martin a drink, and a little for herself. It didn't take much. Then after the drink, in the empty house, trying not to wake the sleeping girls—his girls—came the first kiss, the hand on her breast, her giddy desire. Martin's hands; the living room sofa; the bed that was his own. Teddy could see the chip in her tooth as her mouth came open in something like a smile, and then she was coming, and Teddy was coming, too, and the image was lost in a white burst. When it was over, he lay on his back in his bunk with his mind burning.

Three days before the rumors had them scheduled to attack Japan, the bomb came down on Hiroshima. Teddy's carrier was in the Marianas, waiting, and everyone was surprised. The rumors shifted quickly: there would be no land invasion. The feeling on board was celebratory, but Teddy stood by in awe. There had been no rumors about the bomb, not a word, but now there were descriptions, thirdhand, of its power. The blue, waiting moment Teddy imagined as death couldn't have come to all those people at once. Death had come terribly, without warning. Then the second bomb dropped. Teddy retreated from his shipmates in his mind, and his thoughts of Yvette increased.

A week later they were over Guam, doing training runs over the beach. Teddy flew in low, and dropped his load on empty oil cans, while an officer with a radio watched from a landing craft offshore. Teddy anticipated the second target and dropped early. The officer's voice in his ear, telling him not to anticipate, stopped in midsentence and said, "Japan has surrendered— Japan has surrendered—" There were antiaircraft explosions on the horizon: other carriers celebrating at sea. A B-29 flew overhead and Teddy followed him down to the carrier, buzzing low over the waving men below, and off into the sky again in a giddy victory loop. Teddy thought the surrender might mean he could go home, and his stomach leaped with the ascent of the plane.

The carrier was sent to Tokyo Harbor then, with every other ship in the area. They were there to be a presence, Teddy supposed, and they swung at anchor for ten days. There was nothing to do—no sub patrols, no training exercises, no practice raids. He tried to push the thoughts of Yvette away, but they returned. He tried to be rational. Yvette was a good girl. She liked a highball and she liked to dance—she was just a girl with life in her. But the Yvette in his mind had become decidedly wanton. Teddy knew the fantasies were a sin, and he felt something wrong with his need for them—not just morally, but something wrong with his brain.

They were still waiting in the harbor when a typhoon hit the coast, and they went to sea to avoid it. The seas were so rough that the carrier pitched and dived deep into the troughs of waves, then hawed nose-up again. Teddy stopped thinking of Yvette, the spinning gears in his brain requisitioned by the task of survival.

Neither awe nor victory nor fear of madness or death was any match for the nausea and sleeplessness, the pitching from the bunks at night, and the perpetual cold. The cooks couldn't use the stoves, so there was nothing to eat but sandwiches. Teddy kept a watch cap pulled over his ears and moved through his duties in a miserable dream, then tied himself to his bunk in a waking sleep.

When he was a boy, there was a priest Teddy believed to be part of the family: a man who ate suppers with them, another Father. When Teddy was six, his grandfather died, and the priest stood over the big dirt hole with the white box in it, and said things Teddy didn't understand, and then Teddy's grandmother threw herself like a great bird in her black dress down into the hole, and held the box in her long, thin arms, crying, *"Il est mort! Il est mort!"* still more like a bird, and they had to pull her collapsed body from the grave. Was that what Teddy wanted from Yvette? He thought it was. It had frightened him, but was still his model for devotion. He wouldn't throw himself into Yvette's grave if she died—it was too hysterical for a man—but he would do more. He was quite sure he would do more.

When the storm was over, they evacuated swamped Army troops from the beach onto the carriers. To make room on the hangar deck for makeshift barracks, they moved all the planes up to the flight deck and lashed them down. The Army troops were happy to be out of the mud, cheerful and gregarious now that they were clean. Three officers found Teddy reading in his bunk after his shift, and said Rand had told them Teddy had a beautiful wife. They wanted to see a picture. Rand, behind them, held up his hands in helpless apology. Teddy said he had no pictures, and one of the men smiled.

"I think you're lying," he said.

"I've got nothing to show you."

"Can't hurt to let us see her." The man grinned. "She must really be something." He lifted a corner of Teddy's mattress, as if he might find the photographs there. Teddy caught the man hard under the shoulders and shoved him back against his friends. They stumbled beneath his weight and looked at Teddy with surprise.

"Jesus," the man said when he was upright. "It doesn't matter." He held up his hands. "No trouble," he said.

"You can go now," Teddy said, and his voice sounded strange.

The men left, except Rand. Teddy felt foolish in front of his friend, but the knot of anger in his gut remained.

"Dogfaces," Teddy said.

Rand looked at him.

"I'm losing it, aren't I?" Teddy asked.

Rand said nothing.

"I mean, it shouldn't matter. They just want to see an American girl."

"That's all right," Rand said. "They'll forget about it."

When Rand went away, Teddy sat on his bunk with his face in his hands. He had lied—he had photographs, but he couldn't stand to look at them. He kept them in the folds of a letter Yvette had written him after his first furlough, on yellow paper in violet ink. In the letter she described the way her body looked when she rose from her bath, the water running from her legs, the look of her outstretched arm as she reached for a towel. In most of her letters he had to circle the words that were too scrawled to understand, so he could ask her about them later, but in this one he understood everything. The letter had infuriated Teddy because she didn't know her own power. She might talk and write to other people like that, without knowing it should be only for him, not even for him—it was too much for him, if she had such command of her body that she could express it like that, and so little thought for its sacredness that she *would* express it. He had not written back but waited until he could call, and her voice on the crackling line grew hurt and embarrassed. She said the letter was only for him, to give him pleasure. But that was an easy thing to say. The next furlough he hadn't mentioned the letter at all, but it was the one he kept with him, the one he couldn't let go. He read it sometimes, and looked at the pictures, to make his eyes smart and his chest seize up. To let the Army boys see how much it mattered had been a mistake. Teddy lay back on his bunk, and Yvette began to tell him of an Army officer who had seen her picture and come to find her, and of all they had done.

The next morning his eyes itched from sleeplessness. He sat in his plane on the flight deck, with his head back and his chest strapped tight, but instead of leaving his hands open, he closed his left hand over the throttle and his right hand over the stick. As he did so, he thought: it would be out of his control, the thing that would happen next. It would hardly even be a sin. The impact of the launch would jerk his hands toward him, and the stick and throttle would come with them, and the plane would cartwheel off the short runway until the blue water closed over his head, and Teddy would be done. The crew rigged the plane to the catapult and Teddy waited, feeling the moment fill him up, watching his hands hold the controls tighter than he had ever held them, even in the air, and then he opened his hands and let go. The impact came as usual, and Teddy's stomach felt shot through his spine, and he was airborne above the waves, that still blue moment filled, as always, with another day.

There were no subs, of course, and he returned to the carrier. As Teddy climbed out in his gear he saw Rand standing on deck with their commanding officer, talking seriously. Rand wasn't laughing or gesturing the way he did when he told stories. When Teddy caught his eye, Rand looked away.

Two days later, at Guam, Teddy received transfer orders to a troop carrier on its way to Hawaii and then to California to be stationed at home. Rand wasn't going with him. Teddy cornered his friend in the ready room, before their last mission.

"Why am I going?" he asked, low enough for only Rand to hear.

"Hell if I know," Rand said. "You're a lucky bastard? Half the ship's getting transferred home."

"Where are you going?"

"Back to the Marianas," Rand said. "Not for long, I hope. Go see your wife, go see your kids. Think of me rotting in those stinking islands."

Teddy studied his friend's face, looking for signs the man thought he was losing his mind.

"Is it because of that dogface who wanted to see the pictures?" he asked.

Rand looked genuinely puzzled.

"I mean do they think I'm crazy?"

Rand frowned. "God, no, man," he said. "They will if you keep asking. I thought you were ready to go home."

And he was ready to go home, and he wasn't.

There was the long sea voyage on the new ship, and then there was Hawaii with its bright, sweet smell, and then the transport carrier docked at Long Beach and Teddy was home. He shaved carefully, and straightened the starched creases of his trousers. He put on his hat, and took it off, and put it on again. He was going to see his Yvette, and he was not sure how he would handle himself. He wanted to act like a husband, and a man. He wanted very much not to cry.

The crush on the dock was impossible—all the families in clean American clothes come to see their servicemen home. The sense of congratulation was muted by the urgency of the civilians struggling to find the men they wanted. Teddy pressed among the bodies, carrying his heavy canvas duffel. He could have stayed on board until the throng cleared out, but men with babies were allowed to disembark first, and Teddy had been waiting too long. He scanned the faces of the women as they appeared in the crowd, but none was his: too plain, too blonde, too painted, too old. He had unwrapped the pictures of Yvette as he packed: Yvette on the lawn in a skirt, and on the beach in a white one-piece bathing suit. Yvette glancing over her shoulder in pearls, with her dark hair done up, smiling from the folds of yellow paper and violet scrawl. The pain in his chest had been so acute that he couldn't breathe; he had folded the pictures back into the letter and put them away.

Someone in the press of the crowd knocked his hat off, and he bent to pick it up. When he stood he saw her, standing at the edge of the lot full of cars. She hadn't seen him yet; she had the baby on her hip and was leaning to hear something Margot said, Margot who now stood on her own. Their heads were together in conference, Yvette's dark and Margot's gold-blonde in the sunlight. He walked free of the crowd, then stood at a distance, watching them, afraid to go closer. Yvette looked like the girl he remembered—as pretty as that—but she didn't look like a pinup girl, standing there with his daughters.

Little Margot saw him first, and Yvette swung her dark hair over her shoulder to look where the child looked. She smiled, wide enough for the chip he loved to show through. She said something to Margot and the little girl smiled, too, and stepped forward, reaching for him.

"Oh, sweetheart," he said, and he picked Margot up and held her against his chest, her green dress bunched up under his arm, her miniature Yvette-face beaming down at him. He dropped his bag on the pavement and took his wife in his other arm, as tightly as he could without crushing the baby. Yvette kissed him in their awkward clutch and said she'd missed him terribly, and she'd brought the car, and they should go before the crowd started out of the parking lot.

He studied her face. Was there sex in her hurry? Or did she not know what to say to him and so wanted to rush out of the awkwardness? Margot reached for her mother and Yvette spoke gently to her, leaving her in his arms. Then she smiled at him, shifting Clarissa on her hip.

"I want you to tell me everything," she said.

He stood, next to his bag, Margot in one arm, waiting to be able to step forward into his life. If he could only step forward, then he could keep walking, back to the car, back to the house, back to his bed and a week's leave and then a life at home, with peacetime duties. Yvette smoothed Margot's skirt against his arm, and gave Teddy a curious smile that widened as she watched him, to see what he would do. In a moment he would be ready. In a moment he would pick up his bag, and they would go.

3

WHEN CLARISSA WAS three and a half, the Winstons, five doors down, found her squatting in her yellow dress in the middle of the street, without her older sister.

"Why are you alone?" they asked. "Where's Margot?"

Clarissa stayed crouched in the street. "Oh," she said solemnly. "Margot died last night."

"Died?" The Winstons were alarmed.

"Yes," Clarissa said. "At the hospital."

Then she stood up, tugged at her bunched-up dress, and walked home. A flurry of phone calls determined that Margot wasn't dead—wasn't even sick—and a flurry of scoldings followed. From then on, Clarissa kept her wishes to herself. She went with her parents and Margot to church, frowning at her white gloves. She played with the other children on the street, though the best game was throwing a ball over the whole house, while everyone in the neighborhood ran from the front yard to the back to catch it, shouting wildly, and Clarissa wasn't big enough to get there first. Even in the smaller-children's games, she often stopped playing and only frowned and watched.

In kindergarten, there were boys in Clarissa's class, and it was her favorite year of school. But the next year she was sent to Our Lady of Lourdes, with no boys, and her father was gone, flying his plane. A man took their picture to send to him, but it disturbed Clarissa that her father might need pictures to remember what they looked like. When he came home at Christmas, they had lots of presents, and he was in a rush, kissing them and dancing her mother around the living room, until her mother cried, "Teddy! Stop!" Clarissa was confused by how much she wanted him. She followed him through the house, but drew back when she got his attention.

"What is it, Little?" he would ask. And what could she say? Then he was gone again, flying his plane.

At Our Lady, they raised money to buy pagan babies in Africa, to give them baptisms and Christian names. Clarissa saved all her money for the babies, every penny she found—even if it wasn't technically hers—and by February her class had the most in the whole school, more even than Margot's class. One day Sister Eugene asked to speak to Clarissa alone, and she was proud.

"Clarissa," the nun began. "The Lord tells us never to let our left hand know what the right hand is doing."

Clarissa knew which was which because she had sucked her right thumb for years, so it felt different, swollen and tingly. She felt it now, against her leg, through her uniform skirt.

"Do you know what that means?" Sister Eugene asked.

Clarissa shook her head, blushing.

"It means we give charity without pride, so that our generosity is unknown even to ourselves."

Clarissa frowned, still thinking about her tingly right thumb.

"I believe you've been bragging about the pagan babies," Sister Eugene said.

The flush in Clarissa's cheeks became hot and painful; she felt it in her ears and in her throat. "We have the *most*," she said.

"That's no reason to boast or be proud," Sister Eugene said. "We should think how much more there is to do."

Clarissa glared furiously at her desk. It *was* a reason to be proud. It was a contest, and they had won. Margot's class had lost.

"God understands what you have done for the children," Sister Eugene said. "You don't have to tell anyone for God to know."

Clarissa sat silent and glaring, until Sister Eugene let her go. At home she buried Margot's china doll in the garden, but her mother found it and sat her down, just like Sister Eugene had. Clarissa prepared to wait out the scolding.

Her mother said *she* had an older sister, too—Clarissa's aunt Adele—and that she had always been jealous of Adele getting to do everything first. She said Adele once wore a new dress to a dance, and came home with a pink cocktail spilled all down the front, and the dress smelled like alcohol. Adele hid the dress in the back of their bedroom closet but Yvette found it, and told their mother, who told their father.

Clarissa waited to hear what happened next, but her mother stopped, and wouldn't tell her, and seemed confused about what her point was. Finally she said that she just understood how it felt to be a younger sister. She said that God sees everything we do, the good and the bad, so we shouldn't worry about what other people do. We should try very hard to be good.

"I do try," Clarissa said.

"I know, sweetheart," her mother said, and she put her arms around Clarissa and squeezed her tight.

Margot was confirmed first, in a white dress their mother made, and told Clarissa she was going to be a bride of Christ, and eat His body and drink His blood. Clarissa said it was wine, but Margot smiled, and said how little Clarissa knew. Clarissa said that Margot was a disgusting vampire, and her sister stopped speaking to her for a week. Then Clarissa's own turn came to wear a white dress and take the Host—which was His real body—and she couldn't help being excited, too.

When her father came back from flying in Korea, he was more serious and less predictable. He didn't dance anyone around the house anymore, and he talked about moving the family away. When he found them coming back from the beach with their mother, all sandy in their swimsuits and squinting in the sun, he seemed angry. He'd say the weather was too good in California, and their lives were too easy, and they should see how the rest of the world lived. They were all rotting from the inside, he said. Clarissa kept her distance from him then.

Sometimes, though, he was her wonderful father, exactly what she thought a man should be. "You're my favorite girl . . . in this room," he would say when they were alone, and she knew the first part was true. He had to add the second part because of Margot, but Clarissa understood.

When she was almost fourteen, she finally got what she wanted: Margot went to study in France, and their mother got pregnant again, and went to a convent to rest, and Clarissa stayed home and had her father to herself. There was never another girl in the room. They ate peanut butter sandwiches for dinner, or hamburgers at the Surf Shack, and the good weather didn't make her father angry. They ate Neapolitan ice cream with chocolate sauce and as many maraschino cherries as she wanted. There seemed to be air overhead, with Margot gone.

Clarissa started high school at Sacred Heart that year, and

won a science prize from General Electric. Ronald Reagan, the host of *G. E. Theater* on television on Sunday nights, took her out to lunch. Mr. Reagan seemed brighter than normal people, like a painting, and he asked about the electrical appliances her family had in the house. It was a fancy restaurant with things on the menu she didn't recognize, but Mr. Reagan said they would make her a tuna melt if she wanted one. She had the tuna melt, and a chocolate sundae, too. But not with Neapolitan ice cream—that was hers and her father's.

At Sacred Heart, there were weekly lessons in cotillion and charm. Miss Blair came to the school gym, and the girls partnered up to fox-trot and waltz. They learned to walk like ladies, and offer their hands. Miss Blair was tall and thin, with ash-blonde hair in a French twist, and sometimes she would come around the room giving makeup tips: what colors the girls should wear, and how they could accentuate their looks. The only makeup the nuns allowed was colorless Tangee Natural lip gloss, but the girls took careful notes just the same. Miss Blair said Clarissa should shape her eyebrows with a tweezer, to have less of a frown. Clarissa tried, with a tweezer from her mother's cabinet, but pulling the hairs brought tears to her eyes, and she stopped.

At the beach, she met a boy named Jimmy Vaughan, who didn't seem to mind her eyebrows at all. He went to Hermosa High and had gray-green eyes and curly blond hair, and when he touched her over her swimsuit top, she got shivers in her whole body. Every time she thought about it, the shivers came back. She knew it was a thing to confess—Margot would have confessed it. But in church, when Clarissa heard the priest breathing on the other side of the screen, something rose up in her and closed off her throat. Her mother said God knew everything. But if so, then Clarissa didn't have to tell the priest. She sat thinking in the musty dark, and finally said she had used her mother's good sewing shears to cut paper, and worn pink lipstick to school.

Then her brother, Jamie, was born. When Yvette brought him home, she was distracted all the time, with a burp rag over her shoulder and her hair undone. Her father got angry at the baby's crying and said it was like Clarissa all over again. When Margot came back from school in France, it was even worse. Clarissa was hardly ever alone with her father, and when he began, "You're my favorite girl . . ." she felt a pain in her stomach, waiting for him to say, "in this room."

At swim practice, Sister Inez saw the bikini-strap tan line across Clarissa's back, and scolded her for wearing two-piece suits. After practice that day, Clarissa opened all the empty gym lockers and ran down the length of them, slamming them shut. She was given silent prayer meetings with Sister Inez for a week, during which she thought about Jimmy Vaughan and got shivers.

Jimmy started a four-piece band with some other boys, and he wrote their songs and played in coffeehouses around town. One of the songs was called "Clarissa," and at the Hermosa fair they sold it on a 45. Sometimes, walking down the streets at night, she would hear Jimmy Vaughan's voice through an open window, singing her name. Margot didn't have any songs named after her, but then Margot would never wear a bikini to the beach, or let a boy run his hand over it when they were alone.

4

MARGOT WAS A quick study, and she liked rules and appreciated their function—there wasn't anything more to it than that. She wasn't Saint Margot, as her sister called her, and she wasn't a prig. She liked the rules of church: don't let the sun go down on your anger, do unto others, turn the other cheek. She loved the systems at school: the sonnet form, geometry, and foxtrot. By eighth grade she understood that there was a way to dress and to comport yourself, which affected how others treated you, and she understood how easily she had avoided Clarissa's difficulty with grown-ups and nuns. Her sister knew it, too; it was why Clarissa hated her. It was in Margot's nature to please.

In high school, when Miss Blair and Mr. Tucker came to Sacred Heart to teach dancing lessons, and Miss Blair went round the circle of girls giving makeup tips, she stopped when she got to Margot and shook her head. "I've never seen a girl so perfectly groomed," she said.

Margot smiled at Miss Blair, embarrassed. She slept in curlers to make her hair bob at her shoulders, but her lashes were dark and thick without anything on them, and her eyebrows arched on their own.

"I have nothing to offer," Miss Blair said. "I'm stumped."

Mr. Tucker, who danced like a prince, did not seem to be stumped by Margot at all. When Miss Blair was busy correcting the girls on the other side of the gym, he would cut in, stranding whichever girl Margot was dancing with, and fox-trot Margot all over the floor. Other girls whispered it: she was the perfect partner he deserved. Miss Blair was too tall for him, and too severe. Margot was the right size; the top of her head came right to Mr. Tucker's nose. When they danced, the girls forgot their feet and watched—they only pretended to keep dancing, so Miss Blair wouldn't notice and stop the whole thing.

Once, when the music ended and Miss Blair was still on the other side of the gym, Mr. Tucker smiled at Margot in their finishing pose. "What a sweet, sweet face," he said.

Margot was happy, and could have gone on dancing in the gym once a week till the end of time. The other girls daydreamed about Mr. Tucker, but he had chosen her, and she didn't need to daydream.

Miss Blair and Mr. Tucker emceed the dances at Sacred Heart, when the girls decorated the gym and the boys came from Immaculata. Miss Blair called the dances, and Mr. Tucker gave prizes and made announcements. Mr. Tucker in a tuxedo was a glorious thing, especially compared with the skinny schoolboys. Margot's date for the spring dance at the end of her sophomore year was a boy named Hal Fitzhugh, who played basketball. He was a terrible dancer, his long arms and legs getting in his way. Margot tried to hide her disappointment, and Hal went off with some other Immaculata boys, saying he'd be back.

After a long time alone at a table in her blue chiffon dress, watching the other girls dance with their perfectly competent dates, she went looking for Hal. The air outside was fresh and cool in the dark, after the stuffy gym. She found Hal behind the building, passing a flask to another boy. He smelled like her mother's gin.

"You know that's not allowed," Margot said.

"A guy's gotta have some fun."

"Dancing is fun," Margot said—though it hadn't been with him.

"Not with you, sweetheart," he said. "You're out there keeping score on what I do wrong."

The other boys laughed, and Margot looked around at them, flustered. She had never been brayed at like this before.

"You're like a coach we had," Hal went on. "Grumpy old bastard."

The boys laughed again.

"How dare you!" she said.

Hal grinned at her. "Drink?" He offered the flask.

Margot spun and left them there—not marching off, exactly, as it was hard to march in high heels on soft grass—unable to speak. She was just deciding whether to cry or not, when she rounded the corner of the building and bumped into Mr. Tucker.

"Mr. Tucker!" she said, and they both apologized; he held her elbow to steady her.

What happened then was a confused rush of images, as Margot reconstructed it later, but she remembered being kissed by Mr. Tucker, and her knees nearly giving way beneath her. She remembered following him to his white convertible, and riding in it, and looking over the ocean but not knowing exactly where. She remembered his hands unzipping the blue chiffon dress her mother had made, and the softness of everything he did, and her feeling that all rules in the world had been suspended for this to happen, and how sweet that suspension was.

Mr. Tucker disappeared after that, as he always did when school was out, and Margot did her chores and thought about other things—but by August she couldn't ignore what had happened to her body. She knew what a girl had to do in this situation, and she told her mother. Yvette cried. Then she held Margot and told her it would be all right. She said there were some things you didn't have to tell people; it would only upset them to know, and wouldn't do them a bit of good. Margot thought she should go to confession, at least, and tell her father.

"No," her mother said. "You can leave the priests and your father out of it, and tell God on your own."

Then Yvette packed Margot's suitcase and sent her off to France.

The Planchets were distant cousins of her mother's: no one was sure of the exact connection. They lived in a drafty stone farmhouse in Lisieux in Normandy. Everyone at home thought Margot was just having her junior year abroad, working on her French. It made perfect sense. The Planchets knew the truth, but it didn't seem to bother them at all. They took her in and assigned her chores. She went to the local lycée with Jean-Pierre Planchet, who was fourteen and still a boy, obsessed with his exams.

Jean-Pierre was scornful of Margot's French, and mocked her for it. "She speaks like a baby," he told his parents, and she guessed it was true. He spoke English to her, showing off, whenever the elder Planchets were out of the room. No one at school seemed to notice her condition; everyone knew American girls were *un peu grosse,* and she wore the loose jumpers her mother had sewn in a rush before she left.

M. Planchet loved America, and after a few glasses of wine he would lose his shyness and speak in English. He loved Margot's father, whom he had never met, for flying a fighter plane in the war. He loved to talk about the Chermans.

"Germans," Jean-Pierre would correct him.

"*Oui, ça. Les Boches.* They were building these tanks from 1936. And you Americans started from the neutral, and made so many tanks—it is like a miracle."

"He thinks it's still the Occupation," Mme. Planchet would say in French. "Pay no attention."

"The Germans would come tomorrow if not for the Americans," M. Planchet insisted, in English. "But the atomic bomb: for this we can be thankful."

"Enough," his wife said.

M. Planchet shrugged. "Or you fight, or you lose," he said. "That's the war."

"*Either* you fight or you lose," his son corrected him.

"*Oui!*" he said. "*C'est la guerre.*"

Margot was never sick, and always hungry. She watched M. Planchet arrange the cold meat tray before the evening meal, with his delicate hands. When he said, "Open your mouth and say thank you!" she did. What he popped onto her tongue was sometimes salty, sometimes smooth and rich, sometimes sweet.

"From Spanish pigs, who eat nothing but figs!" M. Planchet would say; or simply, "This is good for you, this!"

In the Planchets' kitchen was an earthenware jug filled with a dark red tissue that looked like raw liver, half submerged in red liquid, called *la mère*. After lunch and dinner, taking the dishes in to wash, Mme. Planchet poured the red wine from the bottom of each glass into the jug, feeding the mother. It was a kind of mushroom, she said, and it cured the wine, and from the spigot in the bottom of the jug came fresh red vinegar. Margot dutifully added the leftover wine, and the sharp vinegar smell pricked her nose, but after the first time she didn't look in at the shiny, organlike growth. It was such a grotesquerie, with that embarrassing name, and she had nothing in common with it and never would.

On Sundays the family went to Mass in the new Basilique dedicated to Thérèse Martin, and the statue of the young saint stared down at them. Mme. Planchet said that Thérèse had entered the convent at fifteen because she knew the temptations faced by young girls.

M. Planchet said, "Bah! To marry the Spouse of Virgins—what a life. You are better off, *chérie*."

After Mass, Margot helped prepare the Sunday meal, and poured the wine. She began to dream in French, and to think it strange that she had ever imagined her life without this detour from normal events. There was no question that it was only a detour—a long, eventful French dream—and that her life would resume its orderly course when it was done.

5

WHEN HIS WIFE told him she was pregnant again, Teddy
was furious. She was supposed to keep track of the days when it
was safe. The girls were both in high school, and Margot had
been flown expensively to France, and Teddy would be paying
for college soon. Yvette was thirty-five and he was forty-one. The
last thing they needed was another baby. He had not yet recov-
ered from his anger when he realized that Yvette was saying she
didn't want another child either.

"That's our baby!" he said.

"You said you didn't want it."

"I said it was an unfortunate *time*."

"Which means you don't want it," Yvette said. "So I'll take
care of it."

"No!" Teddy said. "I mean, yes, take care of the baby. Not the
pregnancy, no. That's murder."

"I didn't say it wasn't," Yvette said.

Teddy raised his hand, and might have struck her, a thing he had never done—but she sat on the edge of the bed and looked at him with absolute calm. He wondered how he had ever thought she belonged to him. She was her own. He knelt at her feet, and took her hands in his.

"It's me, too," he said. "That baby's me, too."

Yvette stood up, and stepped neatly away from him.

"It's not you," she said. "It's a baby we can't afford. It would be selfish to have it." She stopped at the bedroom door and turned to look at him—her pinup girl pose, but she wasn't smiling, and she'd had a dentist fix the chipped tooth he had loved. No chinks in her armor. "I'm going to start dinner," she said.

Teddy stayed kneeling on the carpet he'd laid down himself. He could see the individual fibers, dark and light, which merged from a few feet away into pale greenish-gray. Finally he pulled himself heavily to his feet, to go have a rational discussion about this baby he didn't particularly want. He told himself it might be a boy, it might be good to have a son. Once he had that thought, Yvette's willingness to kill the child, his son, made his eyes go out of focus with rage. He could hear her setting the table in the dining room: the jangle of silverware, the clank of plates.

6

AFTER AN HOUR of fighting about the invented pregnancy, Teddy threw the heavy serving fork across the room—not at Yvette exactly, but hard enough that it left a mark on the wall behind her. As soon as she heard it hit, she knew she had won.

She told Teddy she would agree to have the baby, but she wouldn't live with a man who threw cutlery. She needed time to be alone. Margot was still in France, and Clarissa was self-sufficient now, between school and swim practice and homework. Yvette stocked the freezer with casseroles, and told Teddy that when those ran out, he could get by on his own.

In Santa Rosa, a sister from the Holy Name met her at the train station. She was old and round and effusive, in cheap eyeglasses and a black habit. She gave Yvette a suffocating hug right there on the platform. "You'll do so well here," the nun said. "I can tell already."

She picked up Yvette's suitcase with surprising strength and bustled her into an ancient station wagon. "I hope you've brought a sweater," she said. "The house gets chilly at night."

Yvette rode in the passenger seat and answered the sister's barrage of questions about her supposed breakdown and spiritual crisis. The nun said they had been praying for her since she contacted them, and the vote to let her come had been unanimous. She would be a guest of the convent, during her retreat, giving a small donation for her room and board. They expected her to help with light chores.

"The chores can be a kind of praying," the nun said. "They are for me. They might bring you closer to God."

Yvette said that was what she wanted. A book had circulated when she was a girl in school in Canada: a tiny gray paperback called *Convent Cruelties.* It had belonged to a classmate named Marie Rémy, who had a Protestant cousin in America. The book had pen-and-ink illustrations, and told the story of a young girl from Pennsylvania who was kidnapped by nuns, beaten and starved in a convent basement. She was forced to do endless laundry, drink dirty soup, and sew clothes for the convent to sell.

The Holy Name, when they arrived, was disappointing by comparison. It was a two-story Victorian house, built from a mail-order kit at the turn of the century. The Mother Superior, who was taller than the first nun but just as old, with a long face inside her wimple, showed Yvette to a room with a single bed and a view of the backyard. The curtains were homemade, and Yvette thought of *Convent Cruelties* again—which was silly. It might be good to have sewing to do. She felt suddenly anxious about how she would fill her time.

Most of the nuns were old, but there were two novices who wore white smocks instead of habits: a plump, pretty girl named Maria-José and her shy cousin Teresa, both nineteen. The Mother Superior was proud of them: not every convent had novices anymore. Yvette helped the girls with the laundry, but there wasn't much. Margot and Clarissa, with swim practice and beach towels and uniform shirts and after-school clothes, produced more laundry in a week than all the nuns put together. The laundry room was bright, with a window over the valley, and Yvette lingered there to talk. Maria-José must have recognized her boredom, because she invited Yvette behind the annex, where the gardening tools were stored, to have a cigarette.

At first, Yvette didn't actually smoke. She went behind the annex only for the girlish, illicit pleasure of it—she, a grown woman with teenage daughters of her own. But Maria-José, compelling in her round-faced prettiness, and used to getting her own way, finally talked her into taking a drag. The cigarette felt so delicate between Yvette's fingers, and so dry and papery against her lips, that the hot smoke in her lungs and the warm, bitter taste of the tobacco surprised her. She felt instantly light-headed, and gave the cigarette back, smiling at Maria-José and Teresa, such sweet girls. She met them behind the annex every day, between their chores and prayers, but she had been at the convent two months before she took a whole cigarette of her own.

"You look like a movie star with that," Teresa said.

"A movie star in love, all dreamy," Maria-José said. "Dreamy Yvette."

"I'm very susceptible to drugs," Yvette tried to say, but she stumbled on the words, and the girls just laughed.

"*Drogas!*" Maria-José giggled. "It's just a cigarette!"

Yvette leaned against the annex wall and listened to the girls while she smoked, amazed that they were barely older than her daughters. Maria-José talked about her family: her brother, who was caught robbing a store with a screwdriver, and her little sister's baby. Teresa talked about how much she loved having her own bedroom at the convent after sleeping on her cousin's floor. When the girls kissed her good-bye and went back to their duties, Yvette returned to her room, still dazed from the cigarette. She knelt dizzily before the window that looked out on the churchyard, and tried to pray.

She began at the beginning. She prayed for forgiveness for defying her father in marrying Teddy. Her father loved her, that was all, and he hadn't wanted her to move so far away. She had done it blithely, sure her father would come around, but he never had. He remained frozen in his disapproval, back in Canada, and she in her defiance, and she had lost him, who used to be so central to her life.

She prayed for forgiveness for that awful thing with the photographer, because she knew there was a part of Teddy's mind that still thought her capable of faithlessness. She accepted that the incident had been her fault, but she asked God to understand her regret at telling Teddy. God could see into each heart and mind and would know how the situation had gotten out of hand.

She prayed for forgiveness also because her marriage had distracted her, and she hadn't paid enough attention to the girls. And she prayed because she had lied to Teddy about being pregnant, although she didn't regret it. Offering to get rid of the baby had made him desperate to have it, as she had known it would. She would go back with Margot's baby, and all would be well, and Teddy would be able to love the child, thinking it was his. That was the most important thing—that he be able to love the child wholeheartedly. It trumped everything. She hoped the baby would be a son.

She had just finished praying, still high from Maria-José's Chesterfield, when she felt at once the heaviness of what she had undertaken to keep from Teddy, and a rushing upward in the top of her head. She caught her breath, and looked down, and saw

43

her own kneeling figure at the window below. She could study the part in the dark hair on the top of her head: it was a little crooked. She no longer felt the aching in her knees—she no longer felt anything. She willed her body to look up, but it stayed in the attitude of prayer, while she floated above. The sensation lasted for impossible minutes, and she wondered if she were dying. Then she was back in her body with the confused feeling of waking from a dream.

That evening, in the little dining room off the kitchen, she sat through dinner with no appetite. The old nuns ate quietly and slowly. Sister Joan in her clear, thin voice read aloud from *The Imitation of Christ*. Teresa and Maria-José shot Yvette gleaming conspiratorial looks, as they always did, but she was too agitated to return them. When the plates were cleared, Yvette went to the Mother Superior's office and knocked at the door.

"Yes?" the Mother's voice came, and Yvette slipped inside. She could feel her heart pounding, still full of what had happened. She had expected nothing from God, but He had surprised her, come to her for the first time in her life. She had never felt anything like it, not even the births of her daughters. She had been cradled there, in air.

The Mother Superior looked at her for a long time when she had finished the story, and her long face seemed to grow longer. "You were still attached to your body?" she asked.

"There was still a connection," Yvette said. "That's what pulled me back in."

"And this happened while you were praying?"

Yvette nodded.

"About what?"

"Oh—about everything. I'd never prayed so long before."

"Had you eaten lunch?" the Mother Superior asked.

Yvette looked at her, puzzled. She couldn't remember. "Yes!"

she said finally. "Of course. We had soup. The reading was from Saint Augustine."

The old nun nodded, considering.

"But food has nothing to do with it," Yvette went on. "I was out of my body."

"Yes, I know," the nun snapped. "Please don't do it again."

Yvette sat with her hands in her lap.

"That will be a condition of your staying here," the Mother Superior said. She gathered up some papers on her desk, to show Yvette their meeting was finished. "You can decide whether you want to stay or not."

Yvette stood, slowly. Where else could she go?

"And no more cigarettes with the girls," the nun said. "They admire you. You're a grown woman. It only encourages them."

Yvette stayed mostly in her bedroom after that, for three long months; she didn't speak to the Mother Superior unless it was absolutely necessary, and she was silent at meals. The winter rains set in, and made walks soggy and unpleasant. She felt that she really was pregnant, on bed rest, following orders. She kept her hand on her soft, flat stomach as if she housed something there, and she wrote letters to Teddy about the progress of the baby she imagined. She wasn't exactly lying, because there really was a baby growing as she described—it just happened to be in France. She told Teddy she couldn't come home for Christmas, in her condition—which was also true, in a way—and that he should stay home and provide Clarissa with some stability. She told him what gifts to buy. She had come to understand that Teddy hated secrets, but only when he knew there was something he didn't know. As long as she supplied him with detailed information, and never sounded coy or mysterious, he wouldn't inquire about her with the nuns.

It kept raining, and she read all of the Bible on her bedside table, and was amazed at how much she knew by heart. She took the autobiography of Saint Thérèse of Lisieux from the convent library, and read it over and over. She lingered on Thérèse's vision of the Virgin, which the Carmelites hadn't believed, and on her idea of being a little flower in God's garden, loved as much as the great roses were, in spite of her faults. The girl's anxiety and her doubts felt like Yvette's own, but the girl had mastered them, imagining herself as Jesus' plaything, to do with as he pleased. Yvette began to do the same, and she no longer felt so dejected. She didn't go for cigarettes behind the annex with Maria-José and Teresa, and there was pleasure in the sacrifice. The girls gave her wounded looks at the dinner table, but God had spoken to Yvette, and she would keep His company alone.

When it was time to go to France, she borrowed the money from her sister and told Teddy nothing. She spent the whole transatlantic flight looking out the window of the plane, praying that nothing would happen to give her away.

Margot had grown up during the year, and it was shocking to see her pregnant. But she was beautiful, and Yvette was proud of her. The Planchets clearly adored her, especially the father. Margot—punctual as ever—went into labor three days after Yvette arrived, and Yvette pushed her daughter's hair from her sweating face in the hospital, and spoke rusty French with the calm, flirtatious doctors. Then she went to the *mairie* to give an account of the birth to the unquestioning official there: *"Né du père, SANTERRE, Theodore James, directeur des affaires aéronautiques, de nationalité américaine, et GRENIER, Yvette, épouse SANTERRE, de nationalité canadienne, à Lisieux, Calvados, un fils, James Theodore, ce 4ème jour de février, 1959."*

She went to the Basilica of Saint Thérèse, to give thanks to her Little Flower. When she was sure no one was watching, she kissed the stone feet of the pretty saint. Margot slimmed down at once, and wanted nothing to do with the baby; she wanted to stay and finish out the school year at the lycée, and Yvette was relieved.

When the child was old enough to travel, Yvette said good-bye to the Planchets and went home to Teddy a glowing new mother with a baby boy. The few questions he asked, she answered easily. She arranged for a baptism right away, grateful that she had pulled the thing off, and she returned to the Dominicans with a full heart. God had lifted her up to be with Him, just for a moment, and she was His.

7

CLARISSA LOVED HER new brother—once she got used to the idea—so fiercely it was a revelation to her. She saw light all around him, wherever he was. She had not, she knew now, loved anyone before; this was the love people talked about. The slavish devotion she had for her father was cold and sterile in comparison. Her mother was just her mother, and Margot was impossible to love. Jimmy Vaughan had made her body shiver, but he didn't fill her with sweet, aching warmth this way. She walked Jamie around the house for hours when he was colicky, and the feel of his small head against her shoulder made her heart seem to expand and fill. She gave him his bottles, and later his smooth green and orange food, then his apples and cheese. She played with him on the carpet, building towers out of blocks and pulling a wooden duck on wheels to make the polished egg on the duck's back roll over and over. Margot, on her way to dance class, or study sessions, or reading to the blind, barely glanced at them sitting on the floor. If she did look, it was with confusion and disdain.

When Jamie was three, Clarissa graduated from Sacred Heart in a blue dress and white gloves with her arms full of roses, and gave a Miss Blair curtsy to the bishop in the chapel, without stumbling. She had watched Margot do the same thing the year before, and she imagined her sister watching her now, although Margot had called from the University of San Diego, where she had a full scholarship, to say she couldn't come.

Clarissa had decided, the moment she heard about Margot's scholarship, not to apply to USD or any other Catholic schools. She intended to stand firm even if her parents threw her out in the street, but they hadn't. They were happy, prosperous people; her father had been promoted at work, and her mother was a lector at the church. A handsome, charming, war-hero Catholic, with a beautiful wife, had been elected president, with the help of her parents' first non-Republican votes. When Clarissa applied to UC–San Diego and got in, she thought it would be a slap to her parents, a state school so close to Margot's Catholic one. But everything was going their way, so they shrugged and gave in, and Clarissa was a little disappointed.

Then, on her first day at college, Clarissa met Henry Collins, and her life turned on a pivot. He was a halfback on the football team, a biology major, with sandy hair and green eyes. He picked her out of the registration line, and the force of his convictions got her into bed within the month. She told him they couldn't have actual sex, because she didn't want a baby, which made Henry laugh.

"There are ways around that, you know," he said.

But Clarissa was too embarrassed to talk about it further, and Henry said he could wait.

Henry's rented house had a big claw-foot bathtub with enough room for two. Lying back against his chest in the cooling bath-water, when they were supposed to be doing physics problem sets, Clarissa told him how the nuns had convinced her that the bread really did become the body of Christ, and the wine became his blood. At Sacred Heart, Sister Beatrice had quoted Cardinal Newman to her, from the nineteenth century: "Why should it not be? What's to hinder it? What do I know of substance or matter?"

Henry laughed, and asked if Sister Beatrice was the physics teacher or the chemistry teacher.

"History," she said.

"Did the physics teacher know anything of substance or matter?"

"Yes," she said.

"Which was?"

"Oh, velocity and gravity," she said. "And that the Host becomes the real body of Christ." She leaned forward to turn on the hot-water tap, because the bath was getting cold, and the roar of water kept him from making fun of her. Then she turned it off and settled against him again. "What do you believe in?" she asked.

"This right here," Henry said, running a wet hand over her breast. She caught the hand and held it. It was as big as both of hers.

"I mean really, like faith."

Henry paused, and began slowly. "I have faith," he said, "that given the chance, people can improve their situation."

"When you're out on the football field," Clarissa said, "and three-hundred-pound monsters are running to crush you, then what do you believe in?"

"Velocity," he said. "Gravity."

"Come on."

He was silent, tracing wet patterns on her skin. "My dad was an altar boy," he said.

"He was?" This was startling information, and might be useful with her mother.

"He doesn't believe that stuff now," he said. "He says he's a Great Westerner—he believes in a God like the cowboys had, out where there weren't any churches. You don't owe anything to it, and you can't count on it to do anything for you, but it's the force in things. I guess I believe in something like that."

"Can I be a Great Westerner, too?" Clarissa asked.

"Roll over."

Clarissa did, sloshing water and sliding against him. He drew a circle on her forehead with his wet thumb. "I baptize you in the name of the conservation of energy," he said. "What comes around goes around."

She was smiling too hard to kiss him right. She was a baptized Great Westerner, and she didn't feel like frowning anymore, with Henry. She felt something like she had felt when Jamie was born, plus something like she had felt with Jimmy Vaughan. And then Henry was so rocklike, and it seemed like he would never go away.

She took him home to meet her family, and Jamie fell in love with him, as she'd known he would. Jamie wasn't five yet, but he aspired to teenage status, and saw Henry as a source of male information. Her parents were wary; Henry teased her mother and towered over her father. Margot was indifferent. But the important thing was that Henry didn't fall in love with Margot—he didn't even take her seriously. That was the last straw for Clarissa's virginity, and once it was gone she felt relieved not to have anything to protect anymore, not to have anything to lose.

When June came, Henry found a job in a research lab near her parents' house. Margot was staying in summer school, so Clarissa asked if Henry could have Margot's room. Teddy waited up each night to see that Henry and Clarissa went to bed separately, and they did. Then every night, Clarissa sneaked down the hall to her sister's white, perfect bedroom. She left her nightgown on the floor and climbed under her sister's white chenille bedspread, where Henry was waiting, warm and naked. They wrestled and hushed each other and readjusted, and sometimes the thought that pushed her over the edge was that she was Margot—Margot in clean white bobby socks and nothing else, and her legs were Margot's, smooth and virginal and now defiled. And then afterward she was herself again, behaving outrageously in Margot's bed.

Before dawn each morning she slipped back to her own room, and an hour later Jamie would run in to pounce on Henry, leaping onto the mound of white chenille. Jamie sang when he pounced: "Waaay-ke up in the morning and water your horses and feed them some corn-y-corn-corn!"

"My horses aren't thirsty," Henry would mumble, covers around his ears.

"WAKE UP in the MORNING and WATER your HORSES . . ."

"No corn here."

"Wake UP! In the MORNING!"

One big freckled arm would emerge from the covers to crush the source of the noise. Jamie would dodge and wriggle free, squealing, "WATER your HORSES! And feed them some—" until Henry rolled him into a pile of chenille on the floor.

When Clarissa came out sleepy in a bathrobe, Jamie would be padding after Henry into the kitchen, asking one question on top of another—were the Beatles better than the Rolling Stones? And who was the best guitarist of all? And was candy apple red a better color than British racing green?

"Leave Henry alone," Clarissa's father would say.

"Teddy," her mother would say in a warning voice from the stove.

"Listen to him!" Teddy would counter. "He never stops!"

Henry ignored them, and turned Jamie upside down, then right side up, before dumping him into his chair at the kitchen table, where Jamie scowled, red-faced and pleased. Then Henry would explain: "The Stones imitated the Beatles, who imitated Elvis, who imitated black singers in the South."

"Like who?"

"Kokomo Arnold," he said. "Big Mama Thornton. I'll bring their records up."

"Are they good?"

"They're the best."

"Okay."

"British racing green," Henry would go on, "is particularly suited to certain cars, like the convertible MG, while the Ford Mustang was made to be candy apple red."

Jamie would nod thoughtfully and eat his breakfast, absorbing these incontrovertible facts.

Clarissa's mother still disapproved of Henry, but that was just part of the summer, like the morning routine with Jamie. Henry flirted with Yvette, and made mischief, and Yvette tried to scold him but couldn't help laughing. Everyone laughed more, even Teddy, and he didn't bark at Jamie so much in his Marine Corps voice.

"You're in my house, Henry," Yvette would say, when Henry engaged Jamie's toast soldiers in battle, lining up his own strips of bread for an attack on Jamie's poached egg. But Jamie's soldiers were already fighting back, and buttered-crumb shrapnel was everywhere, and Henry ignored Yvette, intent on his war.

"You let him outshine you," Yvette said, when Clarissa was

alone with her, folding laundry. "He'll put your light under a bushel, and it won't make you happy."

Clarissa sighed and ignored her, folding the clean white sheets she had slept in with Henry, knowing her mother was wrong.

When school started in the fall, Henry promised Jamie a sailing trip, to get him to stop looking at them with heartbroken, abandoned eyes. On a bright windy Friday in November, they drove north to Hermosa Beach to pick him up. Henry opened her parents' front door without knocking, as he always did.

"Ahoy, mateys!" he called. "Where will I find a captain for my pirate ship?"

Jamie came running through the house, shrieking, "ME!"

Clarissa didn't know how to sail, and it became clear that Henry didn't, either. They were crowded and clumsy in a rented fourteen-foot boat, tacking fast across the harbor, when they rammed a cabin cruiser called the *Grocery Boy* and punched a hole in its side. Clarissa nearly went overboard, and the *Grocery Boy*'s skipper shouted obscenities from overhead. Henry was quiet and reasonable, and tried to calm the man down as they limped back to the dock.

When they got home with Jamie, windblown and shaken, the house was silent. Clarissa followed the faint sound of the TV, and found her parents staring at the screen.

"Oh, honey," her mother said. "The president's been shot."

Clarissa watched the flickering screen as the convertible went by, and watched as beautiful Jackie turned. She bundled Jamie out of the room.

The days afterward felt weighted down with sadness. Her parents were devastated, and everyone ate sandwiches for dinner because her mother was too sad to cook.

Margot brought her boyfriend, Owen, home for Thanksgiving, and everyone was still quiet and subdued. Clarissa studied Owen in the kitchen and at the dinner table. She never saw Margot in San Diego, and she had never met the boyfriend. He was a graduate student in chemistry, quiet and polite to her parents, and only spoke when he was asked a question. Yvette asked a lot of questions, trying to draw him out, and he told her he'd grown up in Chicago, and his father was a chemist, too. His parents were Methodists, but he wanted to raise his children Catholic— or at least he nodded when Margot said he did. Margot announced their engagement after the pumpkin pie, and everyone seemed grateful for something to celebrate.

That night Clarissa slipped down the hall to Margot's room, but not to see Henry. Henry was in a sleeping bag on Jamie's floor, and Owen was on the living room couch. Clarissa knocked softly on her sister's door, and Margot folded her reading glasses and closed her book when Clarissa climbed up on the end of the bed.

"Are you in love with him?" Clarissa asked.

"Yes," Margot said.

"Why?"

"Because he's kind and good."

Clarissa hugged her knees in her nightgown.

"I want a baby, and I want to start my life," Margot said. "Owen will be a wonderful father."

Clarissa had never thought about what Henry would be like as a father—she thought mostly about what he was like as a boyfriend. "I feel like I already had a baby," she said.

Margot looked at her sharply.

"Because we were old enough to take care of Jamie," Clarissa said. As she said it, she remembered that Margot hadn't helped with Jamie at all.

"It's not the same as your own," Margot said.

Clarissa shrugged and yawned, suddenly sleepy. She was used to falling asleep in Margot's room, with Henry, but she couldn't fall asleep with Margot. She agreed to be the maid of honor, though she was a little surprised to be asked, and she went back to bed. In the morning Margot left, and Clarissa helped her mother wash sheets and towels.

"I was sure she would marry a Catholic," Yvette said. "I was just sure. But Owen seems like a kind man, doesn't he?"

Clarissa said that he did.

"Margot will be a beautiful bride," her mother said. "I'm still just feeling so shaken and sad."

Clarissa said she understood.

When they packed up Henry's Bug to go back to school, Jamie kept riding his bike with the training wheels up and down the sidewalk. Every time he got to the car, he'd stop and watch them, and say, "Good-bye." Then he'd bike away and back again. "Have a good drive," he'd say. Then to the other corner and back. "Bye."

"You said that already!" Clarissa snapped.

Jamie looked startled. He looked at the ground.

"Oh, sweetie, I'm sorry," Clarissa said. She reached for him, but he pedaled away.

The next time he stopped, he asked, "Can Henry stay here?"

Henry lifted Jamie off the bike and threw him over his shoulder, but Jamie just hung there, limp and sad.

"Tell you what, Bucko," Henry said.

"What?" Jamie's voice was full of suspicion.

"We'll be back before you know it."

"Liar."

"I have to come back for city court." The owner of the *Grocery*

Boy had filed suit against Henry, whose name was on the rental agreement. "You're my star witness," he said.

"No, I'm not."

Henry lowered Jamie to the ground, put his hands on Jamie's shoulders and looked at him. "You want to keep *Meet the Beatles?*" he asked. "You know I'll be back for that."

Jamie thought about it, and nodded, and the two of them wedged themselves solemnly into the backseat of the Bug to flip through Henry's box of LPs. Clarissa sat on the curb feeling guilty, because all she could think about was leaving the house and the street and her little brother on his bike, and her sad parents and the repeating images on the TV, and the neighborhood and the pier and the beach, until she was on the freeway with Henry, mercifully free, going south to weekly quizzes and no TV and a bed where she wasn't Margot, but herself.

When they finally drove away, Henry took his eyes off the road to kiss her, and almost hit a parked car. He grabbed the wheel and looked scared for a second, then smiled and squeezed her hand. She felt the rush of adrenaline fade. He was invincible. He was unflappable. He was hers. He could put her light anywhere he wanted, and for her it would do.

8

YVETTE THOUGHT, when she thought about it, that families change irrevocably with each additional child. As Jamie's mother she was not very much like the woman who had been Margot's mother, or Margot and Clarissa's mother. For example: this Yvette spent her afternoons drinking Thunderbird in the backyard.

Now that she was in her forties, women liked her more, and she had friends from the neighboring houses. They talked and drank and watched the children, until Teddy and the other fathers came home, and it was time to get dinner. Yvette didn't know Thunderbird was for bums; the wives were buying it for themselves, so they bought what was cheap and sweet. It was not very different from Communion wine, and it made each day tumble into the next.

Jamie, the boy she had gone to such lengths for, was not a simple child. It seemed to Yvette that the girls had raised themselves, by comparison. Clarissa had been able to handle him, but when she stopped coming home he ran wild. He learned how locks worked, and how to start cars and steal the best fruit off the neighbors' trees. He rocked his head on his pillow at night in a way that disturbed Yvette: he said he was thinking of music, but he seemed not to be able to control it. He told Yvette solemnly that he knew he'd never get married, because you had to sleep with a woman, and no woman would ever be able to stand his rocking back and forth. He was contrary, and to ask him to do something was to ensure his refusal. He skipped class at Immaculata to throw rocks at birds, and hated going to Mass.

Teddy was no help; he never seemed to connect to Jamie. Jamie was slight and dark, where Teddy was broader faced and blond, and Yvette thought Teddy was put off, without knowing why, by the boy's looks. But he did try. He came home excited one day when Jamie was eight, with a giant cream puff in a paper bag. He put it triumphantly on the table and called Jamie downstairs. Jamie looked at the oversized pastry, uncertain.

"It's a cream puff!" Teddy said.

Jamie sat down in the chair Teddy had pulled out for him, and looked at his father for instructions.

"Well, try it!" Teddy said.

Yvette wanted to give Jamie a fork or a knife, but it wouldn't have helped. It wasn't a good cream puff. The pastry shell was too hard and crusty, and the overwhipped cream stuck to Jamie's fingers and nose. He carried on like a soldier, with a sickly, hopeful smile on his face for Teddy.

"Now, that's about the finest thing there is to eat!" Teddy proclaimed, clapping his son hard on the back. He must have sensed it was a failure, though, because he looked from Yvette to Jamie sadly, before wandering off to his workbench in the garage.

Jamie stared miserably at the ravaged puff. Yvette sat beside him and brushed his dark hair from his forehead.

"Your dad grew up at a time when they didn't have a lot of

treats," she said. "Cream puffs were his favorite, and he wanted you to have one."

Jamie kept staring at the mangled thing.

"Do you see?" she asked. "How he wanted something special for you?"

Jamie nodded.

Yvette leaned close and whispered, "We won't tell him that it wasn't very good."

Jamie smiled, finally—grinned.

Then Teddy took a new job, with more travel, and he was away all the time, and Jamie seemed to get in trouble every time Teddy came home. He was kicked out of Immaculata for offenses the brothers listed apologetically to Yvette, beginning with smoking, unexcused absence, and insubordination. At twelve he drove a car into the ocean, and Teddy said the boy should go to military school.

"Not military school," Yvette said. "Not for him. He just wants your attention."

"Well, he's got it now."

Yvette refused to send Jamie away, and in turn Teddy said the boy was her responsibility, alone. Immaculata wouldn't take him back, and she worried about the trouble he could get into at Hermosa High. Sometimes she confided in Clarissa on the phone, but Clarissa had moved to Hawaii with Henry, and the calls were expensive. Yvette never told Margot that there were problems. Margot was trying to have a baby, and didn't seem to want to know.

One afternoon in the backyard, when the wine had begun to mellow the tension she had felt all morning, someone said the new priest was giving music lessons. The next day Yvette drove Jamie to the church to meet Father Jack, and Jamie pounced on the priest's acoustic guitar in the empty Sunday school room. He could barely speak, he was so excited. He told her on the way home that he hadn't known you could take guitar lessons, and could he take them every day? And why hadn't she told him there were guitar lessons before?

Father Jack was a Jesuit, young and handsome, with dark, unruly hair, and Yvette saw him in town once wearing a black leather jacket and sunglasses, which made her nervous. But Jamie worshiped him. And Jamie changed: instead of breaking into garages, he stayed in his bedroom, practicing chords. He practiced until he was exhausted, and the head-rocking at night stopped because he fell asleep the moment he got into bed.

Then Jamie invited Father Jack to dinner, and Yvette wished he hadn't. Teddy hadn't met the priest yet, and Yvette hadn't told him about the leather jacket: she hoped Father Jack wouldn't wear it. They had priests to dinner all the time, but Father Jack seemed different.

He arrived at the door in vestments, as if he'd understood her worry, and he tucked his sunglasses into a pocket. His hand, when he shook Yvette's, was strong and dry—a guitarist's hand, she imagined—and she felt shy as she led him into the house. He wasn't much older than Margot, and it was silly to get so unsettled.

Jamie jumped up when Father Jack came in, and shook the priest's hand happily. He didn't seem to know what to say then, so Yvette asked the two of them to set the table. She could hear Jamie talking excitedly in the dining room about songs he'd learned, and about a transition between chords that was giving him trouble.

"Come to my room and I'll show you," she heard him say.

"Why don't you bring the guitar out here," Father Jack said, and Yvette was grateful.

"I don't usually practice out here," Jamie said.

"It's fine!" Yvette called, and Jamie ran upstairs to get the guitar. Father Jack came into the kitchen. "He's a great kid," he said. Yvette was trying to work out a reply that wasn't a protest when Jamie came running back down the stairs, guitar in hand. They were hunched over it in the living room, working out the problem, when Teddy came home. The priest stood up right away.

"So this is the famous Father Jack," Teddy said, shaking his hand. "You're the only thing anyone talks about around here."

Jamie blushed, and said, "Dad."

"Your son's a fine guitar player," Father Jack said.

"That's the racket I hear upstairs?" Teddy asked, but Jamie wasn't in the mood to be teased.

"Dad," he said again.

"Oh, right, it's *mu*-sic," Teddy said, drawing out the word.

The evening seemed a disaster, but when they sat down to dinner, Father Jack deferred to Teddy, and drew him out. He had been to the Pacific Islands and Japan before entering the seminary, and he had questions that Yvette had never thought of. They talked about the occupation of Japan, and the future of the royal family. They talked about the role of the geisha in Japanese society, which seemed a bit much for the table, but Yvette was just glad they were talking. Then Father Jack got Jamie going about music, and Teddy didn't make any more wisecracks. He listened, and seemed to have been tamed. Father Jack took second helpings of everything, and said that if Yvette ever wanted to cook for a house full of gray-haired Jesuits, he would take her away from all this. Yvette smiled at him, and glanced at Teddy. He was smiling, too.

"I'd like to hear something on this guitar," Teddy said when the plates were cleared. He followed Jamie to the living room, and Yvette was filled with gratitude.

She carried dishes to the kitchen, and Father Jack came to help. He asked if she would come talk to the catechumens, the learners who were converting to the Church.

She ran hot water from the tap. "Oh, no," she said. "What would I tell them?"

"Anything you wanted," he said. "I guess you'd tell them your experience with faith."

And that was how, standing with her hands in the soapy water, she found herself telling Father Jack what she'd never told anyone except the Mother Superior in Santa Rosa, about praying in the convent and feeling herself lifted out of her body, and knowing that God had spoken to her.

"It was while I was pregnant with Jamie," she said, because being pregnant in Santa Rosa had become part of the story of her life, so much so she almost believed it. "The Mother Superior told me not to do it again."

"Sounds like the old lady was envious," Father Jack said.

Yvette looked up at him, amazed. "Do you think so?"

"Celibacy does things to the brain," he said.

"No," she said.

"Believe me."

Jamie and Teddy came in from the living room with the guitar then, Jamie's face glowing with pride.

That night as she undressed, Yvette thought how glad she was that God had sent her Father Jack.

Teddy, already in bed, put aside his book. "I don't trust that priest," he said.

Yvette was startled. "I thought you liked him."

"He wants you to like him," Teddy said. "Priests shouldn't be charming like that."

"I don't see why not."

"He wants things from people," Teddy said. "He wants something from you."

She didn't tell him what Father Jack had said about celibacy, or about talking to the catechumens. "Like what?"

"I don't know," Teddy said, and his face flushed a little. "I just had this feeling that I didn't want him around you." He looked up at her. "He seems safe because he's a priest but he's not."

"Jamie loves him."

"I want him out of our lives," Teddy said.

They argued the subject up and down for a week, but Teddy held firm. Meanwhile Jamie practiced his guitar constantly, and talked about nothing but Father Jack.

Once again, Yvette devised a plan. Father Jack was leaving for another diocese at the end of the summer, a fact Jamie didn't know. It was a hot summer, with Santa Ana winds out of the desert scorching the air. The little house, which was usually cool, was not. One afternoon when Jamie had collapsed on the couch with the heat, Yvette suggested casually that he visit his sister in Hawaii. Clarissa was teaching high school there, and would be starting summer vacation now.

"Can I really go?" he asked.

Yvette felt a pang at how much he loved Clarissa. It was in his voice. She nodded.

"Can I take my guitar?"

"Of course."

"Is it this hot in Hawaii?"

"I wouldn't think so."

"Cool," Jamie said.

She had already bought his ticket, and she helped him pack his things. He made her promise to tell Father Jack good-bye, and that he'd be back soon. Yvette thought Jamie loved the priest because he needed a man in his life who wouldn't be angry and disappointed. But Clarissa's Henry could be that; he had been it before. And then a visit to Margot would seem only natural, and Owen was so kind—and then Father Jack would be gone, and Teddy's fears, whether founded or not, would be put to rest.

9

THE KENNEDY ASSASSINATION and the ramming of the
Grocery Boy were paired—sacrilegiously, she feared—in Clarissa's
mind, because that day had changed the course of Henry's life,
and so changed hers. Henry had decided to represent himself
against the *Grocery Boy* in city court, and she'd never seen him so
high. He'd been clearly in the wrong, out of control, but he was
under sail and the cabin cruiser was under power, so he won the
case. He changed his major from biology to political science,
and started filling out law school applications that week.

The gap between Clarissa's family and Henry widened: her
parents and Margot returned to the Republicans, but Henry
started stuffing envelopes for the California Democrats. Clarissa
stayed in the lab, where she didn't have to argue about anything:
the Krebs cycle was the Krebs cycle, and cells were cells.

In 1968, when Henry was in law school at UCLA, he took her
to see the people thronging Sunset Boulevard, passing out flowers.

There were boys in robes and moccasins, and perfectly beautiful girls with long, loose hair, barefoot in the median. Henry was talking about the grape strike and Cesar Chavez, but Clarissa was thinking about what her father would say about the vacant-looking, half-dressed girls in the street. Her mother liked the strike leader because his people were so poor and had such faith, but her father said Chavez was a communist. He brought home grapes when he could find them on the shelves. Clarissa wasn't sure, but she felt that Henry was right, that the changes were important and necessary.

Henry went to the Ambassador Hotel the night Bobby Kennedy won the primary, with people who'd been working on the campaign. They thought they might be able to talk to the senator, and were moving through the crowd in the direction he had gone, when they heard shots from the kitchen—though they didn't know it was the kitchen then. Henry stayed for hours, in the hotel and then in the street, while Clarissa waited at his apartment, not knowing where he was. Witnesses were questioned and rumors moved through the crowd, and finally Henry came home with his hands shaking and tears on his face, a thing she had never seen.

It was his last year of law school, and Henry wrote a paper for his ethics class on the inequities of the 2S draft deferment for students. It wasn't fair, he argued, that poor men went to Vietnam while middle-class white boys stayed in school just to stay out of the rice paddies. His professor, who had just approved Henry for Ph.D. work after law school, gave him an A-, and a thoughtful look.

The next year they dropped the student deferment, and announced the draft lottery. Each day of the year would be drawn, and the young men with the first-drawn birthdays would be drafted, whether they were in school or married or not. It was beautifully fair, and Henry told Clarissa he appreciated its fairness, without being happy about it at all.

The week before the lottery was drawn, Henry stood Clarissa up for dinner, drove out to the desert and parked off the road. It wasn't until later that she knew where he had gone. It was December, and getting cold as the light faded, but he walked straight into an empty stretch of sand. When it got dark, he stopped. He thought about what it would be like to go to Mexico or Canada and never come back, and how Clarissa with her war-hero father would never forgive him, and he with his high-minded essay topics would never forgive himself. Then he threw down a sleeping bag and climbed in, and watched the moon come up, slowly, and sink back down. In the last of the moon-light, he got up to pee. He walked away from his sleeping bag, thinking to keep the urine smell out of his camp, but as he walked back he missed the bag. The moon was yellow on the horizon, very faint, and the ground in every direction looked the same: dark patches of waist-high scrub, and lighter patches of sand. He'd left his flashlight in the car and he was naked from the waist down, and the cold was sharp now. He thought it was cold enough to snow, though there were no clouds, which only made it darker. He walked back and forth, crisscrossing the area east and west, north and south, wishing he'd counted his steps at the start, not knowing how he'd overshot his camp. He couldn't tell if he was doubling back too far or not far enough. He scraped his bare legs on scrub he couldn't see. Each place he got to looked like the last.

As the moon disappeared, the idea that he would be freezing alone all night seized his heart. He didn't think he would die, but it was very dark and he had started to shiver. He would spend the night crouched and pantless in the scrub, because he was afraid to be a man and go to war. The shame and self-pity of it made him sick, and he could feel the bile in his throat when he finally stumbled on his sleeping bag. He collapsed on the slippery nylon in relief, and made himself breathe until the nausea went away.

In the morning he woke to harsh sun and the sight of his own lost footprints everywhere. He packed up, hiked back to his car, drove home, and joined the Navy. When he was able to talk about it, he told Clarissa he couldn't stand to take his chances in the lottery, and the Navy would keep him farthest from the war.

Clarissa stayed home with him on the night of the lottery, on the couch in front of the TV. The capsules were drawn from a tall glass jar, with the birthdays on slips of paper inside. There were lottery parties all over campus, people gathered around TV's in dorms and frat houses, and Clarissa and Henry could hear shouting when the first birthdays were drawn—September 14, April 24, December 30. The slips kept coming, but none of them was Henry's. Then the TV stopped reporting the numbers, because everyone knew that none of the last boys would go. When they checked the newspaper the next day, they found Henry's birthday, April 12, at 346 out of 365.

The Navy had him, though, and Clarissa drove him to Watts for an exam, where he stood in a warehouse in a circle with a hundred other naked men, and a doctor came around the room and checked them out. Clarissa waited in the car with the doors locked, and caught herself saying Hail Marys under her breath, hoping Henry would fail the physical and have an honorable way to stay home. But he passed all the tests, as they knew he would. He was ridiculously healthy. When he came back out to the car, Clarissa heard a boy on a pay phone on the street, crying.

"I *told* them about the asthma, Mother," the boy said. "They didn't care! I *knew* we should have tried for CO."

The Navy was slow in deciding what to do with Henry. First

they sent him to boot camp, where he wrote to Clarissa that he felt very old, at twenty-five. Then they put him to work in their legal affairs office, then they sent him to Hawaii. When he finally had his interview in Honolulu, with a trim, pretty lieutenant in a skirted uniform, she cocked her head at him and looked at his shoulders.

"Did you play football?" she asked.

Henry said he had.

"You could sign up for Shore Patrol."

Henry pretended to think about it, but he knew he couldn't be a cop. "I don't think I'd be suited for it," he said.

She tapped her pencil against his file. "What made you go to law school?"

He told her about ramming the *Grocery Boy*, about the lawsuit and changing his major.

"And you chose the Navy?" she said, smiling.

"As long as you're not using sailboats," Henry said, "I'll be fine."

She left the room and was gone for twenty minutes, then came back with a job that she presented to him like a gift. He could stay in Honolulu and do legal work for the generals.

"The *Grocery Boy* just kept you out of Saigon," she said.

She saw him out with a friendly handshake, and he started work for the generals, and sent for Clarissa. They were married quickly by a Navy priest, to satisfy Yvette. Clarissa only cared that the wedding was nothing like Margot's: all that fuss, and Margot ordering bridesmaids around, and the choir and incense and the long Mass, and poor Owen looking propped-up and dazed, and Margot beaming like a princess. Clarissa wore a cotton sundress and sandals to the priest's office, and Henry sent her parents a telegram: HITCHED. THANKS FOR BEAUTIFUL DAUGHTER. PROGENY PROMISED TO POPE.

Teddy and Yvette sent a tablecloth and bed linens, addressed to Mr. and Mrs. Henry Collins, and wished them luck.

"At first I was upset, not to see you married," her mother wrote.

But then I prayed, and I realized I was married in the same way, quickly, before a war. I feel you and I are soulmates, and I wish you the happiness I have had.

Clarissa put the letter away. She didn't want her mother's version of happiness. She had her own. The Navy's married housing in Honolulu was in termite-infested two-story barracks, but Clarissa loved living with Henry, and felt like they'd moved into a palace. She took a job teaching biology at the high school, where her students called her Miss Collins, and she made picnic dinners on the beach, spreading the tablecloth her mother had intended for china and silver out on the sand. Her mother told her not to wear miniskirts to teach in, but she wore them anyway. She wore shorts made of soft cotton rice sacks, and went grocery shopping in her bikini. People might look twice, but not in disapproval. Everyone did it. She had never been so happy in her life.

Henry had a harder time. One of his jobs was writing wills for officers, and so many men were going to Saigon that Henry felt overcome by the weight of their belongings. The officers dispensed with money easily, but they pondered over the *things*, staring at the yellow notebook Henry gave them for making lists. A fly rod to a son, a camera to a nephew, a watch to a newborn baby, a flat-bottomed johnboat to a brother. They never knew what to leave to daughters. Henry said that by the time he saw them to the door, the men smelled like nervous sweat, and so did he.

Clarissa knew Henry thought about death all day, so when

she missed her period she went to the doctor alone, and then offered the news to her husband the way the pretty lieutenant had offered him the job: as a gift, as rescue. Henry said it felt like the closest thing to the existence of God. He gave her a cutout picture of a baby, pasted to a Navy requisition form with a request for: "One (1) Green-eyed Baby Girl."

"I don't want a girl," Clarissa said, more bitterly than she expected to. She was sitting up in their rumpled bed in the converted barracks, looking at the requisition. "Then the next one would have an older sister."

Henry shook his head and looked confused.

"Like Margot," she said.

Henry wrapped his arms around her waist and laughed, burying his face in her growing belly. "She won't be like Margot," he said. "I promise you one firstborn girl baby who is nothing like Margot."

Clarissa hugged his head, but she didn't accept.

10

Hawaii, when he got there, was like a place Jamie made up. Henry had speakers set up on the deck of the barracks for listening to music and watching the blue ocean out over the city. And he still had the best records, Dylan and Cream, and crazy-sounding Hawaiian music and things Jamie had never heard of. They sat together on the deck, and Jamie picked out chords on the guitar, learning the songs—except the Hawaiian ones, which were twelve-string and impossible. Once, when no one else was around, Henry let him have a hit off a joint, and the music was so good, and the water was so blue.

Clarissa had started a garden in a little patch of bare ground, and from the deck they watched her weeding in shorts. She was pregnant but you couldn't really tell yet. Her hair was long and straight to the middle of her back, and she tucked it behind her ears. She wore a shell bracelet on one ankle, and seeing it against her skin sometimes gave Jamie a boner he had to hide. The three of them went for hikes, and Clarissa slid naked down waterfalls into deep green pools, and her breasts looked like fried eggs. Henry showed Jamie how to squeeze the awapuhi plant, and they used the thick goo to wash their hair. They picked moki-hana for necklaces and dried the beads so they wouldn't get a rash, and they played water polo with Navy guys in the pool at the base. Clarissa was good, splashing and fighting for the ball. In a bikini she had a little stomach, because of the baby, but she still looked hot.

They caught fish or bought it from old Hawaiian men, and Henry grilled it, and they drank beer from cans with dinner. They always gave Jamie one, too, even though he was only twelve. Henry was a Great Westerner, which meant there was a force in everything, so they didn't even have to go to church.

Then Jamie found Henry's pot stash and smoked some alone at the barracks, and Henry found out. He didn't shout, like Teddy would have: he asked what Jamie had been thinking, and then he got quiet. He didn't say anything, but his disappoint-ment was in the air like a bad smell. It was everywhere, and Jamie knew it was his fault. Henry didn't tell Clarissa, and Jamie wasn't going to tell her if Henry didn't. He had hoped—and now he was ashamed to admit it—that he might move to Hawaii when he was out of high school, to live with them. Now he knew that was fucked. Henry and Clarissa's life, where grown-ups had the best records and slid down waterfalls, was another thing he couldn't have for himself. Like getting married and sleeping with a woman if you were a chronic head-rocker. He wanted to go home and be with Father Jack, and dress like Father Jack, and play guitar.

When his mother called, he asked her to bring him home, but she said he had to go to Margot's next, and spend the rest of the summer in Louisiana.

"I want to come home," he said. "I have new songs to show Father Jack."

"But Margot wants to see you, honey," Yvette said.

"Do I have to?"

"Honey. What if Margot heard you say that?"

"Tell Father Jack about the songs."

"Of course I will," his mother said.

So he flew to Louisiana, which was hotter than California had ever been, and sticky and wet. At Margot's, you couldn't put your feet up on the furniture, or play loud music, or eat dinner at eleven if no one was hungry before then. Grown-ups at Margot's house didn't smoke pot. They didn't swear. He swam in the backyard pool, but no one skinny-dipped, even though the hedges were so high the neighbors couldn't see in. Margot never even swam, and Jamie didn't have the hots for her. She barely spoke to him. Her husband, Owen, was nice enough but always at work. There was a black woman named Rosa who cleaned and cooked, but Jamie had never known a black person before, and she made him shy when she came through the house in her peach dress, with the vacuum cleaner, smiling at him. He stayed in the guest room and practiced songs to show Father Jack, and waited to go home.

On the plane, with his guitar stashed overhead, he practiced the fingering for "Absolutely Sweet Marie" in the air, and rocked his head against the headrest until the lady beside him got up and moved.

Finally back in his own house, he wanted to call Father Jack right away, but his mother said he should wait. After the enchiladas she made because they were his favorite, and the lime sherbet, she said Father Jack had been called to another diocese, where he was needed more. His father said nothing during this announcement, but looked at his empty ice cream bowl. Jamie asked if Father Jack had left a message for him, and his mother said that he hadn't: no message, no note.

That night Jamie looked back on the summer, and considered it seriously. He tried to think if there was a single person he felt loyalty to, a single one of them who was worth it. He tried to imagine that he was dead, to see if they would be sad. He decided they wouldn't. And he guessed he felt the same about them.

11

MARGOT COULDN'T HAVE a baby. As a married woman, with a kind husband with a good job, she couldn't get pregnant at all: she found it impossible to re-create the thing that had happened so effortlessly in Mr. Tucker's parked car. At twenty-six she was finally pregnant, but miscarried after three months. The next year she carried a baby four months before losing it. She was going to tell the doctor what she thought he must already know: that she had once carried a child to term. She thought the information might help. But in his office, before she spoke, the doctor had looked at her strangely and asked if there was something about pregnancy that made her anxious. She was so angry she changed doctors the next week, and there had been nothing since.

When she was twenty-eight, M. Planchet wrote her a letter from France. "*Chère* Margot," it said:

How did the baby grow up? Do you have more? My son Jean-Pierre has no children, he only makes money, and so I think of yours. Come to see us again. We are just the two of us here. Je t'embrasse.

She hid the letter in her locked diary, and didn't reply.

It didn't help to be living in the South. The wives of Owen's colleagues had all been debutantes together, and were raising their children together, and had no room in their circle for a new childless wife. The women in the church were the same. The only non-Southern wife was a loud, friendly girl from Michigan who had five children: she had created her own circle, and didn't have time for the debs, even if they had wanted her. Margot thought it was brilliant.

Some days her principal companion was her housekeeper, Rosa, but Rosa, too, had children—four, that she couldn't afford—and Margot resented her for it. She felt the desire for a baby in the pit of her stomach. She dreamed about being pregnant, and woke to the disappointment of being awake, alone, with Owen already at work. She wondered if her body were poison to children.

Then her mother called and asked her to let Jamie come stay. That night she dreamed of chasing a two-year-old Jamie through the house. She caught him behind the curtains and was going to eat him, and have him in her belly, and she woke in a sweat.

But she couldn't say no, so Jamie arrived, a thin and sullen twelve-year-old. Having him in her house was torture. If he hadn't been born, she might have a baby now. Or he might have been her baby. She felt a sudden anger at her mother for taking away her only chance, and then remorse for the anger. What would she have done with a baby at sixteen? She hadn't wanted the baby then, and would have been a terrible mother, and it would have ruined her life.

When her path crossed Jamie's in the house, they both seemed startled. She saw Mr. Tucker in his face: the man who'd waltzed her all over the gym floor, and guided her so effortlessly out to his car. Owen was cheerful and friendly to the boy—he had no idea. But she could barely be civil. She knew Jamie was puzzled, but the guilt only made it worse. She was relieved when he finally went away.

12

JAMIE FIRST SAW Gail in 1975, when he was sixteen, after a party on the beach where everyone got shitfaced and paired off. The girl Jamie ended up with got cold and sick, and went home. Jamie slept—or tried to sleep—huddled in the ice plant against the cliff, with his sweatshirt over his head, as far from the water as he could get. When the sun came up, he stumbled down the beach to pee, and there was a girl he didn't recognize, sitting up in the dead coals in the fire pit, black with ash on one side of her face and clothes. She grinned at him.

"Hey," she said.

Jamie was still mostly asleep. The girl's skin was pale where it wasn't smeared with ash, and her hair was dark, and rising up from the fire pit she looked like a ghost.

"Go take your piss," she said. "Don't let me stop you."

Jamie shuffled down to the water.

Before he had finished, the girl was standing next to him, and he quickly zipped his jeans. A big wave came toward their feet, and Jamie stepped back as the water swirled white on the beach. The girl stripped quickly, threw her clothes on dry sand, waded out into the surf, and dived in. Jamie watched her go. Her whole body was white. When Clarissa swam naked, she always had a tan line from her swimsuit. This girl had nothing, not even a shadow around her ass. But she was a good swimmer.

"You coming?" she called. Her face was clean now, the ash all washed away.

Jamie glanced behind him. The few people still on the beach were starting to wake up. The morning was misty and gray and the water looked cold. He knew his chest was skinny. He was still getting his nerve up, deciding which clothes to take off first, when the girl waded back up the sand.

"Too late," she said. "It's freezing out there."

She was so thin and white she looked carved out of soap, and the wet black patch of hair below her belly button was shocking to him. Her breasts were small but they were neat and round as she stooped to pick up her ashy clothes and pulled on her jeans.

"Why'd you sleep in the fire pit?" he asked.

She rolled her eyes. "It was warm there, dopey," she said. She shook out her wet hair over the sand. "Want breakfast?"

At the Surf Shack, Gail ordered pancakes and bacon and ate hungrily. Jamie pushed away a plate of eggs.

"You're Jamie Santerre," she said. "You ran a car into the water once."

Jamie nodded.

"You've never seen me at school," she said.

Jamie shook his head.

"I saw the girl you were with last night," she said.

"She got sick," he said.

Gail grinned. "So did you." She ate some more of her pancakes, then slid out of the vinyl booth, leaving a trail of ash from her jeans.

"C'mere," she said. "I wanna show you something."

Jamie followed her past the kitchen, where the dishwasher was clanking dishes, to the bathrooms in the narrow hallway in the back. She looked into the ladies' room to see if it was empty, then pulled Jamie in and locked the door behind them. For the second time that morning, she pulled off her shirt with no embarrassment at all. She took his hands and slid them down inside her jeans. The jeans were still damp from her swim, but her skin was smooth and warm.

"We have to be quick," she whispered. Then her hands were in his pants, too, and her pants were down, and she had hopped her bare ass up on the edge of the sink and wrapped her legs around him. Jamie, who was only a sophomore, had never expected anything like this.

After that, they were always together. Jamie's mother didn't like Gail; Gail wore scruffy jeans and tank tops with no bra. But he didn't care what his mother thought. He liked the tank tops. Gail made him laugh, and she always knew what he was thinking, and she wanted to have sex all the time. She wanted to do it as much as guys did. She bought him a giant box of rubbers after making him pull out at the Surf Shack, and he tried to imagine her paying for it at the drugstore. They did it in the supply closet in the art hall at school, and in the pottery studio with the smell of clay from the uneven pots on the tables. Gail hung out in the art hall, which was why he'd never seen her before, and she had keys to everything. They did it in the city pool at night, climbing over the fence. They did it on the sink in the Surf Shack ladies' room, for old times' sake. When the drama club put on *Oklahoma!*

they did it backstage in the surrey with the fringe on top. There was a set of reins in the surrey, long thin leather straps; Gail looped them once around his wrists, and held his wrists over his head, and he almost came before he got inside her.

There were bathrobe ties in both their houses, and long-sleeved shirts and belts. There were scarves in his sisters' rooms, and long white evening gloves, and old silk stockings with runs. Jamie had briefly been a Boy Scout—his father's bad idea—but Gail was better at knots than he was. They tied each other to bedposts and chairs and doorknobs and car doors, and if there was nothing to tie, Gail just held his wrists, or he caught her hands in one of his, and either way was enough to send him right over the edge. She gave him a magazine full of girls in leather, as a joke, and he kept it under his mattress. He looked at it so often that the thought of it in class could make his eyes glaze over, and send him looking for Gail in the five-minute passing time, just to kiss her at her locker and know what she was willing to do.

He learned to play the songs Gail liked on the guitar, by listening to records. It made her laugh to have him play something sweet, like "Michelle," and then put down the guitar and tie her up. Sometimes he picked up the guitar again and serenaded her, raising his eyebrows and tilting his head like early Paul McCartney, while she giggled and writhed on the bed. He changed lyrics, and made up new ones for her:

> Gai-il, my snail,
> Is the snail I'm going to nail right now
> Nai-il right now . . .

He made up nicer ones, too, but those didn't make her laugh so much.

When they heard his mother or father pull up in a car, they

scrambled to untie knots and put on clothes and get into some tableau of innocence: playing-guitar-watching-TV-drinking-Cokes-fully-clothed. Condom wrappers and bathrobe ties shoved under the couch. When his father found them that way, Gail gave him these outrageous smiles. Teddy always looked away and mumbled some nervous hello. When she stayed for dinner, she sat next to his father, and Teddy would stumble over the grace. Gail could imitate him perfectly, clasping her hands: "Lord, w-we thank you for this f-food. . . ." At dinner, she'd sneak a socked foot into Jamie's crotch under the table, just past his father's knees.

The amazing thing was that Jamie wasn't ashamed with Gail, ever. It wasn't like being hot for Clarissa in shorts, or getting a boner in school. Gail liked it all. She'd started it. It was like the way she'd stripped on the beach that first morning: she wasn't embarrassed, so after a while he wasn't either. They would graduate in June, and Gail would go to art school, and he would play guitar in a band. They spent hours deciding between Seattle, where she had an aunt, and Louisiana, where Margot might be able to help him out, and Rhode Island, where there was a good art school but they didn't know anyone. They talked about the apartment they would get, the jobs they would take. And they would be together. Jamie couldn't believe his luck.

13

IN APRIL OF Jamie's senior year, Yvette missed her bathrobe tie and found it in Jamie's room, tied expertly to the headboard of his bed. Confused, she made his bed while she thought about it, and under the mattress she found a dog-eared magazine full of girls in leather costumes with whips. She left the magazine on the bed and cleaned the whole house in a fury.

When Jamie came home she gave him some time, then went again to his room. He was lying on his stomach on the smooth bedspread, next to the magazine, his face pressed into the pillows. He looked up, his face flushed and his eyes bright. "What were you doing in here?" he demanded.

"You're only seventeen," she said.

"Eighteen."

"What would that girl think?"

"Her name's Gail," he said. "She knows."

"I'm not going to tell your father about this."

"That's good."

Yvette couldn't help it; she started to cry. "I don't want you to see that girl anymore."

"Her name's Gail."

"I want you to look into your heart," she said. "Into your soul. And see if you think this is right."

That night Jamie refused to come to dinner. His ears were still bright red with shame, and he said his stomach hurt, and he couldn't eat. When Gail called, he refused to speak to her, and said to tell her he wasn't home. Yvette didn't say anything to the girl about the magazine or the bathrobe tie, because what would she say?

Jamie didn't call Gail back that night, or the next night either. There were parties for graduation, but Jamie stayed in his room. Yvette blamed herself for the situation, but she didn't know what to say to make it right.

Then she had to stop thinking about it, because her sister Adele called and said their father, who was ninety, had gone into the bathroom that morning and hadn't come out. When their mother finally went in after him, she found him collapsed over a sink full of blood. Adele asked if Yvette would take the first shift at home, so Yvette was on a plane to Canada the next morning, and found her mother in shock, and her father in a coma. She played solitaire by her father's hospital bed for three days, while her mother sat with her hands in her lap. On the third day her father died, never regaining consciousness. Yvette took her mother home.

They were quiet in the car, but when they arrived at the front door of the little house, Yvette's mother began a tirade in a shrill, hoarse voice that wasn't her own.

"I won't mourn him!" Lenore said. "You don't know what a tyrant he was! He was worn out by the time you came along, but he never let up on your sister! Or on me!"

"Mother," Yvette said.

"It's true! The only women who were pure were his sister Rosalie and the Blessed Virgin. The rest of us were faithless whores. And I could tell you a few things about Rosalie!"

Yvette helped her mother inside the house. She sat her down at the kitchen table, and turned on a light. The kitchen hadn't changed since her childhood, and now it looked like a museum exhibit. Home Life in the Depression: respectability clung to through tidiness and thrift. The weak light didn't help.

"Papa didn't think I was a whore," she said quietly.

"You should've heard him when you married that flyboy!" Lenore said, in the same harridan's voice. "He was good to you, and then you left without a thought, his favorite, so young—just up and left, his little girl. Adele had reason to leave, he was harder on her."

Yvette thought of her father bringing her sister home from dances, and car doors slamming, and her father's rage at the dress with rum punch spilled down the front. She winced, as she always did, at the thought that she had found the dress and turned her sister in. He had stopped speaking to Adele for a month.

"He was hardest on *me*," her mother said, losing steam. "But I never left."

Yvette's earliest clear memory came to her, of her parents' voices downstairs late one night. "It isn't true, Leo! It isn't true!" her mother was crying, and Yvette got out of bed and tore downstairs to their bedroom. She threw herself at her father's legs and said, "Leave her alone!" Her father had looked at her strangely, and said he was sorry, then carried her back to her room in his arms.

"You weren't supposed to leave," Yvette said. "You were his wife, not his daughter."

"Oh, and I loved him!" her mother said. "You should have heard him beg for forgiveness. You'd understand."

The autopsy was performed the next day. It revealed he had no liver left at all; it had slowly eaten itself away, and he had finally hemorrhaged into his esophagus and collapsed from loss of blood. The pathologist asked if her father had ever been jaundiced. Yvette remembered him taking a tonic he called porter—beer mixed with molasses and an egg—for his bad blood. But it had never seemed strange to Yvette. He was her father. Nothing about him seemed strange.

After the outburst, Lenore grew fiercely repentant. She begged Yvette's forgiveness, and said none of it was true, that Yvette's father was a sainted man. Then she retreated into her room, refusing to eat or to discuss his medical history. "Leo was never sick a day," she said, and she shut the door in Yvette's face.

Yvette sat alone at the table in the ancient kitchen, going through his papers and what medical records there were. Leo Grenier, b. 1887, d. 1977. Spouse: Lenore Theveneau Grenier, b. 1889. He'd been in the hospital in 1929, when Yvette was six. Yvette knocked on her mother's door to ask about it, but her mother said, "Go away." So she called Adele, who'd been thirteen.

"Dad had the store then," her sister said. "It was Prohibition in the States, and he sold whiskey out of the basement. Mother likes to point out that he never actually *ran* the whiskey—American bootleggers came over the river from Detroit to pick it up. One night three men tried to rob him, and when Dad stood his ground they shot him in the gut. The bullet must have grazed his liver. Don't you remember how yellow he was?"

"No," Yvette said. "He was always tan."

"Yellow tan," her sister said. "Are you doing all right? Is she all right?"

Yvette decided not to mention the things their mother had said, because it seemed not to be their mother who had said them. She said everything was fine.

Then she called her oldest brother, Joe, who'd had such a hard time with their father. He said the gunshot story was true. But he said Dad had gotten off a shot, too, and hit one of the men in the neck. Only two of the American bootleggers made it back to Detroit that night, so they must've dumped their dead partner in the river.

"Dad had a gun?" Yvette asked.

"Of course," her brother said. "A thirty-eight. I wish I knew what happened to it."

"He's so full of shit," Adele said, when Yvette called back to confirm Joe's story. "Joey didn't even live there then. How would he know?"

Yvette had been trying to accept her father as a killer, and now she was confused. "Dad didn't do it?"

"He might've shot a man over Mother, but not over whiskey. Joey's making that up."

"You think Dad shot a man over Mother?"

"Oh, God," her sister said. "No. I don't know. I just mean he would have."

It was dinnertime, and Yvette made scrambled eggs and toast for her mother, who refused to eat it. So Yvette sat alone in the kitchen, eating the food herself, as the sky grew dark outside. She remembered the cases of whiskey in the basement, and some trouble about them. She thought now that she remembered her father being sick. She tried to remember talking to him about anything important. He'd never said a word to her about his liver, devouring itself all these years, or about her mother, after the day Yvette threw herself at his knees, or about Joe leaving home so young. But still she felt she'd had a bond with him that hadn't needed any words.

Her sister came, brusque and capable, to help with the funeral and take a shift with their mother, and Yvette flew home to find Jamie still in a funk. His girlfriend, Gail, had taken a job waitressing for her aunt in Seattle, and the next day she was gone on a Greyhound bus. Jamie did nothing but lie facedown on his bed, miserable. He let Yvette sit beside him sometimes, if she didn't try to touch him or comfort him.

While Yvette was wondering what to do, her sister called to say that their mother was still refusing food, and Adele had to go back to work. They would have to find a nursing home, but in the meantime Yvette must come back.

Teddy protested. "You can't leave us here again," he said. "We don't know what to eat."

So Yvette was making up a shopping list of things that didn't have to be cooked—bananas and ice cream and sandwich bread—when Clarissa called to say she was unhappy in her marriage and wanted to come home.

Yvette lost all patience, standing there on the phone. She had received no tenderness from anyone since her father had died, and she felt suddenly that they deserved none from her. She had warned Clarissa not to marry that man.

"I won't be here," she said, not believing her own sharp tone. "My mother needs me. My father has died, as you know. I'm very sorry about Henry, but I don't know what I can do about it right now."

There was a silence on the other end of the line. Yvette looked up to see Teddy watching her in astonishment from the living room, and Jamie watching her from the hall. She said good-bye to Clarissa and threw away her shopping list.

"You can go to McDonald's," she told them.

"How can you talk to Clar like that?" Jamie asked.

"Like what?" she snapped, though she knew what he meant.

"Did she want to come stay?"

"She doesn't know what she wants."

"Is she coming?"

"No."

"She could cook for us," Jamie said.

It wasn't a bad idea, but Yvette was too angry now to concede. "She has a husband and child of her own to cook for."

"Can I go there?"

She heard the longing in Jamie's voice, and resented it. "No," she said. "Now I have to go pack."

She stood, not looking at either of them, and tried to edge past Jamie down the dark hall to her room, but Jamie grabbed her as she passed, and shook her hard by the shoulders. She was too surprised to do anything. His face was an angry blur in the half-light.

"You drove her away!" he said, his voice hoarse. "Like you drove Gail away! You drive everyone good away! I hate you! I hate you!"

He was still shaking her, hard, and her head bumped against the wall and she thought she might faint, and then Teddy tackled Jamie, and they all fell in a heap in the hall.

"I hate you, too!" Jamie shouted at Teddy. In kicking himself free of the pile, he caught Teddy under the jaw with his shoe. He scrambled down the hall to his room and slammed the door.

Teddy stood up in silence, rubbing his jaw, went to the kitchen phone, and called the police. Yvette sat in the hallway, dizzy from the shaking, too upset to cry. Jamie came back out of his room with a duffel bag and a jacket, and stepped over Yvette in the hall. He spoke to neither of them, but left the house, got in the old Ford Escort that Teddy let him use, and drove away.

When the police arrived, Yvette smoothed her hair, answered the door, and told the young officer that it had all been a mistake.

PART II

To her master, or rather her father, husband, or rather
brother; his handmaid, or rather his daughter, wife, or
rather sister . . .

—Héloïse to Abelard

Oh! I love Him! . . . My God . . . I love You!

—Last words, Saint Thérèse of Lisieux

14

WHEN THE NAVY was through with Henry, he didn't want to be a lawyer anymore. He told Clarissa he could either sit back and watch men like Nixon run the country, and complain about it, or he could try to change things. So they moved with the baby to Sebastopol, California, north of San Francisco, where he could run for the state legislature in a district that might elect a Democrat. Clarissa had wanted to stay in Hawaii, but Henry didn't stand a chance there, as an outsider.

The Navy packed everything in boxes and moved it to California, including three dead Honolulu cockroaches with wings. The new house in Sebastopol was five miles from Santa Rosa and the convent where Clarissa's mother had spent her third pregnancy, but Yvette, when Clarissa told her, didn't seem interested in that fact, and it wasn't a pilgrimage Clarissa felt like making.

Henry went to every door campaigning, listening to voters'

problems and explaining what he wanted to do. His newspaper ad was a picture of him smiling with their daughter, Abby, in his arms. Clarissa kept it on the refrigerator to remind her there was a time when Henry was around long enough to pick Abby up and smile at her. He had gotten the green-eyed baby girl he wanted, like he got everything he wanted, and then he won his election and went off to Sacramento for the session, leaving Clarissa alone in a strange town with his child.

Clarissa had always had a sense of possibilities, of many versions of life available to her, and now she seemed to be stuck with the one. When she had gone with Henry to Hawaii, it didn't feel like giving anything up. It felt like all new possibilities: waterfalls and picking moki-hana and flirting with high school students and drawing up lesson plans. When Abby was born, Clarissa had stopped teaching, but having a baby seemed like a new life, too. She learned about breast-feeding, and read books about brain development. She made notes about her own childhood, comparisons. She knew she'd been given formula and got colic, and when she'd screamed, her father had pushed her bassinet out on the service porch. And Jamie had colic on a bottle. So she breast-fed for nearly two years, and it worked. Abby never had colic—never once. But then Abby began to announce in public, "I want your nittle," and it got embarrassing to have a breast-feeding child who could speak and overhear things. "The milk is fucked," Abby said once, when she couldn't get any more. Clarissa knew her parents would be appalled.

About the time she stopped breast-feeding, Clarissa became afraid, to the point of panic, that God would call her to be a nun, and she would have to leave her baby behind. She hadn't baptized Abby, and hadn't gone to Mass since she left home, but she couldn't ignore God's call. What would she do? She told herself it wasn't rational. She missed having the baby at her breast, and was looking for a new intimacy, a new set of things to know: prayers and matins to replace the constant feedings. But she couldn't explain it away. The fear spread physically from behind her breastbone, and she was overcome. It came one afternoon while she hung sheets outside on the line. She dropped the clothespins and touched her chest; it was so strong she thought the fear itself might be the call. She looked at Abby, riding a wooden wagon across the lawn, with infinite sadness. How would she say good-bye?

When the panic subsided, Clarissa put Abby in the car and drove to Santa Rosa. She found a Catholic church, and asked the man practicing the organ if there was a convent in town, then followed his directions to an old Victorian house on a quiet street. With Abby on her hip, she knocked on the door. A woman answered, wearing blue jeans and an embroidered blouse; her hair curled around her face, the color of honey.

"Oh," Clarissa said. "I thought—I was looking for nuns."

"I'm so sorry," the woman said. "Did you know them?"

"No."

"They were old," the woman said, as if apologizing. "Most of them had died when we bought the house. A few went to rest homes, and one went to a convent in Detroit, I think. That was in sixty-nine."

Clarissa nodded.

"You must be Catholic," the woman said. "I always feel awful, when someone comes looking. Do you want to come in?"

She showed Clarissa all the rooms, and explained how she'd found period wallpaper for the walls, and furniture built before 1910.

"The nuns had terrible furniture," the woman said. "I guess they have to. It came with the house, so I had it all taken out. The place had a funny smell, too. But they had a great laundry room, with a great view." She flipped on the light to brighten the yellow walls of the room with the washer and dryer. The window looked over the houses and green trees beyond.

At home, Clarissa wrote a letter on a legal pad of Henry's that Abby had been using for drawing paper. "Mom," she wrote.

I saw your old convent today, but it isn't a convent now. The order sold it to a Lutheran family named Hansen. I don't think you ever said how beautiful it was. What was it like there? I've been thinking about the call. Did you ever think you might get it?

She waited for a response, checking the mailbox every day, and putting off laundry in case the fear at the clothesline came over her again.

"Honey," her mother wrote back, on pale pink stationery. The penciled handwriting was nearly illegible; on the delicate paper it looked like a pattern for lace.

I went to the convent because your Dad and I were having difficulties, and I was nervous about the baby. I was very far from God then, but He came to me in the convent, and showed me that our purpose on this earth is to love Him. He loves us so, even with our flaws.

I think from your letter that you're worried about the Call. But God knows that Abby needs you, honey. He's not going to take you away. You can serve Him every day, in your life with your family. That's your vocation.

There was more at the end of the page, but her mother had erased it. Clarissa held the paper up to the light, and made out something about a priest, and celibacy being difficult. She reflected that celibacy wouldn't be much different from what she had now. Over the top of the erasure was written, "Love from your Dad and from me, Mom."

Clarissa spent a long time looking at the letter, thinking how much easier her mother's life seemed than her own, how content and fulfilled. The panic stopped coming; she was able to hang the laundry in peace, while Abby trucked along on the wagon. But then she felt bereft, because all of her possibilities seemed gone, swallowed up in washing diapers and finger painting and cooking carrots, the little details that made up her one life. She tried to make the details elaborate and purposeful, and full of ritual: she made her own yogurt, saving some to start the next batch. She baked her own bread, while Abby skated across the kitchen floor with her socked feet in the bread pans. She used cloth diapers instead of disposables. But she didn't feel like she was serving God. She felt like she was serving Henry and Abby, and it didn't feel anything like a vocation.

When Henry came home, with drafts of bills to read, she said that if they were going to make this marriage work, they couldn't live apart. He was too busy and too tired to argue very long, so she went with him to Sacramento, and moved into the tiny apartment he kept there. She took Abby to watch the debates, and made friends with Henry's colleagues, and met lobbyists in the halls. Henry accused her of flirting with them, but she was only talking about the bills—and if the lobbyists liked her, so what? It could be useful. They said she had good ideas. She thought about becoming a lobbyist, too; she might be good at the research and the persuasion. But on three different afternoons she wanted to listen to important hearings, so she left Abby playing on the lobby carpet, just outside the chambers, perfectly safe. And each time, someone found Abby crying in a marble hallway somewhere else, with a full cloth diaper, and took her to Henry in committee, and Henry came out of his committee to find Clarissa. The first time it happened he smiled and said, "I have a job, Clar, and it's to stay in that meeting." The second time he just said, "Diaper." The third time he handed Abby over silently, with a dark look, and that was the end of Clarissa's lobbying career. She moved back to Sebastopol, less happy than ever. She believed Henry was fighting the good fight, but neither he nor the good fight seemed to need her.

It wasn't until Abby was seven that Clarissa got her nerve up to leave. She had no money of her own, and no job, so she couldn't move out of the house; she would have to ask Henry to let her have it. She thought it might have been easier if she'd had an affair, but while she was married to Henry she didn't have the energy. An affair might be as disappointing as her marriage, and she couldn't face that. So she told him at the kitchen table, one rare summer night when he was home. Henry rubbed his eyes with his palms and then stared at her, red-eyed, and said nothing. She waited for questions, but none came, and finally she went to bed. Henry followed, hours later, and didn't touch her or speak. She understood: he had to work in the morning, and just needed a place to sleep.

She helped him pack, cleaning his things out of the desk they shared, and found a photographer's business card, from before Margot's wedding. The photographer had been her parents' age and military-looking, and said he'd known their mother once, which wasn't surprising—everyone knew Yvette. He'd been excited about taking a picture of the two sisters, and asked if Clarissa had ever thought about modeling. He gave her the creeps, and Margot had gone with someone else. Now, looking at his card, Clarissa thought about the phone call she might make. She would explain that she'd been too busy for modeling when she was twenty, but she was ready now. She had one bra, she would tell him, and a haircut so bad it had freaked out her seven-year-old, and some crow's-feet starting. She hadn't worn makeup, not even Tangee Natural lip gloss, since 1972. Otherwise, she was ready. She smiled at her own joke and felt paralyzed with grief.

That night she called Margot in Baton Rouge. Margot's husband, Owen, was an executive at a pharmaceutical company, as Clarissa's parents liked to report, and came home at five-thirty every day. But it wasn't Margot or Owen that Clarissa wanted to see, it was Jamie. After high school, Jamie had shown up at Margot's house, strangely unannounced. He had taken a job on an oil rig, and stayed in Louisiana.

"Can I come see you?" she asked Margot.

"Of course," Margot said. "Owen will send you a ticket."

It annoyed Clarissa that her sister assumed she was broke, though she was. And it annoyed her that Owen was so rich and kind. "That's all right," she said. "I'd want to bring Abby."

"He'll send Abby a ticket."

"All I want is to visit," she said. "You don't have to get us there."

There was a silence on the line. "Then please come," Margot said.

In the morning, Clarissa made poached eggs on toast, and Abby studied the road map.

"Louisiana is too far to drive," Abby said.

"We'll see the Southwest."

"I think seeing Louisiana would be enough," Abby said.

Clarissa put Abby's plate on the table and considered her daughter. Abby, at seven, had come into rational thought like it had been hers all along. Even without a younger sister, Abby acted like an older sister, which was the one thing Clarissa had wanted to avoid. But Clarissa won, by saying, "Eat your breakfast." She was the adult, after all.

They took the diesel Rabbit that Henry had bought for the

energy crisis. Clarissa didn't know how to use a stick shift when he bought it, but Henry had said, "You'll learn." Then he was off to Sacramento again, leaving her with a fuel-efficient car she couldn't drive. She had learned on the way to the doctor's office, stalling out while Abby screamed with an ear infection in the backseat. She was better at it now. They took four tapes: *The Muppet Movie,* Holly Near's *Imagine My Surprise,* Linda Ronstadt's *Heart Like a Wheel,* and the Eagles' *Hotel California.* Somewhere in Arizona they started figuring the distance of a destination—the camp that night, or a lake to swim in—by how many tapes it would take to get there:

"How long till we stop for lunch?" Abby would ask.

"Two *Muppet Movie*s and a Linda Ronstadt."

"How long till the lake?"

"One *Hotel California* and a Holly Near."

"No more Holly Near."

"Two *Hotel California*s, then."

Abby studied the cassette cases for hours in silence. "Why can you check out of the hotel but never leave?" she asked.

Clarissa said she didn't know. On campground registers, she was signing her maiden name, *Clarissa Santerre,* but it didn't feel real to her. She feared she would be Clarissa Collins forever. She also feared being Clarissa Santerre again: a frowning girl scolded by nuns. She thought the hotel in the song had something to do with both those fears, the one of being stuck in her marriage, and the one of being stuck in her childhood, but she didn't know how to explain it to Abby.

When it got too hot, Abby stood on the seat and put her head out the sunroof. Henry would say it wasn't safe, but the Rabbit had no air-conditioning, and Clarissa wanted to do it herself. When Abby came down, her hair was wild from the wind.

"I think I got a bug in my tooth. How long till dinner?"

Texas was flatter and bigger than anything Clarissa had ever seen, and the freeway was so bright and unchanging she had trouble focusing. The air felt burnt. Her eyes felt burnt. Near the Louisiana border, she stopped at a gas station and called her sister.

"Where am I?" she cried. "Tell me I'm close!"

Margot's house in Baton Rouge had a hush to it. Everywhere, expensive attention had been paid to be sure the fabrics were smooth and heavy, the windows shut out air, the walls fused solidly to the floor. There were two empty guest rooms, one for Clarissa and one for Abby. Abby was thrilled. The campground the night before had been badly lit, and a man camping alone had watched them walk back from brushing their teeth, so they'd slept in the car: Abby in the back, and Clarissa with the passenger seat rolled down as far as it would go.

Clarissa collapsed back on the smooth expanse of bedspread, in her sweaty tank top and shorts, and she could feel her sister wince. She remembered that she hadn't shaved her armpits in months.

"Jamie is coming for dinner," Margot said. "You can use the pool if you want, and the bathroom to clean up."

"You have a pool?"

"Everyone here has a pool."

Clarissa kicked off her sandals. "Does Jamie?"

Margot gave her a look. "No," she said.

Owen grilled enormous steaks for dinner, and Jamie showed up late. Clarissa, clean from a swim, jumped up to hug her brother, but he seemed shy of her touch. He was twenty, and thin, and smelled like cigarette smoke, both stale and fresh. Margot pulled out a chair for him, and Jamie slid into it, not meeting anyone's eye.

Abby was clumsy with the steak knife, but when Clarissa reached to help her, Abby shot her a glare and Clarissa withdrew. They had eaten mostly rice and beans on the drive, cooked over a Coleman stove. Margot talked about the volunteer work she was doing, reading to children at the hospital, and Clarissa watched her little brother, no longer little, pick up Abby's knife and fork and cut the giant steak into small pieces.

Abby sat quietly while Jamie did it, and when he put down the knife and slouched back in his chair, she kept watching him. When she caught his eye, Abby brightened.

"Why do elephants wear tennies?" she asked.

Jamie looked surprised. "I don't know," he said.

Abby took a breath, suddenly shy. Clarissa waited for the answer.

"Because nine-ies are too small and eleven-ies are too big," Abby said, rushing the words together. The two of them looked at each other. Then Jamie cracked a smile, and Abby collapsed into giggles.

"That's her favorite joke," Clarissa said.

When Abby had gone to bed, Jamie sat in the hot tub, smoking. Clarissa took another swim in the pool, then climbed in with him, under the trees, her feet tingling in the hot water.

"Margot did well, didn't she?" she asked him.

"Did you think she wouldn't?"

"I thought she might surprise us," Clarissa said. "Go wild."

Jamie grinned a quick, humorless grin, then stubbed out his cigarette on the side of the tub. "Margot picked the only place in America more weird and Catholic than Teddy and Yvette's house," he said. "And I followed her here. I'm a fucking genius."

"She has a beautiful house."

"She wants kids so bad she can taste them."

Clarissa leaned back in the tub until her hair drifted in the water, and looked up at the sky. She thought how much easier life would be without a kid. Then, by way of apology, she thought how much she loved Abby. The sky seemed dense and close. "Is it lights or clouds that block out the stars here?" she asked.

Jamie didn't look up. "Both, I guess. Margot tell you I got fired?"

Clarissa sat back up and shook her head.

"I woke up one morning and didn't want to go risk my life with a bunch of convicts. So I didn't show up."

"Oh—"

"I went back the next day to apologize, and get my job back, and the whole oil rig was gone."

"Gone where?"

"Who knows? No trace. Weirdest thing I've ever seen."

There was a silence for a while.

"I'm leaving Henry," Clarissa offered.

Jamie sighed. "That's too bad," he said.

Clarissa shrugged and looked away into the trees. She should have asked more about his job, but she was hungry for sympathy. "It has to be better than staying together," she said.

"Maybe."

"What will you do now?"

"Go risk my neck on a different rig."

"Dad would pay for college," she said. "You're so young."

Jamie lit another cigarette, his eyes sharp in the butane light. "I'm not taking Teddy's money," he said.

Clarissa studied him. Her father had paid for Margot's college, beyond the scholarship, and for hers. But Jamie didn't seem to want to discuss it further. She remembered her mother saying that Jamie had been unhappy before he left home.

"Mom said something about a girlfriend," she said.

Jamie said he didn't want to talk about it, and then he got out of the hot tub and went home. Her darling baby brother, the one who had taught her what love was, and he treated her like a prying grown-up, which she guessed she was.

Clarissa slept hard in the big, clean bed that night, and on the nights that followed. She was overwhelmed by Margot's house: it was so spotless and huge. It was like their parents' house in Hermosa Beach, but much bigger, and even cleaner, because of Rosa. Clarissa thought she would be too embarrassed to hire a black woman—or any woman—even if she'd had the money. But it would help so much. As a child, she'd looked down on the Winstons, five doors down, because they didn't clean their electric frying pan after breakfast but left congealed grease in it all day. That was not a stone she could cast now. She was glad Margot had never seen her house. Rosa kept Margot's frying pan faultlessly clean.

At some point she would have to go back, she knew. She would have to face Henry and file for divorce. But first she would have to drive across Louisiana, Texas, New Mexico, Arizona, and most of California. Divorce would be a piece of cake after that. The thought of the drive exhausted her, and she knew it horrified Abby.

They had been at Margot's a week, and Clarissa was taking a night swim in the pool, when she heard voices from her sister's room. It was cool outside, and the windows were open to let in the air. Clarissa stopped swimming and let the water go still.

"He should have come to me," Margot's voice said, on the other side of the window screen.

"He's afraid of you," Owen said.

"I don't know why he moved here."

There was a pause that seemed to Clarissa to be uncomfortable.

"It's our children's money," Margot said. "You should consider that."

Owen sighed. "We don't have children."

"We might, still."

There was another pause.

"Jamie's your brother," Owen finally said. "He just needs some help."

"Clarissa will be asking next," Margot said. "With a divorce, and with Abby . . ."

In the pool, Clarissa drew back, and thought about starting to swim again, but was afraid they would hear the splashing.

"If she's next, she's next," Owen said.

"If she'd just taken the plane tickets," Margot said, "she'd be staying a reasonable length of time. That insane drive. She could be here all summer."

"She's no trouble. And she's leaving next week."

"We don't know that," Margot said.

"Oh, Margot," Owen said.

In the pool, Clarissa moved silently to the stairs in the shallow end, crept out, and wrapped herself in one of Margot's thick white towels. She felt her eyes start to sting, but she wouldn't cry over Margot. The slate pool deck was still warm from the day's sun, and she sat down on the stones to wait, watching the window lights in the pool's dark surface go out, until the house was quiet.

That night Clarissa didn't really sleep at all. She thought of her grandmother Lenore, who was ninety, and had passed on good French peasant genes that would last a century. But Clarissa didn't want to live a century. She felt depleted and unhappy after thirty years, and the idea of seventy more was too much to stand. Lying in Margot's immaculate guest bedroom, with her pile of grubby clothes in the corner, she thought—not for the first time—that she would be happy becoming part of the earth, fertilizer for a garden somewhere. But you couldn't turn into fertilizer when you had a kid.

In the morning she called Jamie at his apartment. "We're driving back today," she said.

"That was quick."

"I wanted to say," she said, "that you could come live with me in California, and help with Abby."

Jamie said nothing. She had been sure he would say no, but when she heard the suggestion out loud it sounded plausible. She took his silence as encouragement to go on.

"Henry's moving out, and I have to get a job now," she said. "And sitters cost a fortune."

Still Jamie said nothing.

"I mean, I couldn't pay you," she said. "But I'd feed you, and you wouldn't have rent. You couldn't smoke in the house, I guess. And it's small."

"I'll think about it," Jamie finally said. "Thanks, Clar."

"You could come with us now!" she said. She felt immensely relieved. It would be so good to have a second driver. He could bring new tapes, and talk to her in the car, another grown-up. He could scare off the weird men in the campgrounds, and help light the tricky stove.

"I've got an apartment full of stuff," he said. "I can't go now."

"Of course," she said—of course he couldn't come now. "But come soon."

"I'll think about it."

"Okay." She couldn't help smiling. He would come.

"Clar, do you know why I was born in France?" Jamie asked out of the blue.

Clarissa had twirled Margot's phone cord around her wrist in her happiness, and now she tried to untangle it without stretching the coils. "You were born in Santa Rosa."

"France," he said. "I needed a birth certificate for insurance, so I called the records office in Hermosa. It's all in French, except my name, and Mom and Dad's names."

"How weird. Did you ask Mom?"

"I asked Teddy, he didn't know."

"I don't either," she said, getting her wrist free. "We're getting on the road. Do you promise you'll think about it?"

"Sure," he said.

She packed and settled Abby into the car with a happy sense that Jamie would come, and that she had edged out Margot. As they headed back on the freeway, Abby sang along with the Muppets: *Movin' right along, footloose and fancy-free* . . . They were on their way home.

15

NINETY-ONE YEARS was a long time to live, and it was late in life to have to sit through another birthday party. Lenore said so at her morning card game on the sunporch. Everyone was so amazed you were alive at that age that they showed up in droves, and kept asking you questions.

"Oh, it's so difficult to be popular," Edith Cadieux said, smiling, arranging the cards in her hand. "At least they throw you a party."

"Next year, you can be me, and cut the cake and answer the questions," Lenore said. "They'll never notice."

"I'll take you up on that," Edith said.

"Birthday cakes are the worst cakes anyway," Mr. Osbert said. Mr. Osbert had not received a visitor or had a party for years. "Like eating a kitchen sponge with silver-polish frosting."

"How do you know about silver polish?" Edith asked him. "When did you ever polish silver?"

"I did," Mr. Osbert said. "My wife hated to do it, and I loved to see that tarnish come away."

"That discard's yours if you want it, Mr. Osbert," Lenore said.

Mr. Osbert covered the card with one from the stack and passed them both, which was what Lenore wanted. She tucked them into her hand. The best party she could remember was New Year's Eve, 1899, when she stood on the porch of her grandfather's house, banging a pot with a spoon. She was ten years old, and she'd never seen everyone so excited before. Everyone except her uncle Eugene, who said it wasn't really the new century until 1901, was dancing and kissing and shouting and lighting things on fire. Then even Uncle Eugene got caught up in the frenzy, lifted Lenore to his shoulders, and waltzed into the street. Birthdays were bound to be a letdown after that.

This year, her great-grandchild Abby had arrived with the boy Jamie, because Clarissa was occupied with a divorce. It was something, she thought, how blithely girls now divorced. You lost your husband and your church and your friends all at once, and then what did you have? Children you couldn't afford to feed. She would never have left Leo, even though women always went for him, and he went right back. He was a womanizer, a roué, she could say it now. But so many men were, and she had loved him. When Jamie asked her to tell her wedding story to Abby, she remembered every detail, like it had been the day before.

Leo had been working across the river in Detroit, for the Ford Motor Company, and on the day of the wedding, he came to the house in a Ford motorcar, a Model T, shined up so it gleamed. Everyone ran out on the porch to look. Lenore's mother said it was bad luck to see the bride before the wedding, but Leo wanted to take Lenore to the church in style. They drove out of town, and stopped in a yellow field in the morning sunshine. Leo said he wanted to kiss Lenore Theveneau one more time, before she became Lenore Grenier. When the children asked about her wedding, she didn't describe that kiss, the last kiss she'd had as an unmarried girl. It was hers alone. Leo's kisses made her feel the floor was dropping out from under her, like a terrible dream, only it was wonderful.

By the time they got to church, everyone was waiting, and her mother hustled her into a back room and put her in the dress they'd made together. Lenore felt dazed, from the speed of the car and the effect of Leo's kisses, and also—though she had told no one, not even Leo—from the baby that had started inside her. She walked up the nave, in the dress that was a little tight now, and repeated the priest's words, and Leo kissed her again. It was a sweet, public kiss, but still she thought she might faint. And then she became that different girl, a married woman, Lenore Theveneau Grenier. She was twenty-one years old, and her life had started.

"Your turn to discard, *arrière-grand-mère*," Edith said. She was teasing, because Lenore was just herself at the card table, plain old Lenore, the part that didn't exist in relation to all those children and grandchildren and great-grandchildren. It was a shrunken part, but it was there. She threw down a useless eight of clubs.

"What good is that to me?" Mr. Felix said, on her left. He covered the card and passed it on to Edith. The men had asked Lenore to call them by their Christian names, but she never had. It was enough that she was playing cards with them, unattended. Leo would have gone crazy if he'd been alive, but she figured he could give her some rein now that he was dead.

Leo hadn't had a happy childhood; that was why he had been so jealous. His mother had died when he was twelve, and a housekeeper had moved in to help. His father was a railroad man, always off in the provinces, and when he came home he slept with the housekeeper. Leo and the other children all knew where he slept, but no one said a word about it, except some small jokes his father made at breakfast. The jokes seemed to include only the housekeeper, who shushed him. Matronly and coarse, even in her best dress, she took the children to Mass every Sunday to pray to the Virgin, and Leo grew up confused, desperate to protect his sister Rosalie from the tawdriness of the world.

Lenore never did tell her husband that the first baby, the boy, Joseph, hadn't been born early at all. She had never told anyone; her doctor must have known, but he kept her secret. Leo was the baby's father, certainly, but he might have treated the child differently if he'd known the boy was evidence of their sin. She hadn't wanted to take the chance.

Lenore put her cards down first, laying out a run of four spades on the table, plus an extra spade for good measure, and three nines, and three sixes she didn't even need. That left only her discard, and she dropped it, sticking them all with the cards they held in their hands.

"How do you do it, Lenore?" Edith asked. "How do you always do it?"

The others tallied up their hands for the points against them, and Mr. Felix wrote down the scores. Lenore watched Mr. Osbert perform his slow, thorough bridge shuffle, over and over. He offered it to Lenore, who cut it to please him.

There was the kind of man who would be jealous no matter what, and you just had to accept it in him, and that was Leo. Then there was the kind who could become jealous under the right circumstances, and that was Teddy. Lenore had known it the first time her daughter brought him home, just as she had known that Yvette was the kind of girl who could pull jealousy from a stone. Yvette had to be the center of attention, so she made sure she was. She wasn't a bad girl, she just had a way of checking on the people in a room to be sure they were watching—a glance would do. It worked on her father the most. He couldn't bear her leaving. One moment this Teddy was a cocky college flyboy, picking Yvette up in a sixty-dollar car; the next he was calling her long-distance with catarrh, saying the illness had put him behind in his flight training, and they could get married in California in the time he'd gained. And then she was gone. It was a break between Leo and Yvette, as it had to be with fathers and daughters who were so close.

"Oh, what a hand," Edith said, sighing and rearranging her cards. "Thank you very much, Mr. Osbert."

Yvette had never talked about her marriage—she was a smart girl, and she knew you had no right to complain about someone you got all the way to the altar with. You made that choice, even if you were a child when you did it, and the marriage vow was sacred. When Leo got angry because Lenore played cards with the other wives, she had moved the card games into the back of his grocery store. If he was afraid of what he couldn't see, let him see it.

"You dealt me a hand of stinkers, sir," Edith said. "You really did."

She had been sure she would go right after Leo, when he collapsed in the sink full of blood. Her daughters said she was foolish—especially Adele, who knew Leo had had other women. But Lenore couldn't imagine her life without Leo, couldn't imagine that he would never kiss her again or say her name. She couldn't sleep in her empty bed, couldn't take food. The girls took turns coming to stay with her, scolding her for failing to eat, but she was ready to follow Leo wherever he'd gone.

After two weeks of little sleep and no food—only the water into which Yvette stirred sugar to spite her—Lenore saw him standing at the foot of her bed. He told her to go to the kitchen and eat. She reached out to touch her husband, to pull him to her, but her hand went through him and hit the brass bedstead, bruising her wrist.

She lay against the bedstead after he left, gathering her strength, and then she went to the kitchen in her dressing gown. She sliced a hard salami into thin circles, and ate the circles with bread and milk. She threw up that first meal, but after that she was able to eat, as Leo had told her to.

The girls found her the nursing home, and it wasn't a bad one: it overlooked Lake Superior, and the long, protected sun-porch ran the length of the building. Lenore surveyed the bored old men and women on the sunporch the first day, and asked if they could get up a round of cards.

She looked around at her friends now, at Edith and Mr. Felix and Mr. Osbert. She laid down her discard, one round away from going out again and catching them all with a mitt full of points. Playing cards on the sunporch, she had first discovered she could be happy without Leo. The games—her mother's rummy and her uncle Eugene's penny poker—started after breakfast, as soon as she came down from her room. She could play all day and never account to anyone for where she'd been.

So she was glad she had been too hardy to die before Leo brought her the message that she should live, and glad she had seen their family continue, Yvette to Clarissa to Abby. Abby would have children of her own, and they would have some of Leo in them, and some of Lenore. And she didn't have to wait long to join him; he couldn't expect her to carry on much longer. She sat quietly watching Edith fuss over which card to put down, and she waited like a cat for her chance to go out.

16

YVETTE HAD NEVER felt truly close to her mother. She had loved her, in a general way, but she couldn't help considering Lenore a rival for her father's affection. So it came as a surprise to her, at fifty-seven, that her mother's death shook her the way it did. When a person lived so long—lucidly, in fair health, still winning at cards—you were expected to celebrate her life, not morbidly mourn her death. So Yvette mourned in private. She might be carrying a stack of sheets, warm from the clothes dryer, down the hall, and burst into unexpected, choking sobs. She talked to God while weeding her garden, and said she didn't want to forget her mother, but she did hope it would get easier, because it was so difficult to live from day to day.

That she had lived away from her mother for so long, and still felt her absence so strongly, made her think about her own children, so far away. As she went down the hall, dusting each of their old bedrooms, she expected to bump into one of them at every corner: Margot in white socks, Clarissa in braids, Jamie in a baseball cap, dashing down the stairs. Teddy still had his work to distract him, so he didn't notice so much. But Yvette had less to do, with the children gone, and more time to feel sad.

Her granddaughter, Abby, had once asked what Yvette had wanted to be when she grew up. Yvette had explained that it was different when she was a little girl: everyone wanted to be a wife and a mother then, and no one knew they could be anything else. To be a wife and mother had seemed a glorious purpose, and that's what she had become. Abby had seemed embarrassed about the answer, but Yvette said she had been very happy with her life. The girls her daughters' age, who had so many options, didn't seem to be happy with any of them—though Yvette didn't tell Abby that.

What worried her more was Teddy's impending retirement. She didn't know what he would do at home all day. Since Jamie left, their marriage had gone more smoothly, but it seemed important to her that a couple maintain some distance, and not see each other all day long. He talked about the walks he would take, the books he would read, the work he would do for the church—but she worried that he would want to keep tabs on her, that restlessness would lead to suspicion, as it had in her father, until she couldn't go to the market without his getting jumpy. Teddy wasn't like her father—he had been the most jealous when he had been away at war—but Yvette was nervous, and thought Teddy was nervous, too. He began to plan projects for the weekends, as if to prove that he would keep himself occupied when he retired, and wouldn't be underfoot.

One Saturday Teddy was cleaning out his storage closet, in his campaign to be useful, and he came to Yvette with a sheen of sweat on his forehead, and a manila envelope in his hands. He gave it to her, saying nothing.

She took the heavy prints from the faded envelope and there they were: Margot in perfect order, Clarissa with crooked teeth and a crooked hem, and Yvette, so young, with her black hair set and her tipsy smile. Yvette touched her hair, now white and cropped around her ears, and waited.

Teddy said, "There wasn't anything with that photographer, was there?"

She shook her head. "No," she said.

He stood silent a minute, as if absorbing the fact.

"I want to ask you something else," he said.

Yvette knew the question that would come. She stacked the photographs and lined up the edges, waiting for Teddy to organize his words.

"Jamie," he finally said. "He was born in France."

Yvette nodded.

"When I asked you last year, when Jamie asked me, you said you'd gone to see Margot."

"I did go to see her."

"But you didn't have a baby there."

Yvette hesitated, then said, "No."

"Margot did."

Yvette said nothing.

"Does anyone else know?" he asked.

"Only the Planchets in France."

Teddy stood for a minute, thinking. His voice was thick when he spoke. "I had this feeling, this feeling . . ." he said, and then he stopped. "Maybe Jamie should know."

"I promised Margot," she said. "People don't have to know everything. If I hadn't told you about the photographer, you'd never have worried."

"Yes, I would."

"Not as much," she said.

Teddy looked at the floor. "They kept secrets in the war," he said, as if he were trying out an idea. "They had to do that."

"Yes," Yvette said.

"Confession is secret."

Yvette nodded.

"We keep secrets at work. That's business."

"Yes," she said again.

"I don't think we should keep this from our family. I think Jamie should know."

"He's our son," Yvette said. "I won't tell him he's not."

She waited for Teddy to argue, but he returned to the storage closet, and didn't bring the subject up again.

17

WHEN CLARISSA LEFT Louisiana, asking Jamie to come to California, Jamie had stalled for a day or two. He didn't need anybody's help, he told himself—but finally the idea that Clarissa needed *his* help won him over. He gave notice on his apartment, packed up the red Ford Escort, drove to California, and moved in with his sister. Clarissa had filed for divorce, and she was a nursing-home ombudsman for the state, driving from town to town talking to old people, getting them things they needed. Jamie thought it was a good job for her: he loved his sister, but he thought other people's problems were a good thing for her to have to deal with.

Clarissa had a little shingled bungalow, with a clothesline and a sunny patio with a bank of roses, and no Henry anymore. She put a borrowed bed in the playroom next to Abby's room, and moved Abby's books and toys off the shelves for Jamie's things. He practiced his guitar on the patio, singing

"Tangled Up in Blue" to Abby and showing her how to make chords.

In September, he enrolled in an engineering course at the community college. The class cost six dollars a credit and met twice a week, and he took Abby with him to class. Abby read her own books, or listened while Jamie took notes, and the professors never seemed to mind. She sat at the kitchen table with him while he did his homework, and when he got bored they played cards. The only game she knew was his grandmother's rummy, which was boring as hell with two people, so he taught her five-card stud. Abby was a careful bettor, playing it safe even when she had a good hand. He said he'd give her all the pennies after the game if she risked it, but she'd still see his bets and never raise them, and fold the minute she thought she'd lost.

He taught her basic odds, the ones he thought would be useful. If the teacher asked them to pick a number between one and ten, and her classmate picked three, Abby should pick . . .

"Four," she said.

If her classmate picked seven?

"Six." They practiced in the car, where she also held her breath past cemeteries, and touched glass going under yellow lights.

"Lose the superstition," Jamie told her. "Play the averages."

But Abby would only shake her head a little, still holding her breath or touching the window, appeasing the magical powers. Driving home one day from his engineering class, Abby asked why Teddy's car wasn't drawn magnetically to Dairy Queen anymore.

"Say what?" Jamie asked.

The red flush of embarrassment spread up from her cheeks to the roots of her hair. "It used to go to Dairy Queen when it left the house," she said.

"When my dad had it?"

Abby nodded.

"It doesn't do that now," he said. "I'm too broke."

Abby was silent.

"Remember we studied magnets?" he asked. "There's no magnetic pull in ice cream."

"I know that," Abby said.

"Anyway, there's no Dairy Queen here."

"There's a Foster's Freeze."

So the red car found its way to Foster's Freeze, and they bought a third cone for Clarissa and raced home before it melted.

On the patio, ice cream dripping down her thumb, Clarissa said, "I love having you here, Jamie. I do. I drove all the way to Louisiana to see Margot, and she's never come here."

"Who loves you, baby?" Jamie said.

Jamie got a B in his engineering class, but he didn't sign up for another. Taking one class a semester, it would take him sixteen years to get a bachelor's degree. And four classes at once would kill him. His parents called from time to time, to see what he was doing. Teddy wanted him to try a job in sales. Jamie felt increasingly grateful to Clarissa and Abby because they didn't care. He walked Abby to and from school every day, and made dinner, even if it was only grilled cheese sandwiches with Worcestershire-sauce smiley faces on the bread. He mowed the lawn and cleaned the gutters of leaves. At Christmas he strung the tree with lights, and played carols on the guitar, and dragged the tree out to the alley when the needles started falling off. He felt useful, and was happy.

Full of New Year's ambition, he alphabetized Clarissa's records. Henry seemed to have taken all the Beatles and Stones, but Clarissa had held on to the Dylan somehow. There was plenty of Linda

Ronstadt and Donovan, and some Christian children's records Yvette had sent to Abby. Behind everything, shoved to the back of the shelf, was a battered 45 with a homemade label. Jamie changed the speed on the turntable, and after dinner he brought Abby and Clarissa into the living room and rolled back the throw rug. He dimmed the lights, and made his sister close her eyes while he dropped the needle. A reedy male voice started singing her name.

"Oh, no!" Clarissa cried, her eyes popping open.

Abby said, "What?"

Jamie took his sister in his arms and danced her around the living room, singing along as much as he'd learned: *"Da-dee-dee-da, Miss Clarissa . . ."*

"Oh, how embarrassing," Clarissa said, but she let herself be danced.

"Love you truly, Miss Clarissa," Jamie sang.

"I should have married Jimmy Vaughan," she said.

"Abby might have something to say about that."

The B-side was a dance cut, and Jamie and his sister jitter-bugged, then showed Abby how. She wanted to be spun around, and didn't care much about the beat. When the record ran out for the fifteenth time, the needle arm dropping itself home, they all collapsed on the couch. Jamie was sweating.

"Miss Blair would never let us jitterbug," Clarissa said. "Too risqué."

"Who's Miss Blair?" Abby asked.

"The dancing teacher at Sacred Heart," Clarissa said. "She only taught us the fox-trot and waltz. She used to teach with Mr. Tucker, before he left. God, I wonder if they were sleeping together."

"They sound like adulterers," Jamie said. "Flaunting their sin at a nice Catholic school."

"No, I should never have said that," Clarissa said. "Miss Blair was so prim."

"It's always the prim ones."

"What's an adulterer?" Abby asked.

"It's an adult," he said.

"Don't you have to be married?" Clarissa asked.

"It's a married adult." He dropped the needle back on the record.

"I'm sure I'm wrong, I'm sure they weren't," Clarissa said.

"I'm sure they *were*," he said, as the music began.

One day in early spring, Henry stopped by the house. Jamie was having a cigarette on the patio, and he stubbed it out in a flowerpot. Usually Henry picked Abby up at school and dropped her off later at the front gate, so Jamie hadn't seen him yet. He acted happy to find Jamie there.

"What are you doing now?" he asked.

"Living here," Jamie said.

"That's all?"

"That's what my dad says."

"Oh, don't pay any attention to your dad," Henry said. "It's great for Abby."

"I hope so," Jamie said.

"Sure it is."

They seemed to have run out of things to say.

"I still have your *Meet the Beatles* record," Jamie offered.

Henry's gaze clouded over in confusion, then cleared. "Hey!" he said. "That might be worth something now."

Jamie frowned. "You mean because Lennon's dead?"

"Oh—no," Henry said. "I didn't mean that. I just meant because it's old."

"I don't think I'd sell it," Jamie said. "Do you want it back?"

"Nah," Henry said. "I guess I haven't missed it yet."

"How's the Assembly?"

"Oh, crazy. I think I'm through with it."

Jamie felt suddenly wary. "Yeah?"

"I'll find something closer to home, I guess," Henry said. "I want to be here for Abby. She needs a dad."

Jamie nodded.

Henry was looking at the cigarette in the flowerpot. "You don't smoke around Abby, right?"

Jamie shook his head.

"She inside?"

Jamie knew Henry didn't want to go inside the house that had once been his, so he went to get Abby, and he sat on the patio after father and daughter had driven away to Foster's Freeze. He closed his eyes and felt the winter sun on his face, and thought that other people must have an easier time than he did, knowing what their place was in the world.

18

AFTER HER FATHER left the Assembly and Jamie left town, Abby's mother was lonely. Abby understood that much. Clarissa had boyfriends, and some of them walked Abby home from school and cooked dinner and brought her presents. Others didn't show up until Abby had gone to bed, but still she had a sense of someone in the house: a man's jacket draped over the couch when she got up for a glass of water, a deep voice from her mother's bedroom, through the wall.

The boyfriends came along in a series, without overlap, as far as Abby knew, and each was different from the one before. There was a builder from the new development south of town, and a stand-up comic who had come for a gig and stayed longer than he expected. There was a paramedic who had a talking parrot, and a counselor from the teen rehab center where her mother had started working. When Abby was twelve there was an Argentine painter named Luís, whose Jewish family had left Germany before the war. He spoke English, German, Spanish, and Italian, and was a practicing Buddhist. He would meditate at the kitchen table, while Abby did her homework, by lifting his water glass slowly to his lips, taking a sip, and slowly lowering the glass to the table. He explained to Abby that you had to pay close attention to every step of the process, to every muscle contraction and every movement of object and hand, for the meditation to be successful. It was true that Luís didn't notice anything else going on in the kitchen: the kettle could whistle, the phone could ring, Abby could ask her mother how to spell "tomorrow," a pot could boil over and her mother could swear—and Luís would slowly raise and lower the glass, noticing only the tightening of his wrist, the squeezing and releasing of the water in his throat.

Jamie wrote letters, and Abby saved them. The letters were never long—a few lines on a card—but they assumed an understanding between them, which she liked. Jamie had gone back to Louisiana for a year, and then to Colorado. He'd gone to school in Boulder, then quit again, and had jobs that never gave him time off, because he was always new. "I work clearing brush off ski trails in the daytime, and play loud, obnoxious rock 'n' roll at night," he wrote when Abby was thirteen. "But it don't last forever, or so they tell me." He was twenty-six: not quite an adult in her mind, and not a child.

Then Jamie wrote that he was coming to visit, and Abby looked around her bedroom. She had chosen the pale blue wall paint years before, and her mother said it looked like the inside of a freezer. With the furniture back in place it was fine, but it was obviously a little girl's room. There were stuffed animals on the bed, and a glass unicorn under a glass shield. There was a poster listing the attributes of the sign of Aquarius. There was a framed watercolor by Abby—an immature work, she felt—and there were old children's books on the shelves.

She took down the Aquarius poster and the watercolor, and moved the children's books into the closet with the stuffed animals. She paused over the glass unicorn, aware that it was something a grown-up might have, but the wrong kind of grown-up, and not a teenager. She put the unicorn in the closet, too.

From an issue of *Tiger Beat* magazine from the grocery store, she cut page-sized posters of musicians that the girls at school liked: Corey Hart, Duran Duran, and Rick Springfield. The posters went up with Scotch tape, beside her bed and on her closet door, glossy and dark with black backgrounds. When she finished, she was satisfied that it looked like a teenager's room. Also at the grocery store she bought a pink disposable razor and shaved her legs to the knee, which was what the girls at school (who were allowed) were allowed.

Luís the Argentine Buddhist had been living at the house, but her mother asked him to leave for a while, so he packed his backpack and left. Abby knew that if Jamie saw the water-glass meditation, he would say Luís was crazy. Luís wasn't crazy, but she was glad he was gone. Her mother stocked the refrigerator with groceries and Neapolitan ice cream, and cut flowers from the garden for the table. She pulled Abby's wet hair into two long French braids, so it came out in tight brown waves when it was dry. And then Jamie arrived, still driving Teddy's old Ford Escort, with the red paint fading in a Rorschach shape on the hood. He hugged Abby so hard her feet came off the ground.

"Your hair's all bendy," he said.

That night the three of them ate burgers at the picnic table on the patio, and talked about Jamie's job at the ski area, and his quitting smoking, and Clarissa's job at the teen rehab center, where all the kids smoked.

"Working there makes her paranoid about kids," Abby said.

Clarissa said, "They all have withdrawal symptoms and tattoos."

"*I* don't."

"Give it time," Jamie said.

They talked about Abby's social studies teacher, who had been Methodist and Baha'i and Taoist—everything except Jewish because she thought she wouldn't be accepted. She'd finally settled on Catholicism as the most elaborate religion that would take her.

"Wacko," Jamie said. "That's like boning up on political history and deciding to be a Stalinist."

"Well," Clarissa said.

"She could have been a Great Westerner," Jamie said.

"Oh, God," Clarissa said. "Not that again."

After dark, Jamie got out his guitar and sang songs, real ones and made-up ones. It was the summer of Springsteen's wedding, and Jamie sang, *"This gun's for hi-ire, but not anymore 'cause I'm mar-ried."*

"You seem happy," Clarissa said, when he stopped.

"I am," Jamie said, playing a little three-chord progression. "Teddy thinks my job is beneath me, but it's not, really. And I like my band. There were some dark days, after losing my old girlfriend, and then after leaving here. But I'm pretty happy." He strummed a quick flourish to end his speech, and slapped a hand on the strings to make them quiet. "You?"

Clarissa sighed. "I don't think I know how to be happy," she said.

Jamie slept in the playroom, like he had when Abby was seven and eight, and in the morning he came into her room singing, "Waaaa-ake UP in the morning and water your horses and feed them some corny-corn-corn!" He threw himself on top of the bedcovers, and only then seemed to notice the room.

"Oh, my God," he said. He rolled so he wasn't crushing her so much, and looked at the walls. "What is this, *Tiger Beat*?"

Abby pretended to be asleep, though she was wide-awake and could feel her face burning.

"Corey Hart?" Jamie asked. "Rick *Springfield*? Oh, Abby, I've neglected your musical training. This is all my fault." He wrapped his arms around her, bedcovers and all, in a tight cocoon. She kept her hot face turned away.

"I'll make amends," he said. "I promise."

When Jamie left the room, Abby got up and took the posters down, not looking at them: when she did her vision went out of focus, clouded over with shame.

Jamie stayed a week, playing tapes in the car, and handing each one off to Abby when it was finished. "Radio-Free Sebastopol," he called it. They went to all the movies in town, and Abby got in for half-price to the PG-rated ones, pretending she was still twelve. Then Jamie bought her a ticket for the R, and Abby hid behind him so the girl who'd sold her a child's ticket the day before wouldn't see her.

On the hottest day they drove to the beach, where kids Abby's age were sitting on towels together, with sodas and radios. If Abby had been with her mother, she'd have been embarrassed, but with Jamie she wasn't. It was part of the way Jamie wasn't really an adult. She had a new blue swimsuit with white trim, and she could feel invisible prickles if she ran her hand along her lower leg. She wondered how often you were supposed to shave. It had taken a long time to do it. They swam in the freezing water, and Jamie showed her how to bodysurf until it got too cold, and they lay on the sandy towels with their eyes half closed against the sun.

"Who was the girlfriend you lost?" she asked him.

"Which one? I've lost count."

"The one you said gave you dark days."

Jamie propped himself on his elbow. "You listen too closely for a kid."

"I'm not a kid."

"No, I forgot. You're a *Tiger Beat* Teen."

"Jamie!"

"Okay," he said. "The girlfriend's name was Gail. She was really cool and smart. We had sex all the time, which I can tell you since you're not a kid, and which was very cool for a fucked-up seventeen-year-old who mostly played guitar alone in his room."

Abby hadn't expected so much information and said nothing.

"But I was a *Catholic* fucked-up seventeen-year-old, and completely tormented by guilt. Gail got fed up and moved to her aunt's place in Seattle to be a waitress, and that was that. Haven't seen her since. The dark days began."

"Did you try to find her?"

"I didn't think she wanted me to. I hope she went to art school. That was what she wanted. We had this whole plan." His voice faded out and he brushed sand off his towel and seemed to be thinking. Finally he said, "I don't think you should decide that a thing in the past would have made you happy. If we'd married we might've thrown pots at each other's heads." He smiled.

"Let's go," he said. "You're turning into a lobster."

They found a bar that was cool and dark inside, and empty in the middle of the afternoon, and Jamie bought her a Coke and racked the balls on the pool table. He corrected her shot and squared her hips to the table, and showed her how to figure the angle for a bank shot. When they had played eight ball twice, he lined four balls up next to a side pocket, hit the line in the center, and sank each ball in a different pocket. Abby tried three times, but could get only one ball in.

"Give it a few wasted years," Jamie said.

He put "The Ballad of El Paso" on the jukebox and polka'd her around the empty bar, singing in a mock baritone, ". . . *with wicked Abbina, the girl I adore.*"

When Jamie left, Clarissa cried, and Abby tried not to. Her mother kept working with juvies in pajamas, and asked if Abby was having sex, which she wasn't, and if she knew about birth control, which she did. She asked where Abby's stuffed animals had gone, and why her walls were blank, and if she was depressed. Abby snuck out her window one night, just to walk down the street while her mother didn't know where she was. She walked back in through the front door, but her mother was on the phone in the kitchen and didn't notice.

One night when Luís the Buddhist was back, Abby came into the kitchen and asked if she could go to the roller rink.

Her mother said, "Kids sell drugs at that rink."

"They do?" This was news to Abby. She'd been going to the roller rink since third grade. Girls had birthday parties there, and wore blue pom-poms on their skates. "We just want to go skating."

"Who wants to go?"

"Tara."

"Who's driving?"

"Her mom."

Clarissa seemed to think about it, then shook her head. "I don't want you in that environment."

Luís, sitting quietly at the kitchen table, said, "I think you should let her go."

"They might drink there."

"We don't drink," Abby said. "They sell Pepsi and Sprite. And you let Jamie drink beer when he was twelve."

"That was the sixties."

"It was the seventies," Abby said. "You were pregnant with me."

"You know what I mean. End of discussion."

But it wasn't the end, and Luís backed her. Her mother gave in, but insisted on picking them up at nine-thirty. In the dark, disco-lit room, in rented skates, Abby skated around the rink to "Another One Bites the Dust." She wondered which of the ordinary-looking kids there were selling drugs, and which were buying.

At nine-thirty, she and Tara returned their skates and waited by the front door for Clarissa to pick them up. They talked about how strange their shoes felt, how soft and stuck to the ground, after gliding around, three inches taller. Other cars came and picked up other kids. Tara and Abby talked about the boy Tara liked at school. His name was Jason and he had braces, but was cute anyway. At ten the rink closed, and the last skaters came outside. Then they were gone, too, and the street was quiet, and still no Clarissa.

"She's always late," Abby said.

The owner came outside, a tall Vietnamese man with lights on his skate wheels. He had once picked Abby up after a bad fall, when she was much smaller, and skated her off the rink to recover. Now he asked if they were all right.

"We're fine," Abby said.

Tara looked at her watch and made an apologetic face. "I have to call my mom," she said. "I'm already so late."

The owner let them back inside to use the pay phone, and the place was unrecognizable in the bright overhead fluorescent lights with no music playing. A woman was running a floor polisher over the rink. Tara had to pry the nickels out of her penny loafers to make the call.

Tara's mother was in front of the rink in her Subaru in ten minutes, and she didn't say anything, but Abby could feel her disapproval. When they dropped Abby off, the house was dark, and

Abby pushed the door open quietly. She took off her shoes and her coat, and crept past her mother's open bedroom door. A dark silhouette sat up sharply in bed, and a deep, threatening voice that was barely her mother's said, "Who's there?"

Abby froze. "It's me," she said.

"Oh," Clarissa breathed, and she lay back against the pillows in the dark room. Luís didn't seem to be there. "Oh, God," Clarissa said. "I was asleep. I thought it was someone breaking in. I thought I had to protect you."

Abby stood where she was.

"Why are you so late?" Clarissa asked.

Abby said nothing.

"Oh. Oh, *no*," Clarissa said. She sat up in bed again. "Oh, Abby, I forgot. I just— Luís and I had an argument, and he left, and I just totally forgot."

"It's okay," Abby said, and she went to her own room to bed.

Tara said that by California law, fourteen-year-olds could choose which parent they wanted to live with. Over pizza with her father, Abby crossed her fingers for luck and brought this question up. She would be fourteen in four months, and she would like to live with him. He was living in town, and had joined a law firm.

He studied her. "What's up with your mom?" he asked.

"Nothing," she said. "I just thought it was time. There's a law."

Her father clasped his hands together, as if he were talking to a client. "See, that law doesn't apply in general," he said. "In a custody case, without any complicating factors, the wishes of children over fourteen might be considered. But if the case isn't in court, if it's already settled, being fourteen doesn't mean you can change anything just out of the blue."

"You could ask a judge for custody," she said.

Her father sighed. "I don't take other people's divorce cases," he said. "I'm not going to drag up my own again. Think how your mother would feel."

Abby had thought of that, and knew it would be bad. "You could just ask her for custody," she said.

"Wouldn't that have the same effect?"

"I can't live there anymore."

"Have you talked to her about it?"

"She'd just cry."

Her father rubbed his hands over his face.

"You have your room and your life there," he said. "You can walk to school. I work late. It wouldn't be a good life for you."

Abby stared at her pizza and said nothing. She didn't argue, though she knew she would argue with her mother in the same situation. She wasn't in the habit of conflict with her father: it was one reason a life with him seemed so appealing. He drove her back to her mother's house in silence, and she sat a minute in his car at the gate, wishing everything were different. Then she kissed him good-bye and went inside.

A few weeks later, her mother dropped the morning paper on the kitchen table at breakfast. Abby read that her father would run for the open U.S. congressional seat and was mounting a campaign. The article cited his environmental work over the last decade, and his pro bono work in private practice. It said he had not seen combat in Vietnam but had performed essential military service in the Navy.

"Did he tell you he was going to do that?" her mother asked. "Did he ask how you felt about having a father in Washington?"

"Yes," Abby lied.

Her mother stared at her. "He did?"

"Of course," Abby said.

"Why didn't you tell me?"

"I didn't think you would care."

"We have a child together. His decisions affect me."

"They're still his decisions," Abby said, taking her breakfast bowl to the sink.

"I hate that tone of voice," her mother said.

"I'm late for school."

As she walked, with her backpack slung over one shoulder in the way her father said would ruin her spine, she watched the sidewalk, thinking about each step on the pavement, the friction beneath her shoes, and the swinging forward of her legs that made each step possible. Luís the Buddhist was right: if you concentrated on a repeated action, you didn't have to think of anything else. She tried not to step on cracks, out of habit. She had once played a game with a friend in which they stomped on all the cracks, shrieking, "You'll *break* your mother's back!" (She was glad for everyone's sake that no one had caught them.) But since then she had avoided the seams in the pavement; it had become one of her automatic gestures against bad luck, like crossing her fingers. Jamie would say it wasn't rational, but she had tried to be rational, and appeal to the law, and it hadn't worked. So she would keep on crossing her fingers, and stepping over the cracks.

19

WHEN YVETTE GREW sad about what had happened to her family, she went outside to the garden to pray. In the garden she felt close to God, with His works all around her, and she could tell Him what worried her while she got the new plants in before it rained. As she worked, she told Him about Margot, still childless, and Jamie without a career, and Clarissa always with a new boyfriend, and Abby growing up in that environment. She didn't speak out loud; her words were louder when she spoke them in her heart.

She was in the garden with God one day when Jamie drove up in Teddy's old Ford. Jamie hardly ever came home. Since he stormed out that night when he was eighteen, and moved away, he had been home twice for Christmas, and once in the summer—only when Clarissa was coming. He'd never showed up unannounced. He got out of the car and stretched, and said he was driving home from Clarissa's, and he'd stopped for a bathroom break and a drink. Yvette put aside her pruning shears and poured him a glass of orange juice.

"The house looks great," Jamie said, not looking at the house.

"We have a girl who comes," she said. She was glad to see Jamie, but she felt uneasy, as she always did. She had forgiven him for shaking her in the hallway and leaving—she had forgiven him the moment it had happened—but it had changed the way they were together, made them both cautious. She put the orange juice carton back in the icebox.

"Mom," he said, "why does my birth certificate say I was born in France?"

Yvette kept her hand on the carton, as if looking for something on the icebox shelves, then she closed the door. Her hand was damp with condensation, and she wiped it against the other. She had prepared an answer to this question when Jamie had first raised it with Teddy—but that was years ago, and Jamie had never asked again.

"Margot was homesick," she heard herself saying.

"In France?"

"In France. I went to see her. The doctors had calculated the due date wrong, or maybe it was the flying. Anyway, I went into labor in Normandy, looking at the Bayeux tapestry." She wondered where that detail had come from: she had never thought of it before, and never lied so actively; she had always let people assume.

"That's so cool," Jamie said. "How come you never told me?"

"I thought I had put you in danger by flying," she said. "I didn't want you to think I wasn't careful with you. I felt guilty."

"Mom, you're such a Catholic."

She smiled at him, sensing with relief that he believed her. The lie was permissible, necessary—it was in the service of letting Jamie know he was loved, and his family was whole, and he had always been wanted. "I didn't think I was much of a Catholic then," she said.

"So, do I have French citizenship?"

"We arranged it so you would be American. That seemed important."

Jamie shrugged. "I could never speak French anyway," he said. "But I might have studied more if I'd known."

"I'm sorry," she said, and she knew how truthful she sounded, because she was—she was sorry for everything, including these new lies. But it was too late to undo them. "We thought it was best not to tell you," she said. "Parents make so many decisions, and not all of them are right."

"That's okay," he said. He rinsed his glass in the sink and hugged her. "Thank you for telling me the truth."

She put a hand on his cheek, as if he were still a little boy.

"I have to go," he said.

She walked him out to Teddy's old Ford, and knew Teddy would have wanted her to confess to Jamie, and would be disappointed. There had been a rough spot, after Teddy learned the truth, but now things were better between them. He would argue that she could achieve the same thing with Jamie. But she couldn't tell Jamie; he might turn against her for good. The car coughed and then started, and Jamie rolled down the window.

"*A bientôt!*" he called, grinning, and he pulled away down the street.

When he was gone Yvette went back out to her garden and stood a moment, gripped with sorrow. A lie wasn't terrible as long as it hurt no one, but she wasn't sure it had hurt no one. But she did know that if it was 1958 again, and Margot came to her, she would do exactly what she had done. She picked up her shears and began to work again, asking God to help her live with the consequences.

She pruned the roses that climbed the east wall, and watched the clippers shear the deadheads away, just above each new grouping of five leaves, leaving the buds that would grow into new flowers and live out their lives. She talked to her Lord, and told Him everything, and He listened, as He always did, and kept her in His love.

20

ABBY ARRIVED AT legal adulthood without aim or direction. After her father rejected her bid to live with him, and was in the newspapers and on TV, running for Congress, her life had begun to feel less real to her. Jamie joked that he'd go public about smoking Henry's pot at twelve, but he wouldn't really. She went as her father's date to fund-raisers and campaign parties, and sat quietly while he talked to everyone else. Then he won his election and moved to Washington, and Abby stayed home with Clarissa. Luís the Buddhist moved back in for a while, then left, followed by a cabinetmaker, a teacher from the middle school, and a shrink. Abby tried not to pay too much attention.

She went out with boys but stayed a virgin, because her mother kept saying it was okay if she wasn't. The first boy who kissed her was Catholic, and felt guilty if he did more than kiss her, but the next was older and given to coaching, and taught her things. Then he moved away, and the next boy was suspicious and sullen because she knew too much for a girl, for a virgin, and they drifted apart.

People said she should go to Georgetown for college, to be near her father, but she knew he was busy, and it would be more painful than it was worth. Her teachers told her she might go to Bates or Bowdoin, but she couldn't understand why she would do that. They were so far away, places she'd never heard of before the teachers suggested them. She applied to UCSD, where her parents had met, because it seemed like a plausible place to go, and got in. She took a job in a bar near campus that was quiet most nights. When she described it to her parents, they didn't remember it. Her mother said there had always been parties on campus, and that the bars had seemed seedy. Her father said he could get her a job in the dean's office instead, but she liked the bar. She spent more time playing pool there than in class, and she mastered Jamie's trick shot, with the four balls lined up by the side pocket. She was taking survey courses for the breadth requirement—"The Symphonic Century" and "Rise and Fall of the Russian Avant-Garde"—and considered the four-ball shot to be her main accomplishment.

When Baghdad was bombed, she watched it on TV. Her father called, full of sadness about the war, and she heard her voice become full of sadness, too. Her mother sent a newspaper photo of a woman in army fatigues leaving her three-year-old daughter to go to Saudi Arabia. Abby guessed Clarissa identified with the woman, but she didn't understand why. She pinned the photo to the bulletin board in the bar.

The pope condemned the American bombing, saying war was an adventure with no return, so Abby's grandparents did, too, although they could talk for hours about the Pacific theater and Korea. Her friends marched through campus and town, shouting, *"One, two, three, four! We don't want your oil war!"* They came into the bar with faces flushed from excitement, then ordered beers and put quarters on the pool table and forgot about it. The conflict felt as remote from Abby's life as everything else did. Only Jamie's letters felt real. He was in school again, way up in Northern California, and working nights. "Man, did I luck out," he wrote. "Too young for Vietnam, and too old & decrepit (sp?) for this one. How did I get so old, Abby! Wasn't it your job to stop it?"

Then the war ended and faded out of the news.

In Abby's sophomore year, just after her twentieth birthday, Teddy and Yvette announced that for their fiftieth wedding anniversary they would renew their vows in the Mission church where they'd married, in Santa Barbara. Abby told her mother she would skip it, but Jamie sent her a postcard of Marcel Duchamp holding a sign saying, I AM NOT A ROLE MODEL. On the back Jamie had written, "I'll go if you will."

"Santa Barbara!" he said on the phone when she called. "Couldn't they have gotten married somewhere cheap? Like Tijuana?"

"We could boycott in protest."

"I'll just share your mom's hotel room and baby-sit you," he said. "Like old times."

Abby had refused all trips with her mother since the drive to Louisiana when she was seven, dodging strange men in campsites and sleeping in the car. But her reward for that drive had been Jamie coming to stay, and she loved Jamie. She wanted to see him now.

Teddy and Yvette had a bungalow at the Biltmore in Montecito, where they'd lived in forty-two, but everyone else was in the Sea Air Motel in town. The motel was blue and white, and nowhere near the sea. Abby was supposed to share a bed with her mother so Jamie could have the other. Her mother's family made her feel shy, and she started to wish she hadn't come. She had borrowed a sundress from her mother, not knowing what to wear.

They rode in her mother's car to the church, and Jamie sat across the backseat looking out at the palm trees and rows of banks. He sang, *"Two banks for ev'ry millionaire,"* meditatively, to the tune of the Beach Boys' song.

"I thought you might bring a girlfriend," Clarissa said, glancing at him in the rearview mirror.

"The last one didn't pan out," he said. "Never hook up with a girl whose parents divorced when she was seven."

"Ha," Abby said.

"Oh," Clarissa said. "Did I ruin you, Abby?"

"Mother."

"Yep," Jamie said. "It's too late now."

The roses in front of the Mission were in full bloom, and Yvette was greeting people on the steps. She wore a tailored cream-colored suit and looked like a queen. Abby felt underdressed. Yvette brushed a strand of hair from Abby's face and tucked it behind her ear.

"I'm so glad you could come, sweetheart," she said. "You look beautiful."

"So do you," Abby said. It was true.

"People tell me that, honey," her grandmother said. "And you know what I say? It's because I'm happy with the man I married. That's why."

They both looked at Teddy in his dark suit, talking to Margot.

"It's the truth," Yvette said. "I knew it would be when I married him. There was a time afterward when I had doubts—about so many things." Her face was concerned and serious, then broke into a brilliant and grateful-looking smile. "But now I know how right it was," she said. "That's why I wanted to do this today. I'm so glad you're all here."

Jamie had brought his guitar, and he played "All You Need Is Love," as people from Teddy and Yvette's whole life showed up. The Winstons came: they'd moved to Carmel, but everyone still called them "the Winstons five doors down." Teddy's old pilot friend Rand came, and Yvette's French cousin Planchet, the one Margot had stayed with in France. His son had helped him buy a used Airstream RV to see America, now that his wife had died and he was alone, and he had just turned up in California. Margot seemed offended by his presumption; she avoided him, and wouldn't meet his eye.

When everyone had settled in the church, a bearded priest began the wedding Mass. Yvette held the silver chalice for Communion, and Abby watched as people filed up the nave. The frescoes on the walls were coral pink. Her mother didn't take Communion, but Jamie did. Beautiful Yvette smiled at Jamie from the altar, and kissed his cheek, and wiped the chalice with a folded piece of linen.

The reception was at the beach club, by the blue pool looking over the water, with ten cases of champagne from Margot and Owen. Clarissa had brought a thick-sided green bowl made by a local potter in Sebastopol. It wasn't perfectly round, but you wouldn't notice unless you looked close.

"Oh, God," Clarissa said, when she heard about Margot's champagne. "The bowl isn't even their style. Will they mind if I don't give them anything?"

"Just give it to them," Abby said.

Her mother put the package with the other presents, frowning. A waiter brought her a glass of champagne and she took it.

"They're happy, aren't they?" Clarissa asked, still looking at the table of presents. "Sometimes I think if I'd stayed with your dad, it might have worked out."

"You shouldn't have stayed with my dad," Abby said.

"I know," Clarissa said. "It just might have been easier."

"It wouldn't have been easier."

"I know." Clarissa sipped her champagne and looked out over the pool.

When the sun got pink and low over the ocean, Abby saw her mother dancing on the pool deck with a man with a leathery tan and graying, sun-bleached hair.

"That's my son Jimmy," an old man near Abby said. "He wrote a song for your mother. He builds boats."

Abby remembered the record, now lost, and her mother describing a boy who had touched her over her swimsuit, which she hadn't confessed because of the way the priest was breathing on the other side of the screen. Jimmy Vaughan was a good dancer, and her mother was laughing in his arms.

"Your mother should've married him," Mr. Vaughan said. "No offense, Abby."

Jamie came over and pulled Abby out to dance the jitterbug he'd taught her when she was eight. Then Jamie danced with Yvette, and Teddy danced with Margot. Then Margot dragged Owen onto the floor, and Abby danced with her grandfather. He missed the beat only a few times, when his balance was off. Then Clarissa danced with Teddy, and Abby danced with the songwriter and swimsuit-toucher Jimmy Vaughan, who had tan lines in the wrinkles around his eyes.

"Do I have permission to marry your mother?" Jimmy asked her. He'd been drinking Margot's champagne, and they were dangerously close to the pool's edge.

"Did you ask her?" Abby asked.

"Thirty years ago."

"I don't think she's the marrying kind," Abby said. "But you can ask again."

So Jimmy cut in on Clarissa, and Abby danced with her

grandfather again. She heard old M. Planchet ask Margot, *"Mais où est ton enfant?"* Margot frowned and shook her head at him. Abby thought it was clumsy and cruel to ask Margot about children.

There was a full-blown wedding cake covered with flowers, and the woman from the bakery stood watching the party for a while, in a white T-shirt and jeans. No one swam, but Clarissa took off her shoes and dangled her feet in the pool.

It was late when the guests went home, and the family moved to Yvette and Teddy's bungalow. Teddy was telling a story about a case of whiskey and a gun, to loud laughter and interjections.

"Honey, that's not true!" Yvette cried, but she had tears in her eyes from laughing. "I don't know where you get this stuff about my father!"

"I can't go in there," Jamie said, outside the screened door. "I need a break."

Abby was relieved. The champagne was starting to fade and leave her headachy. She walked with Jamie down the dark beach, digging her toes into the sand.

"I guess I'm supposed to ask what's your major," Jamie said.

"I don't have one yet."

"Me neither," Jamie said. "And I'm pushing thirty-four."

"You have your band."

"All my band does is drink beer and think of new names for itself."

"Do you still do the head-rocking?"

He looked at her. "How do you know about the head-rocking?"

"You slept in my playroom," she said. "You said it was why you'd never marry."

"Because I slept in your playroom?"

"Because of the head-rocking."

"It's true," he said. "I'll never marry."

They sat on the sand and watched the low waves roll in, a carpet of white in the dark water, then slide back out. And then Jamie kissed her, or she kissed him: her memory of who started it was immediately hazy. She had looked up at him, and he was looking at her, and it was dark, and then there was the kiss. And it was warm and sweet, with the ocean smell and the sand between her toes, and she felt better than she had all day. When they stopped, she could see his face close to hers in the dark.

"That felt decadent," he said.

She didn't know what to say, so she said nothing, but she wanted to be kissed again, and then she was. She lay back on the sand, and Jamie lay beside her. He tucked behind her ear the same strand of hair Yvette had pushed away. Then he looked up at the glow of lights from the hotel.

"It would be bad to get caught here," he said.

"They won't come out."

He ran a hand across the cloth over her breast, lightly. "What are we doing?" he asked.

"Just kissing," she said. She didn't want to think too hard, because she wanted it not to stop, and anything that would stop it seemed like something to avoid. "It's okay," she said.

He kissed her again, and the glow of lights up the beach disappeared when she closed her eyes. There was only the cool air, and his hands still careful on her breasts and rib cage and waist, and then under the sundress where she wasn't wearing underwear because they made a line beneath the dress.

"Oh, Jesus," Jamie said.

"They made a line," she said. "It's okay."

Jamie lay his head on her chest and she could feel her heart beating. "I took Communion today," he said. "And my own niece makes me horny."

146

His hand was still on her thigh and she felt strongly that it was okay, but she didn't say it again. Suddenly Jamie stood up.

"I think I'm going swimming," he said. "To cool off." He walked resolutely down the beach.

Abby sat up on her elbows and watched him go. He stripped quickly at the edge of the surf, dropping the chinos and the pressed shirt in which he had played "All You Need Is Love" at her grandmother's request. His skin was pale and smooth, and he looked like a boy. He waded in, and Abby watched his arms splash through the dark in a quick, clumsy crawl. Finally she stood and pulled the sundress over her head. The water got deep quickly, and she dived under the cold surf to where he treaded the flat water.

"You remind me of a girl I knew," Jamie said, his breath short. "Taking off your clothes like that. She was a good swimmer, too."

"I don't want to be another girl," Abby said, feeling the cold water against her legs.

A surge came and lifted them, and dropped them down again, farther apart. They treaded closer, and she felt her leg slide against his, and his hand slid over her breast, and he kissed her again. They both caught their breath at once.

"We should stop this," Jamie said.

Abby nodded, but what had happened already would change everything between them anyway. It wasn't fair to have to stop now: in for a penny.

"Should stop," he said again, as if to convince himself. They swam in with the waves, shook the sand from their clothes and dressed, not looking at each other. The sand was cool under their feet, and they found their shoes outside Yvette and Teddy's dark bungalow. Clarissa's car was in the parking lot, and Abby felt inside the rear bumper and found her mother's keys.

"She must have gotten a ride home," she said, unlocking the car. But when they got back to the motel room, Clarissa wasn't there.

"Where's your mom?" Jamie whispered in the dark. Abby heard fear in his voice.

"With Jimmy Vaughan, I guess. I think he proposed."

She rinsed off the salt in the shower, thinking about her mother. That Clarissa hadn't come home annoyed her. But she was also glad the room was empty. And if she was glad to come home alone with Jamie, then she was no better than her mother spending the night with Jimmy Vaughan—worse, of course, it being Jamie. Her head was still fuzzy from champagne.

Out of the shower, she took two aspirin from Jamie's zippered bag on the side of the sink. In the bag were three condoms wrapped in blue, attached at perforated folds. She swallowed the aspirin with the milky, aerated water from the bathroom sink and studied her face in the mirror. Jamie must have bought the condoms for someone else, and the thought made her jealous. She didn't want him to have bought them for her, but she didn't want him planning for another girl. She put the aspirin bottle back, burying the condoms in the dark of the zippered bag, and told herself she was being ridiculous. She crossed her fingers in the hope that whatever happened next would not make her sad, and she went out into the room.

The lights were out and Jamie was in the bed by the window, the one that was his. She stood waiting for her eyes to adjust to the dark, and he seemed to be waiting, too. Then he held the covers aside for her, and she slipped in beside him. It was the easiest thing in the world, and felt the most right, though her heart was pounding as he pulled her close.

*

In the morning, they woke to a knock at the door, and Jamie wrapped a towel around his waist. He pulled aside the covers on the smooth second bed, shoved the unused pillows around, and opened the door. Abby heard Teddy's voice.

"Breakfast at the hotel," her grandfather said.

"Sure," Jamie said.

"We stopped on the way back from Mass."

Abby pretended to be asleep, but she could feel Teddy looking past Jamie's shoulder, at the one bed that had clearly been slept in, and the one that clearly had not.

"Where's Clarissa?"

"Out somewhere," Jamie said.

Teddy said, "Jimmy Vaughan," in an irritated voice, and left the room.

When the door clicked shut, Jamie came back to bed and lay on the covers, on top of Abby, wrapping his arms around her.

"Well," he said. "That's over with."

While he showered, she dressed reluctantly, wanting to stay in the room as it had been before her grandfather knocked, not wanting anything to change. It took a great effort to put on her socks and shoes.

Clarissa wasn't at breakfast when they arrived, but she showed up at the Biltmore late and pulled a chair to the crowded table, cheerful and a little abashed. "You didn't worry?" she whispered.

"Of course not," Abby said. She studied her mother. "Jimmy Vaughan?" she asked.

"Oh, God," Clarissa said. "Of course not."

Abby thought about who else there was—old M. Planchet?—but didn't ask.

Across the table, Teddy was explaining about DDT in the Marianas during the war, and how they didn't know it was bad back then, but they knew they didn't want malaria, so they took showers in the stuff. He seemed to have decided everything was all right—Clarissa was back, and Abby and Jamie were sitting apart, scrubbed and punctual. Yvette was describing the most beautiful green bowl Clarissa had given them, and where she was going to put it in the house. Margot ordered Belgian waffles, then frowned when she saw Abby's fruit plate. Abby passed her aunt slices of melon, and took half a waffle in exchange. She helped Owen fill in the morning crossword. It was an easy one, and she knew the answers. She thought that everything might be, amazingly, fine. Jamie reached across the table to pour Abby coffee, and he smiled at her. The smile seemed a little sly.

Yvette, down at the end, said, "I just love this family. I do."

21

JAMIE LEFT SANTA BARBARA more determined than ever to straighten out his life. He would finish his degree, finally. He would quit the band and take a job with a retirement plan. He would find a nice, responsible girl and marry, and become part of a couple like Teddy and Yvette, Margot and Owen. He would not sit around drinking beer and renaming the band. He would not sleep with the wrong girls: for example, his niece. He would stop fucking around.

But then his determination faltered. He wasn't sure he could change. He thought it might be in his nature to be wrongheaded and corrupt, and he brooded on Santa Barbara in despair.

He had felt—he explained it to himself—excluded from his family, and had turned to Abby, who knew and understood him. Then he had been briefly at the center of the universe, until his father came to the motel door and he understood the mistake he had made. He'd sat at breakfast that day—while Abby so blithely did the crossword and traded waffles—feeling physically ill: surrounded by his family's warmth and chatter, knowing he'd betrayed them, and they would cast him out if they knew. He'd felt sick when he tried to smile.

At home again he got blind drunk with his band, and told them he was quitting, and put his guitar away in a closet. When he didn't play, the head-rocking got worse, so he lay in bed without sleeping, shaking his head at the ceiling to a beat that wouldn't go away. He guessed it was part of his penance. He hadn't smoked in ten years, but he bought a pack of cigarettes and left them out to tempt himself, to prove that he was strong. September came, and he signed up for the six classes he needed to graduate, and worked so late on problem sets that he fell asleep at the kitchen table. Then the head-rocking wasn't an issue. He didn't smoke the cigarettes, and finally threw the pack away.

In early November, Abby called him. They hadn't spoken since saying good-bye in the July sun, in a parking lot of polished, gleaming cars, surrounded by their family.

"It's me," she said on the phone.

"Hi." He was afraid to add anything else.

"I wondered what you were doing for Thanksgiving."

"Studying," he said. It was true. "Is there some family thing?"

"Oh—" she said. "I don't know. Maybe. I wondered if I could come have dinner with you."

He waited, thinking this didn't fit his plan for straightening out.

"Jamie?" she said.

"I wasn't going to cook."

"Don't cook. I have a break from school. I could drive up."

"Okay," he said, not knowing what he was agreeing to. "What about Clarissa?"

"She's going to see the cake decorator from Santa Barbara, who did the wedding cake. Her name is Véra."

"Wait, what?"

"That's where she was that night. She says she's tired of things never working out with men. Maybe wait and let her tell you."

"Jesus."

"I'll drive up on the Thursday," Abby said. "Don't cook."

Jamie threw himself back into his problem sets, and tried not to think about his sister or his niece or the holiday's approach. He imagined buying a turkey, calling Yvette for advice on how to stuff it. He had once, under a girlfriend's supervision, made a pumpkin pie. But the Thursday of Thanksgiving came, and he had made nothing. His schoolbooks were spread out over the kitchen table, as usual, when Abby drove up in the late afternoon. She wore denim overalls and a baseball cap, and she looked very young.

"I did what you said," he said, leading her into the cluttered kitchen. "I didn't cook."

"Good," she said. "Let's get Chinese."

Yvette would have made three pies the day before, two pumpkin and an apple. She would have been up at dawn peeling potatoes and roasting yams. She would have invited a favorite priest to dinner, and Margot and Owen, and Clarissa, who wouldn't go because of the cake decorator. Teddy would say grace: "Dear Lord, some of our family can't be with us today. They are in our hearts and prayers."

The Golden Plum restaurant was open, with Chinese families at a few of the tables. Jamie and Abby studied the plastic menu at the counter.

"Mu-shu chicken is kind of like turkey," he said.

"Fried rice is like stuffing."

"Plum sauce for cranberries?"

"I think so. And snow peas for string beans."

They ate in a booth in the back, and asked each other about school, and answered vaguely. The owner refilled their water glasses, and when he had withdrawn to the kitchen, Abby took a breath and said she was having a baby.

Jamie looked at her and felt himself blinking. "Why?" he asked, knowing it was not the right question to ask.

"The usual reason," she said.

"Since when?"

"Santa Barbara," she said. She seemed weirdly calm.

He waited for this fact to sink in, but it seemed impossible that it ever would. He had started to sweat. He felt like a cartoon. "Is it still early enough?" he asked.

"I'm going to have it."

"There could be problems." He tried to keep all the objections straight in his head. "Genetic things."

"I've had all the tests," she said. "I've seen it on the sonogram. Ten fingers, one head. I wish I hadn't seen the pictures. That might have made it easier." She smiled suddenly. "You should see the sonogram. He dances."

Jamie stared at her. It was a boy. "Dances?" he asked, feeling too stupid to do anything but repeat the word.

"He moves all over," she said, her smile widening, then vanishing. She looked down at her plate. "I'm starting to show. I'll tell people it was a one-night stand, which is true."

He understood the overalls. "You're too young to have a baby," he said.

"Not according to the sonogram."

"According to common sense. What kind of secret is that to keep?"

"A big one," she admitted. "But I'm not keeping it from you. And I'm not asking you for anything."

"Yes, you are! The kid will know something's weird. He'll sense it."

"My parents don't speak to each other," she said, pushing a forkful of food across her plate. "Teddy wanted to send you to military school. This baby won't sense anything weirder than any kid does."

"We both started with normal, married parents," he said. "You don't have any money, you don't have a job."

"I have a job."

"In a bar." Suddenly this struck him. "You have to quit that job. People smoke there."

"Now you're protecting the baby?"

"Oh, Abby," he said. "What are you doing?"

"I've thought about it," she said. "Every second of every day. I've dreamed about it. I really, really wanted to get rid of it, but then I couldn't. I can't."

"Abby, please."

She shook her head. The restaurant owner came back with the water pitcher and asked if they wanted dessert. Abby shook her head again, staring into her lap.

"Thank you very much," the owner said. "Happy Thanksgiving." He filled their glasses and shuffled away.

22

WHEN TEDDY FIRST heard that his granddaughter was having a baby in April, he did the math in his head out of habit, the way everyone used to when he was young, because babies were all born so early—if you believed they'd been conceived on the wedding night. With Abby there was no wedding date to figure, which upset Teddy more than he cared to think about, but he counted the months anyway. Nine months before April would be July, the month he'd married Yvette in forty-two. Yvette hadn't been pregnant yet, but it wouldn't have been impossible; that memory still brought a reflexive flush of shame.

As he figured, he stumbled on the fact that he'd married Yvette again last July, and on the memory of Jamie coming to the door of Clarissa's motel room in a towel, and Clarissa not in the room. Of sweet Abby asleep in one bed, and the covers on the second bed thrown back, but flat and smooth.

For three days he thought about what he now knew. It was

not surprise he felt, exactly. He had bombed men on the ground below him, and he had tormented his wife for a transgression he had imagined: he understood that people did things they had not expected to do. He didn't know why he was sure Abby hadn't slept with anyone else, but he felt it in his bones. And he thought it would help Jamie now, to know the truth about himself. He had always thought it would help Jamie: a man should have all the available information about his situation. It was secrecy and subterfuge that clouded judgment and caused mistakes. Now he was doubly sure, because the information would be useful to Jamie: Abby was Jamie's cousin, not his niece. It was important medical information. It would be unethical to withhold it. He had known second cousins who married, with a dispensation from the Church, and their children had been fine.

On his third day of deliberating, Teddy called Clarissa's house, where the boy he still thought of as his son was staying. At every moment—picking up the phone, dialing, waiting for the rings—he was aware that he could stop now and not interfere. Yvette had gone to a meeting at the church, to talk to prospective members.

"Jamie," Teddy said.

"Dad. Hi." Jamie sounded tired. "Is everything okay?"

"Fine, fine," Teddy said. "Your mother's out recruiting." It was a joke between them, but Jamie didn't laugh.

"Okay," Jamie said.

"How's Abby coming along?" There was a silence on the other end, which confirmed what Teddy knew.

"Fine," Jamie said.

"I want to tell you something," Teddy said. "It never seemed important before." This was a lie. He sometimes thought it was the most important thing in his life, more important than the war.

"Okay, shoot," Jamie said, but his voice was wary.

"I'd like to keep it between us," Teddy said. "If that's possible."

"Okay," Jamie said.

"Your mom and Margot wouldn't want me to say anything," Teddy said. He had planned to get right to the point, but now he seemed to need an introduction. He had practiced this moment over the years, and in his mind he had told it simply and directly, but now he found he didn't know what to say. "Your mother and Margot—" he began again.

"Oh, my God," Jamie said suddenly. "Oh, my God. Stop." Teddy heard something crash in the background. "Don't tell me, Dad," Jamie said. "Please."

23

MARGOT ANSWERED her bedside phone in the middle of the night, still half asleep, to hear her sister in hysterics on the other end. It took a long time to work out what was being said, because Clarissa couldn't breathe properly, and kept choking on her sobs.

When Margot had first heard that Abby was pregnant, she had thought it unfair that young girls were so fertile, when no one wanted them to be. The last time Margot had been pregnant, at thirty-six, she had tried to remain calm. She did meditation, ate baked eggs with cream, and stayed in bed. In her sixth month, she dared to name the baby after her grandmother Lenore. She spoke to the baby Lenore and sang to her, and asked her please to stay. But then she lost that baby like the others, and lost so much blood she was in the hospital for a week. After that, Owen asked her not to try anymore, and she agreed. She didn't think she could go through it all again. So when Abby got pregnant, so young, and everyone said how unfortunate it was, Margot had little sympathy. Abby would have a child, and wouldn't grow old without children or grandchildren. Margot knew it must cross Owen's mind that with a different wife he might have had a fuller, better life.

But Clarissa on the phone was saying something different. There was something wrong with Abby. Abby had refused treatment for it because of the baby. Clarissa wanted her daughter to reconsider, and she thought Margot might talk to her.

"Please stop crying," Margot said. "When you're crying, I can't understand."

"Owen's a doctor!" Clarissa said, when she could speak again.

"He's a chemist," Margot said. "He makes thyroid drugs."

"He might know something!"

"He knows how to make thyroid drugs."

"Abby wants to be baptized," Clarissa said. "That's why she said I could tell you. She thought you might know how."

"How what?"

"To be baptized. Do I just call a priest or does she have to take classes?"

"You didn't baptize your daughter?"

There was a pause on the line, and Clarissa hiccuped: half leftover sob, half sigh. "I thought you knew that," she said finally. "Henry thought it was ridiculous, and I thought the Church had made me repressed."

"Oh, Clarissa," Margot said.

"Don't fucking 'oh, Clarissa' me!" her sister screamed. "My daughter might die and you're getting self-righteous because I didn't put water on her head! Jesus fucking Christ!"

Margot was awake now, but she still didn't understand what Clarissa was saying, and she made her sister tell her again.

24

WHEN ABBY ARRIVED home for Christmas, before everything went wrong, she told her mother about the baby. Her mother cried for about a minute and a half, and then seemed to get excited. She didn't seem troubled or suspicious about the absent father.

"I've missed having a baby," she said happily.

"You'll have a baby *around*," Abby said. "You won't have a baby."

Her mother shrugged, as if there were no difference. "Véra's coming for the holiday," she said. "Can I tell her?"

"Okay," Abby said.

"I hope you'll like her."

"I'm sure I will. You seem happy."

"I think I am," Clarissa said. "But it's not just Véra." She dropped her voice to a whisper, although they were alone: "It's the drugs."

"Oh," Abby said, not sure what her mother meant.

"They really work," Clarissa said. "I was just chemically *off*, and it's better now—I mean I think it is." She frowned. "Sometimes I'm not as sure."

"Okay," Abby said. Her mind was a little fuzzy. The doctors said that was normal for pregnancy, but it made it hard to concentrate.

"But Véra makes me happy, too," her mother said.

Véra was Hungarian, and Abby, who had vague ideas about occupations and revolutions, was expecting someone more conflicted than the straightforward woman who arrived. But Véra seemed entirely ungloomy; she seemed optimistic and resourceful. She had abandoned a math degree to make cakes. Her father had taught her Esperanto, and it had helped her learn Spanish in the bakery. She was pretty, with short blondish hair, and she had strong forearms from lifting heavy bags of flour.

Abby wanted to sleep all the time, and she had dreams about small, specific things that then happened the next morning. She dreamed on Christmas Eve that her mother gave her a green pottery bowl like the one for Teddy and Yvette, and in the morning there it was, packed in tissue and wrapped in recycled paper from the Christmas before. She dreamed that her father was in the newspaper discussing water quality, and in the morning he was—with no mention of his unwed pregnant daughter, to her relief. New Year's Day she woke in her childhood bed, from a dream of a missing tooth, with a toothache. She called her childhood dentist and went in.

"Whattya been doing, eating rocks?" he asked cheerfully in the examining room. Then he noticed her stomach.

"Oh," he said.

She wished she had waited and gone to a dentist at school. She would find one when she went back.

"Swallow a cantaloupe?" he asked.

She smiled at him, willing the visit to be over.

"All right, open up," he said, and she told him where it hurt, and then his manner changed. All the jokiness left him. He sat down in his chair and asked how long she had had the toothache, and if she had any other pain, and how far along her pregnancy was, until she, too, became alarmed.

The dentist sent her to a doctor, who told her with little ceremony that she had cancer in her jaw. He was brusque and white-haired, and said she had two choices, as he saw it. She could begin radiation immediately, stand a good chance against the cancer, and lose the baby. It would be dangerous to miscarry at five months, but not as dangerous as letting the cancer go untreated. Or she could have the baby, which would be unaffected by the cancer, but she would have to delay the radiation. Then the cancer would have four months to grow, and he could guarantee nothing about controlling it. Some chemotherapy might be possible without harming the fetus, but it wouldn't be effective alone without the radiation.

Abby thought she must still be in a dream. She thought she might begin to laugh at how ridiculous it was, and she held a hand over her mouth. Realizing how awful it would be to laugh made her realize that the situation was not a dream, and she stared at the doctor.

"You might want some time to decide," he said.

Abby nodded.

"If you decide to do radiation, we could start it tomorrow," he said. "You don't want to wait on this."

Abby nodded again.

"You want to talk to the father?" the doctor asked.

Abby nodded, then shook her head. "The father isn't around," she said.

She left the examining room and called Jamie from the pay phone in the hall, and told him what the doctor had said.

"Okay," Jamie said. "This is your message from God. The god of crossed fingers, the Great Western spirit, whichever god you want. Start the radiation."

"I'd lose the baby."

"It does the baby no good if you're dead."

"I won't die," she said. "I'll start the radiation when he's born."

"Abby," he said. "I should be part of this decision. Go tell the doctor to start the treatment."

"I can't." There was a long silence, which she broke: "Do you think I'm being punished?"

"No!" he said, after a hesitation so brief it was barely detectable. But it was there. He did think she was being punished—he thought they both were.

She told the doctor she wanted to sleep on it, and she went home and lay in bed, in her old blue room in her mother's house, imagining the baby growing in her belly and the cancer growing in her jaw. The baby moved, and her mouth ached. She had seen him yawning on the ultrasound, with all his bones and ribs, and the four-chambered heart beating, and the little bladder already full. He was part of her. If she lost him at five months for her own sake, she would bleed to death out of sorrow.

When she finally slept, her mind felt blank, as if any information there had been erased, and she woke at dawn knowing what to do. The sign in her empty dreams was that there was no sign, and she had to act on faith. She went to the kitchen, where her mother was making coffee, and said she wanted to be baptized.

"Catholic?" her mother asked, the kettle poised in the air.

Abby nodded. She wanted rituals and candles and rules.

"You've got to be kidding."

"I'm not."

"Sit down," her mother said. "Tell me what's going on."

25

JAMIE LEFT SCHOOL and moved into the playroom in Sebastopol, just like old times, and drove Abby to church every morning. She was baptized after eight o'clock Mass on a Tuesday, and Jamie stayed: it was the two of them alone with the priest, and a few stragglers who liked to watch.

"I want to confess," Abby whispered afterward, her forehead still damp with holy water.

"Oh no, you don't."

"I have to."

"Tell God on your own."

"I *have*," she said. "It's not the same."

"They're just men," Jamie said. "They're not magic. They don't need to know."

But Abby spoke quietly to the priest, who nodded and walked with her to the confessional. Jamie waited outside in the sunlight so he wouldn't have to see the expression on the man's face when Abby was through. When she came outside, she seemed calm and sure.

The calm stayed: Jamie had considered her conversion to be a symptom of trauma, but Abby seemed permanently changed. It was like a vacuum suddenly filled in her. He hoped her old secular sensibility—or basic selfishness—might return and change her mind, and make her start the treatments. But she wouldn't risk killing the baby, and she was unshakable in her decision.

Clarissa was furious. "Is she keeping it because of God?" she asked Jamie.

"I don't know."

"You said choosing to be Catholic was like deciding to be a Stalinist," Clarissa said.

"Did I say that?" he asked, though it sounded like something he would say.

Henry came to the house, when Jamie was already moved into the playroom, and found everything out all at once. His twenty-year-old daughter was having a fatherless baby, and was letting cancer go untreated, and had become a fervent Catholic, and his ex-wife was sleeping with a woman who made wedding cakes. He threatened the doctors with lawsuits for not insisting on treatment, and he raged at Clarissa for not providing a stable home environment. Clarissa talked to her therapist, and they agreed to increase her dosage until things got under control. She left the orange pill bottle by the kitchen sink, and Jamie eyed it, but decided that a few borrowed pills weren't going to help.

Then Teddy called, to stammer out the truth about Jamie's own birth, and Jamie had knocked over the blender in Clarissa's kitchen with the phone cord, and shattered the glass pitcher on the floor. Instead of relief that the baby was a safer genetic bet, Jamie felt a gulf yawning beneath his feet: nothing was stable, no footing he had ever had was sure, nothing he had known about himself was true. Margot, who had always ignored him, was his mother. Yvette with her story of contractions at the Bayeux tapestry was his grandmother, and Clarissa his favorite sister was his aunt. Abby was his cousin. Teddy was the baby's great-grandfather, twice.

After long thought, Jamie went to Abby, to tell her what Teddy had said. He thought she might feel less inclined to punish herself if she knew he wasn't her uncle. She was resting in bed in her old powder blue room, with Thomas Merton's memoir propped against her knees. She listened as he told her, and then she looked at him a long time.

"You're still my uncle," she finally said. "Poor Margot."

"Margot's tough as nails, keeping her mouth shut all this time."

"She must have wanted you back," Abby said.

Jamie felt a welling up of something that he pushed back down.

"First cousins can marry in California," he said. "I asked your dad."

"You *what*?"

He laughed; it felt strangely good to laugh, and he tried to remember the last time he had. "I didn't," he said. "I looked it up."

Abby tried to push him off the bed, but she was laughing, too.

"But it's true about cousins," he said. "We could set up house like anyone else."

"Everyone thinks I've lost my mind," she said. "*You've* lost your mind."

He hugged her knees through the bedcovers. "Please, Abby," he said. "Will you start the treatments?"

The laugh vanished, and she shook her head in the way he'd grown used to. "I'm sorry," she said. "I can't."

The cancer moved fast. One doctor said it was because she was pregnant—the cancer grew the way her hair and nails grew; everything about her seemed aggressively alive. The baby was on time, delivered without complications, a healthy eight pounds. The father was recorded as "No Information Available." While Abby slept, Jamie watched his son through the glass nursery wall, in the crib labeled BABY BOY COLLINS—Abby's name, Henry's name—and tried to feel warmth.

Abby named him Theodore James, and then the surgeons took out the left side of her jaw, and began radiation and intensive chemo, so Abby couldn't speak and was sick and exhausted all the time. They gave her antinausea drugs because she wasn't supposed to throw up, but the drugs gave her massive headaches. She cried only once, that Jamie saw, out of frustration that she couldn't breast-feed. Jamie and Clarissa took shifts with the baby, and Abby held him when she could. She wrote them notes on a pad by the bed about how beautiful he was.

The TV was always on somewhere in the hospital, and Jamie watched the news while Abby slept. He tried to concentrate on the siege in Waco or the killings in Bosnia, but it all seemed too far away, and too unreal. He took a book on evolutionary biology from Clarissa's shelf to read, but it just made him angry that Abby had signed up for Heaven and Earth, Adam and Eve. Then the baby would wake, or someone in his family would call about what they could do, and he would have to tell them there was nothing.

Yvette, unstoppable as ever, planned the baptism, and brought Jamie's old christening gown for the baby to wear. A kindly old priest—not the one Abby had confessed to—came to the hospital. Abby gave up her red bandanna, in which she looked like a gang member after a fight, and wore a soft blue hat Yvette had brought. Jamie stood as godfather, not listening to the words, until the priest asked him, "Do you renounce Satan?"

Jamie didn't answer, confronted with the image of a demon with a pitchfork. He wanted to say that evil might be part of human existence. He wanted time. The old priest smiled and asked the question again, as if Jamie might not have heard.

"Sure," Jamie said.

Yvette, at his elbow, whispered, "You have to say the whole thing."

"Yes, I renounce Satan," Jamie said, looking at Abby in the hospital bed. She couldn't smile, because of her jaw, but she managed to look like she was sorry for him, and laughing at him, and grateful to him, all at once.

Clarissa refused to take part. She said she would do anything else, but she would not go through the hocus-pocus. *"It's the hocus-pocus that I want,"* Abby had written on the notepad by the bed. So Clarissa sat to one side, frowning, while the priest wet the baby's forehead and pronounced him Theodore James, a child of God.

"Another Teddy," Yvette said, twisting the wire off a bottle of champagne.

"It's T.J.," Jamie said.

Yvette handed him the bottle. "My hands are too weak," she said. "T.J. sounds like a hoodlum."

"So he'll be a hoodlum," Jamie said. He popped the cork and poured her a glass.

Tipsy on champagne, Yvette sat by Abby's bed and held her hand in both of hers. She said the Lord would stay with Abby through everything, because she had sought Him, and trusted Him, and the child would be blessed. Abby nodded with her collapsed and bandaged face, and Clarissa left the hospital room in disgust.

When the lawyers completed Jamie's guardianship of the baby, Abby wrote him a message on the notepad by her bed. She had been hallucinating on the morphine, so she had the drip stopped long enough to write, in a more tired scrawl than usual:

Jamie, I don't regret anything. I wish I could have all the years you will have with T.J.—I wish I could have those years with you both. But he will be wonderful, he will be good like you and he will make a difference in the world. So please don't regret it either.

Then she died on morphine in the night. Jamie burned the note in the hospital parking lot, with the cigarette lighter in his car. It might suggest his paternity, and his sleep was so disrupted that his memory was slipping. He couldn't keep track of secret letters any more than he could stop regretting; he already regretted everything. He had a three-month-old baby, and Abby was dead.

The head-rocking came back with a vengeance, and at night Jamie lay in Abby's old room in Sebastopol, shaking his head at the ceiling: no, no, no. He heated formula, and changed diapers, and felt homesick for something he'd never had: a normal life, with a wife, a nine-to-five job, and the distant hope of a child. He missed Abby, and resented her, and was afraid to miss or resent her. Clarissa said the baby needed them to be present, and happy and attentive, or its development would be delayed. Jamie couldn't avoid being present; it was being happy he couldn't do.

26

REPORTERS FOUND OUT about Abby and called Henry for interviews, but they were told the congressman couldn't talk to them. Henry had thought he understood grief, but nothing had ever shaken him like Abby's death. He had been away in Washington for so long that it was hard to understand she was really gone. He kept expecting to pick up the phone and hear her voice. But then he would remember. A father's job, at its most basic, was to keep his child alive, and he had failed.

His relationship with Abby had always felt like an adult relationship: she had taken the divorce calmly, and made dinner dates with him, and campaigned with him. He thought Abby's childhood had been taken from her, and he blamed Clarissa for leaving him when they might have worked it out. He had looked forward, he realized now, to knowing his daughter as an adult, when her age would suit her manner. He had thought she might go to law school, and go into practice with him someday.

They had once seen a movie about a father and daughter, both lawyers, arguing opposite sides of a case and then coming together at the end—ditching the scoundrel boyfriend—and it had thrilled him. He had watched it again on tape.

But none of that would ever happen now. When he first heard about Abby's situation, he had wanted to kill the baby's father. He wanted to kill him still. It wasn't a passing desire; it was sustained and profound. He thought he could put his hands around the boy's neck and crush his windpipe and watch him die. He had been lucky during Vietnam; he'd been miles across the ocean from the war. He was ashamed of his luck, but he had thought his soul, or something like it—his sanity maybe—had been preserved when he hadn't gone over. Now he knew that his soul was just as black as anyone's, and he would happily murder the punk who had left Abby pregnant and then dead.

Clarissa had claimed that Abby was dying because of her conversion, that being Catholic was keeping her from having the treatments. Henry had been ready to believe it, but then he had talked to his daughter, and some of his rage had subsided. He thought he understood her better than Clarissa did. She had made her own choices, and she didn't think she was anyone's victim. She had been dealt a bad hand, but she was going to play it out. That was her right, to take the gamble. She was a natural strategist, his Abby. She hadn't lost because she'd converted; she'd converted because she was likely to lose.

But oh, he had wanted her to win.

Yvette planned the funeral Mass, and Henry wasn't sure he could stand it, but he went. In the church, he sat apart from Clarissa's family, and watched Jamie holding Abby's baby, and felt very much alone. They had asked him to give a homily, but he couldn't; what he felt was for himself, not for everyone. He tried to keep his sadness under control, and left quickly when it was over.

A month later, Clarissa came to his office in Sebastopol, unannounced. She hadn't been to his office since they were married. He had a picture of Abby laughing on the wall, and Clarissa stared at it, then looked away. She wore a smocklike dress, and her hair was cut short, and she sat across from him with her knees together and her hands in her lap.

"I want to talk about custody," she said.

"I don't do custody."

"You don't?"

"No."

Clarissa frowned. "But you know the law."

"Not really. Are we talking about Jamie?"

Clarissa took a breath. "My mother's French cousin gave Jamie an Airstream RV," she said. "The cousin's visa ran out and he went home. Now Jamie wants to take the baby in the Airstream to see Margot."

Henry tried to get this straight. "Why Margot?"

Clarissa shook her head. "He went there after high school, too, and it didn't do him any good. But he says he has to. He says it's why Planchet gave him the Airstream."

"How's the engine?"

"How do I know?"

"Jamie is the legal guardian," Henry said.

"Only because he was willing to be the godfather—and renounce Satan. He's never raised a child before. And he's alone. I have a partner."

"Well," Henry said.

"I do!"

"Does she know you're here?"

Clarissa didn't answer.

"Abby made a choice," he said. "I think she thought it through. Jamie's the guardian. We should give him a chance."

Clarissa glared at him. "The baby's your grandson," she said.

"I know."

"You don't want him to have lesbian parents."

"That's not it," he said—though he guessed it was that, too.

"You could get custody yourself," she said.

"Do you really want that?"

Clarissa stared at her lap and said nothing.

When she was gone, Henry sat at his desk with his face in his hands. He wondered how he would work again, really work, like he had before. In the past weeks he had done nothing but sign a few checks. He had always felt he was working for Abby. For her generation, but especially for Abby: to have cleaner air for her, and safer water, and better-paid teachers—those were things to work for. But it was hard to love a generation, especially Abby's, without Abby in it. He used to tease Yvette for her worship of the Kennedys, but now he remembered reading about old Joe Senior, when asked about his plans to bury his daughter. "I have no plans," he had said. "No plans."

His face was still in his hands, his desk still covered with month-old papers, and he didn't know how much time had passed when his secretary said Clarissa was on the phone. He picked up the receiver, stars flashing in his eyes from the released pressure of his palms, and Clarissa said that Jamie, the Airstream, a case of formula, a box of diapers, and the baby were gone.

PART III

Come, thou shalt go home, and we'll have flesh for
holidays, fish for fasting-days, and moreo'er pudding
and flap-jacks, and thou shalt be welcome.
                              —SHAKESPEARE, *Pericles*

This may be true, Cratylus. On the other hand, it may
very well not be.
                              —SOCRATES

27

For the first two days on the road to Louisiana, the baby had cried a lot, and puked up formula, and Jamie wondered what the hell he was doing. But midway through Texas, T.J. turned into a road baby. Whenever they stopped, he woke hungry; he would cry, then eat and smile and give Jamie an unnerving, questioning look. Then as soon as the Airstream started up, he was out for the count.

Jamie thought, as he drove, about the first time he had driven to Louisiana, in a blind fury at his parents. He had hoped Margot would take him in and get him a job, like he and Gail had planned, but she found him an apartment instead, and he wound up on the oil rigs. Then he had driven the same route back to Sebastopol to move in with Clarissa and Abby, and changed the course of his life. Now he was driving it again, with Abby's baby. He thought about fate, and wondered if it would have been possible to avoid coming to this point in his life. It must have been, once. He might have stayed in Louisiana rough-necking, or married his sweet, dirty-minded Gail. But each choice he had made had seemed like the only one possible. And the question made him think of Abby, not pregnant, not dying, which hurt too much to think about.

Then he was parked in front of the address he had for Margot, on a wide, quiet street hung with willows, and he was nervous. It was a bigger house than the one he'd been exiled to at twelve, the one where he'd gone to dinner at twenty, sullen and unhappy, and Abby had told him an elephant joke. He'd been imagining that first house, and now he felt disoriented. He had asked Planchet what to say to Margot.

"You say, 'I understand, I forgive you, I love you, I want to talk, please,'" the old Frenchman had said. *"C'est tout."*

But she might deny it. He didn't know how to think of her: as his mother? His sister? His mother. But he couldn't just sit on the street and do *Chinatown*. He had driven all the way across the country, and he had to do something. So he pulled T.J. out of the Airstream, carrying the car seat like a basket, and walked in the sticky heat to the front door.

They sat in her front room over iced tea and cookies arranged on a tray. T.J. kicked and smiled in his seat on the floor. Margot wore a pressed white shirt, and her hair was still blonde, pulled back at the base of her neck. She looked young for fifty, in the way rich women do, but she also looked like she had always been an adult, which was how Jamie thought of her. She seemed distracted by the baby, but composed. She talked about how different it had been in 1959 for a middle-class Catholic sixteen-year-old. "I was very young," she said.

Jamie said he understood. He was conscious of trying to

behave properly. "What was he like?" he asked. "My—" He didn't say "father," because he still thought of Teddy as his father.

"He was a wonderful dancer," she said. "The girls all had crushes on him. He had a white convertible. He wasn't tall."

"What was his first name?"

Margot set her tea glass on a coaster on the table. "We called him Mr. Tucker," she said.

"You never saw him after that?"

She shook her head. "He left the school."

He had thought about telling Margot the baby was his—he was asking honesty from her, and he could be honest, too. T.J. was her grandson. But she seemed to want the conversation to be over.

"What are your plans?" she asked.

Jamie said he wasn't sure.

"Why don't you stay a few days, until you decide."

"We can sleep in the Airstream."

"Please," Margot said. "Let me give you a room."

So Jamie and the baby moved into a guest room with a yellow and white bedspread and a carafe of water on the night table. There was a desk with stationery and envelopes: heavy cream paper with a weeping willow engraved at the top of each page, and a fountain pen with ink in a pot. In the bathroom were thick towels, and in the closet a bathrobe.

"You'll join us for supper," Margot said.

"Sure."

But Margot didn't come to supper. She went to her room after getting him settled, and she was still there when her husband came home from work. Owen seemed happy to see Jamie and the baby, but he was puzzled about Margot's retreat.

"She get dinner on?" Owen asked.

Jamie thought she hadn't, but said it didn't matter.

Owen went to Margot's room. When he came back, he looked pale and nervous.

"Margot's not feeling well," he said. "I'll grill us some steaks."

"Can I see her?" Jamie asked.

Owen glanced upstairs, toward the bedroom. "I don't think so," he said. He started the grill, and tried to make a salad, but it seemed beyond him. He finally dropped the mangled lettuce in the garbage, and forked the steaks onto plates.

Jamie tried to make conversation. "Great steaks," he said.

Owen said nothing.

"Great lawns here, too," Jamie said. "How come there aren't kids playing on them?"

As soon as he asked it, he knew he shouldn't have. Owen gave him a stricken look. "It's too hot," he said in a flat voice. He opened the freezer, plunked a hard carton of ice cream on the kitchen counter, and went back upstairs to Margot's room.

"Oh, fuck," Jamie said. "Don't let me say everything that pops into my head," he told T.J.

T.J. kicked and smiled.

Jamie served himself a bowl of ice cream and ate it while voices from upstairs came muffled through the heavy doors, and down the carpeted hallways, and then subsided again. He thought the faint sounds must be cries and shouts; the house absorbed all normal speech. He fed T.J. his bottle and put him down in the guest room. When the baby fell asleep he was suddenly tired, and went to bed.

For three days he stayed at Margot's, waiting for her to come out of her room. He watched TV, and played guitar for T.J., and ate take-out food with Owen. Finally Owen asked him to go.

"She's not going to come out," he said.

"Is she okay?"

Owen shook his head. He had dark hollows under his eyes,

and he looked weary and old. "This happened the last time she was pregnant, after she lost the baby. She cried a lot, and wouldn't eat, and we fought." He rubbed his face. "She told me, then, about having a baby before."

Jamie nodded.

"I didn't believe her at first. I thought she'd made it up."

Jamie didn't say anything.

"I'm sorry—" Owen began, then he stopped. "You were probably better off with Yvette, at the time."

"Sure," Jamie said.

"I think it's hard for Margot, with you in the house. And the baby."

"Of course."

"I want to give you some money," Owen said. "I'm not paying you to leave. But Margot would want to help you out."

Jamie shook his head, but he needed the cash. Even to get back to Clarissa's, he would need more diapers, and food and gas, and it would be better if he didn't have to go back to Clarissa's. He hadn't had a plan beyond getting to Margot's. He hadn't expected Margot to melt down. He took the money and started packing, but when Owen left for work, he crept upstairs.

"Margot?" he said at her bedroom door. She didn't answer, but he knew she was there. He listened for any movement, but heard nothing.

"I haven't told anyone else this," he said finally, to the door. "It's kind of a long story, but the baby is mine. He's your grandson—biologically, I mean." There was silence, and he went on. "I'm having a hard time with that fact, but I wanted you to know it."

He waited. This was his trump card, and he felt dizzy from playing it. He was sure she would come out. He was sure she must have questions.

"So Mr. Tucker is his grandfather," he said.

The door stayed closed. He sat down in the hallway and waited, until he heard T.J. start to cry in the guest room, and he went back downstairs.

He fed and changed T.J., and finished packing the Airstream. On his last trip to the guest room he saw a figure in a nightgown disappear down the hall and behind a bathroom door.

"Margot?" he called, but she didn't answer. She had looked thin and hardly there, like a ghost.

In the guest room, T.J. sat smiling in his car seat. Tucked in beneath his feet was one of the thick cream envelopes from the desk.

Jamie waited until he was driving through the quiet streets, with the baby nodding off to the vibration of the engine, to open the envelope against the steering wheel. He tried not to tear the weeping willow engraved on the flap. Inside was a slip of paper, not the cream stationery but a torn piece of blue-lined loose-leaf. In red ballpoint, in Margot's neat, nun-trained hand, it said "Frederick J. Tucker, 1306 Old Pine Road, Lewiston, New Mexico."

28

MARGOT SAT ALONE in her room. Owen was at work. Jamie had gone. The corners were pulled smooth on the bed and the pillows were stacked at the head of it. Jamie had brought her a baby, his baby, her grandson. Her baby's orphaned baby, and she didn't want anything to do with it. She didn't want to see it, didn't want it around. The discovery took her breath away.

She had accepted long ago that having given up her child, gratefully, she was to be given no more children. That was God's will. She had decided there were other ways for her to contribute to the world. But Jamie's return had erased them all from her mind, and brought on waves of sickness and misery. Even now that he was gone, she couldn't think of what the things she contributed were. She couldn't concentrate, and realized she was starving. She hadn't eaten in three days, except a few crackers to stave off the nausea that Jamie's presence with the baby made her feel.

She went downstairs—her house once more blessedly empty—and pulled the refrigerator door. Her arm felt weak against the seal of the gasket. She hadn't been shopping since Jamie arrived, and the fridge was all glaring white shelves. There were six eggs in the egg tray. There was a small piece of cheese in the snack bin, a half-finished jar of marmalade in the door, and a bottle of cranberry juice. There were wilted vegetables in the crisper drawers, but she didn't want to look at those.

She opened the cranberry juice and drank straight from the bottle, then set it on the counter and realized she had never done that before. It was cold, and bitter, and sweet.

She would make a cheese soufflé—she turned on the oven and separated the eggs, and whisked the whites into peaks. Then she grated the cheese, but when it came out on the cutting board in a white, blossoming pile, she took a handful and ate it straight. It was so soft, and salty, and good. She grated some more, and ate that, too. The oven made a ticking noise, the air inside it expanding with the heat. Then the cheese was gone. She drank from the juice bottle and thought about what to do. Mme. Planchet, back in France, had once made a jam soufflé for her husband, who had kissed her loudly on the mouth for it. Margot took the marmalade from the fridge, folded it into the stiffened eggs, and slid the baking dish onto the oven rack.

"What did one chick say to the other chick?" she heard Abby's seven-year-old voice asking in her head. Margot hadn't known.

"Look at the orange marmalade."

She heard again Abby's giggling laugh. But Margot hadn't understood the joke, so Abby had repeated it for her, then explained that there was an orange in the nest with the two chicks. Look at the orange Marma-laid. Abby had dissolved into giggles again. Margot had thought the orange should be in the question part of the joke, and she hadn't thought it was very funny either way, but now that Abby was dead it seemed unbearably sad. The oven made another expanding noise. She could smell the soufflé beginning to cook, and she was ravenous. She finished off the juice and started a list of her small contributions. On a lined piece of notepaper from the kitchen drawer she wrote: *Wife.* She thought of long-suffering Owen, who had been so loyal and good. She doodled a series of slanting ovals, left over from the nuns' handwriting exercises at Our Lady of Lourdes, and then a series of slanting lines. She was going to go on, and write *Daughter. Sister.* But instead she put down the pen, and stopped making the list. She didn't want to see the rest.

Owen came home early from work to find her at the table with a spoon and the soufflé dish, eating the last scrap of sweet, orange-flavored eggs. He looked ready to collapse with relief, and dropped his briefcase at his side.

"Are you back?" he asked.

She had soufflé on her fingers and her eyelids felt swollen and tired. "Look at the orange marmalade," she said.

Owen looked concerned again.

"I'm back," she said.

Her husband kissed her, sticky lips and all, lifted her carefully in his arms, and carried her upstairs to bed.

29

AFTER JAMIE TOOK the baby, Clarissa had the shrink increase her dosage again. She wrote to Abby about how she felt an ache in her heart all the time, like she couldn't go on. She burned the letters with a candle to deliver them, until Véra said she was going to burn the house down. Véra was getting concerned.

Then Jamie called from the road and told her about Margot and the dance teacher. She made him explain it all slowly, from the start.

Margot had been pregnant in France. Margot had slept with the dance teacher when she was fifteen. Margot had given her baby to Yvette, and kept it a secret, and could never have another; her sister's childlessness was much crueler than Clarissa had thought. She tried to call, not knowing what to say, but Owen said Margot wasn't feeling well and wasn't taking calls.

For the next few days, Clarissa thought about her parents. She thought that if they knew about Margot, they might be able to handle the news of Véra—it didn't seem like much more of a transgression. If they met Véra, they would like her. That might help them understand.

"Why do they have to know this?" Véra asked, in the garden, cutting the last of the oregano. Véra's accent wasn't strong, but the precision of her English made her sound overwhelmingly rational. On the phone to Budapest speaking Hungarian a mile a minute, she sounded like any daughter—impulsive and perturbable—and Clarissa wished she sounded that way now.

"I want them to accept who I am," Clarissa said.

"I think they do."

"Not if they don't know about you. I can't take you home."

"To me, this is okay."

"But I should be able to take you, that's the point," Clarissa said. "It's nothing compared to what Margot put them through."

"I don't think this is true," Véra said. "Not to them."

"Really?"

"Really," Véra said. "I don't think it would be nothing to them at all."

Clarissa stood with a fistful of oregano and thought that maybe Véra was right. But she couldn't stand to assume that they would disapprove. Véra couldn't really understand. Her father had loved and accepted her, girlfriends and all, since she was twenty.

So without telling Véra, she took a day off work and drove south to Hermosa Beach. Her mother was in the backyard, transplanting pink lobelia from plastic flats. The garden was overcrowded already, but Yvette had found one more spot.

"I've been trying to get these in all week," she said. "Something keeps coming up." She kissed Clarissa with her gardening gloves still on. "Your father wanted to be here when you got here," she said. "You look wonderful."

"I'm okay."

"What did you want to talk about?"

"Can we sit down?" Clarissa asked. "Can you take off your gloves?"

They sat at the mottled glass table under the green deck umbrella, with her mother's flowered work gloves between them, and Clarissa told her mother about Véra.

Her mother blinked, and then looked sad, and looked down at her clasped hands on the table.

"I don't think you should tell your father," she finally said.

"He knows about Margot's baby."

Her mother looked at her.

"*I* know about Margot's baby," Clarissa added.

"But that's a different thing," Yvette said. "Teddy loves you so much, Clarissa. I think it would only make you both terribly sad."

Clarissa ran her hand over the surface of the table. The glass was smooth on top; the mottled texture was underneath.

"I don't think you'll get what you want," her mother said. "You're his favorite, you know."

Clarissa looked up. "Really?"

"Of course."

"Maybe he'll understand, then."

Her mother shook her head. "I know him so well, honey. I've lived with him so long. I love you, and I would be happy to meet your Véra. But I don't think you should tell him."

They sat in silence for a long time.

"I'll get you something to drink," her mother said, and she went inside and left Clarissa alone.

Clarissa heard the clinking of ice cubes through the screen, and then she heard her father drive up and park on the street. He came around the back of the house with a paper grocery bag, walking a little tilted to keep his balance.

"There's my girl!" he said. "I just ran out to the store."

"Can I talk to you a minute?" she asked. She had to say it quickly, before her mother came back outside.

Her father nodded.

"I'm living with a woman," she said.

He looked confused, standing on the deck with his groceries, as if he didn't know what she was saying. She had to say it again, in different words, before he understood. Then he set the paper bag on the table and walked, straight-backed, into the house. Clarissa sat alone on the deck, and her mother didn't bring her a drink. Finally Clarissa checked the grocery bag. There was a carton of Neapolitan ice cream, a bottle of chocolate syrup, and a jar of maraschino cherries, for the sundaes they had eaten together when Margot and her mother were away. Clarissa sat back down on the deck and her eyes were dry and aching.

Finally she took the bag inside. The kitchen was empty and her parents' bedroom door was closed. She stood in the living room, wondering what to do. The books on the shelves were about gardening, Korea, and World War II, plus a shelf about being a good Catholic. Novels went to the church book sales as soon as her parents had read them. There was a long-faced, Modigliani-like statue of the Virgin on the side table next to the sofa. In the dining room was the old polished table, and the china cupboard, and the bar. She went back to the kitchen, and still there was no sound from the bedroom. She thought about simply driving back home to Véra, but then her mother came out and closed the door behind her.

"I think you should give him time with this," her mother said quietly.

Clarissa started to speak, to say that she wanted to see him. She wanted to hold his hand and talk to him. She wanted to have Neapolitan sundaes together, and tell him she would do anything for him. But her mother stood between her and the bedroom door, and said they both loved her so very, very much, and to give it time.

Clarissa said nothing, and went back to the car and drove home.

30

LEWISTON, NEW MEXICO, when Jamie arrived, had a population of 2,117. He'd driven through the town of Truth or Consequences to get there, and he'd made some jokes aloud to T.J.
about that. Lewiston had one street called Fiesta, which was
noisy with children playing, one street called Siesta, which was
silent and empty, and four traffic lights. There was a small school,
a grocery store, a hardware store, a coffee shop, and a pawnshop.

When he'd driven every street in town, delaying, Jamie drove
out on Old Pine Road. The road was on the edge of town, and
1306 was a tiny wooden structure with ordinary houses on either
side, and a dry grass field behind. Jamie sat in the Airstream and
looked at the house. It was like standing on top of the high dive
when he was a kid. The longer you waited the harder it was; you
just had to jump. But he had been debating with himself all
through Louisiana, Texas, and half of New Mexico, and he still
wasn't sure.

Finally he got out of the RV, walked up the stone pathway, and knocked on the pinewood door. He listened for movement in the house, but there was none, so he waited a minute, then knocked again. Still nothing. He walked around the perimeter, over a crabgrass lawn, and looked through a window in the back. The house seemed to be one L-shaped room, the kitchen set off from the bedroom by turning a corner around what must be a bathroom. Two white taper candles stood on the kitchen table, and books and videos lay scattered near the bed. A pair of red cowboy boots stood by the front door. Jamie walked around the rest of the house, past a high window with shower-curtain rings visible through it, back to the front. In the Airstream, T.J. was just waking up, and gave him that unsettling, questioning look.

So Jamie tried the neighbors: he knocked at the squat stucco house at 1304, and a woman with pale blue eyes and a long gray braid came to the door. Jamie asked if Mr. Tucker was on vacation, or if he would be home soon.

"Vacation from what?" she asked with a harsh laugh. "No, Freddie's around. Try the coffee shop." She started to retreat into the house.

"Could you tell me what he looks like?" Jamie asked.

The pale eyes narrowed. "No." She shut the door.

T.J. had begun to wail, so Jamie had to get formula into a bottle quick, and he saw the woman watching him through the curtains.

In the coffee shop parking lot were a faded orange pickup, a white Honda, a blue Buick, and a golf cart. Jamie wondered which one he would choose for his father, and carried T.J.'s car seat inside by the handle.

The shop was air-conditioned and smelled of roasting coffee. The walls and tables were of stained pine, and the glass case next to the cash register was full of pastries. Watercolors by local artists, of local landscapes, hung on the walls. Jamie didn't look at the customers sitting at the tables. He didn't want to get attached to any of them prematurely. He walked straight to the counter and said, "I'm looking for Frederick Tucker."

The girl working there was a cute blonde with curled bangs, about sixteen, who kept her shoulders back in consideration of her sixteen-year-old's breasts. She was putting coffee cups away, and she pointed with her chin over Jamie's shoulder. "That's Freddie," she said.

Jamie turned and saw a man staring out the window. His hair was long and white, pulled back in a ponytail with a fuzzy turquoise elastic band at the base of his neck. His face was old but not wrinkled. He wore black snakeskin cowboy boots and a canvas ranch jacket. Margot had been right: he wasn't tall. He sat without moving, as if in a trance. Then he turned to Jamie. His eyes were dark and shining, and his front teeth were missing.

"You wouldn't want to sell that Airstream, would you?" he asked.

Unprepared for the question, Jamie shook his head.

The blonde coffee girl said, "This man's looking for you, Grandpa."

Jamie did the calculations that would make the girl—his father's granddaughter—another niece. He felt he had jumped off the high dive into something that wasn't air.

"He's your grandfather?" he asked her.

"I just call him that," she said cheerfully. "We adopted each other. I'm Lauren." She held out her hand, and Jamie shook it. Her hands were small and strong.

Jamie approached Freddie Tucker's little table, set T.J.'s seat on a wooden chair, and sat down. He took a breath. Mr. Tucker smiled at him: a friendly smile, despite the missing teeth.

"Did you know a girl named Margot Santerre," Jamie asked, "at Sacred Heart High School in Hermosa Beach in 1958?"

Freddie frowned. "Questions like these are what I'm worst at," he said. "My memory of the fifties is not what it was."

"Really pretty blonde," Jamie offered.

"Then I hope I knew her."

"You taught dance lessons at the school, right? With Miss Blair?"

Freddie brightened. "Sure!" he said. "I was no Fred Astaire, I can tell you. I was more like a—whattya call it—I knew all the steps, like a toy you wind up. That was before I began to expand my mind." He nodded sagely. "The expansion caused me to forget some things. My brain wasn't able to contain them."

"So, no Margot," Jamie said.

"If you say I knew her, I'm sure I did. I've been healing myself lately, and remembering more. I heal others, too. That's what I do. It's my craft."

"I saw your house," Jamie said. "Margot gave me your address."

Freddie smiled, toothless and proud. "That's my other craft," he said. "I'm an architect. Self-taught. It's eighteen feet by twenty-four feet, if you measure the outside."

Jamie nodded. "I wonder how Margot got your address."

"Can't say," Freddie said. "I'm in the book."

"Margot is my mother."

Freddie tilted his head to one side. "You're not such a pretty blonde."

"I think you might be my father."

Freddie didn't blink. "Lauren, honey," he called to the coffee girl, and she came to the table. She wore white shorts under her apron, and her legs were smooth and tan. Her hands were wet from the sink, and she dried them on the apron. "Does this young man look like me?" Freddie asked.

They both looked up at Lauren while she studied them. Jamie thought about the fact that he was being examined by a teenaged coffee girl to determine his parentage, and how funny Abby would think it was, and he felt a stab of sadness that he didn't have her to tell it to.

"I've been teaching Lauren my craft," Freddie said, still looking up at the girl as if she were taking their picture. "She has insight."

"I think he does look like you, Grandpa," Lauren said. "Yes, I think he does."

"Thank you, sweetheart," Freddie said, and Lauren went back to washing cups behind the counter.

"She's a bright girl," Freddie confided in a low voice. "Terrible home life, no dad. I drive her to school every day, to help her out. She's a junior varsity cheerleader now, gets straight A's."

"Great," Jamie said.

"So." Freddie slapped a hand on the table. "If you're my kid, you've got six ex-stepmothers, two half brothers, and a half sister. I don't suppose you want to meet any of them."

Jamie shook his head.

"Good decision," Freddie said. "I can't give you any money."

"I don't want money."

"I could teach you my craft," Freddie said. "If you're sticking around. What you have to remember is that reality is perception. It's been proven by science. If you control the way you think about matter, matter behaves differently. Particles and waves."

"I have a baby," Jamie said.

Freddie eyed T.J., who was awake and playing with a teething ring. "Is he sick?" he asked. "I could heal him."

"I just thought you'd like to meet him," Jamie said. "He's your grandson."

Freddie patted the baby's head. "I have two granddaughters," he told Jamie. "Besides Lauren. But I don't have a grandson. I'd like to see the Airstream, too. Can I see him in the Airstream?"

They walked out into the dry heat and across to the RV.

"This is a fine vehicle," Freddie said inside. "Not much smaller than my house, and you could have a life of freedom here. I tell you, I've found a community in this town, but this vehicle would be a temptation."

Jamie realized he was staring at Freddie's teeth, and Freddie touched his empty gums with one finger.

"It's like this Margot person," he said. "The memory slipped away from me. I told you I did some expanding of my mind—well, one day I woke up with more room for expansion. Three teeth's worth." He laughed at his own joke, as if he'd never made it before. "For a while I had some fake ones on a bridge," he said, "but I've sworn off vanity. And the people who love me, like Lauren, they don't care."

Jamie nodded.

"Tell you what," Freddie said. "This is a nice town. You park the Airstream at my house and stay awhile. Then I can pretend it's mine to drive off in whenever I want. I won't drive off, though. You don't have to worry about that."

Jamie looked at T.J., as if he might get an answer there. He didn't have anywhere else to go. T.J. didn't look questioning, he just looked like a baby.

"We can stay awhile, I guess," Jamie said.

So he parked the Airstream in front of the house, and pushed the population to 2,119. Days went by, some of them too hot to think, and nights went by, each getting colder. He helped Lauren with her algebra, at Freddie's request, talking her through the story problems. *If a train is going* X *speed toward another going* Y *speed, starting* Z *distance apart, how long* . . . T.J. grew out of his clothes, and Lauren collected hand-me-downs from the families on Fiesta Street: onesies and booties and a T-shirt that said HECHO EN MEXICO across the front. She showed Jamie where the nearest clinic was, for the baby's checkup, and she held T.J. while Jamie filled out forms. The nurse raised an eyebrow at Lauren, who looked so young, but Lauren smiled cheerfully at her and said, "I'm not the mom." She nodded at Jamie. "I'm his niece."

Jamie avoided the nurse's eye and tried to concentrate on the forms. They asked the child's name. It was Collins on the birth certificate, but a man alone with a baby was untrustworthy enough without having a different name. He sat with the pen in his hand, and thought about the elaborate French lie on his own birth certificate, and had a flash of understanding for Yvette, doing what she thought she had to do from moment to moment. Finally he gave T.J. his own last name, writing "Theodore James Santerre" in ballpoint capitals on the form.

Freddie Tucker designed lessons for Jamie in controlling reality: he hid index cards that said FOCUS and STRENGTH in the dry grass field behind the house, and sent Jamie blindfolded to search for them. He sat Jamie down in the darkened living room, lit the two white candles on the kitchen table, and told Jamie to focus on the exact point between them. He showed him how to increase the oxygen supply to his brain by forcing his breath out through his teeth, and he explained that when true focus was achieved, a person could walk through a wall.

Jamie went along with the exercises because they gave shape to his days and distracted him from his thoughts—so in that way, they did control reality. But by late fall he couldn't take it anymore and got a job in the hardware store, where they let him keep T.J. behind the counter. Sorting screws by size was like talking to Freddie; it distracted him from the sick feeling that came when he thought about Abby, and helped keep the head-rocking under control. He tried to learn Spanish from the other employees.

Some nights he drove up into the mountains and camped under stars so dense he could hardly see between them, and that helped, too. It didn't matter whether what was out there was chaos or God: it made his own life seem small enough to handle. Freddie had told him there were people on other planets; he said the probability was too great for there not to be. But even with infinite probability, Jamie couldn't see the evolution of man from single-celled creatures repeating. It was like the monkeys writing *King Lear,* and he didn't believe that one either. In town with Freddie he wasn't sure, but up in the mountains he was.

More days went by, and more nights, and T.J. grew until he wasn't a baby anymore, but walked and spoke. Jamie sent a picture to Teddy and Yvette, and one to Clarissa, and a note saying he was fine. He guessed Margot knew where he was. He didn't know how to explain the current Mr. Tucker to her, and didn't want to try.

Everyone in town flirted with Lauren, but she remained sweet and oblivious. Before cheer competitions, she recruited Jamie to spot her for handsprings, tugging down her spandex tank top and beaming when she got it right, looking crushed when she fell, then demanding to try it again. He tried to maintain his monklike composure with her, with her smooth, tan, flexible body leaping past him, but mostly he found it easier to avoid her, go up into the mountains. She made him hip-hop mix tapes—"Your music taste is *so* old-fashioned," she said—and he left them in the Airstream. He read her college application essay, and suggested that it shouldn't be so much about the things she'd learned from Freddie. She got into New Mexico State on a cheerleading scholarship, but she came home on weekends, bringing picture books and toys for T.J., who loved her passionately. She won first runner-up in the Miss Teen New Mexico contest when T.J. was three, and gave him her tiara. T.J. was thrilled.

One night when Lauren was a sophomore, Jamie sat at the

banquette table in the Airstream with her and with Freddie, playing Yvette's mother's rummy. He had taught Lauren the game one slow, hot afternoon, when her math homework was finished. Her dormant mean streak came out when she played cards, and she loved to win. When they played poker, she bluffed and raised and took risks—nothing like Abby's guarded play—but he still couldn't help thinking of Abby when he watched her arranging her hand. If he only looked out the corner of his eye, it was Abby: the ponytail, the intense concentration. T.J. was asleep in the back.

At college Lauren had learned to drink beer, though she wasn't twenty-one yet, and there were half-empty bottles on the table, none of them Freddie's. Freddie didn't drink anymore; it interfered with his healing. Lauren wore a short white dress that said NMSU across the chest, and Jamie kept discarding the cards she needed to win. She snatched each one with glee. Throughout the game she slid closer to him on the bench, until her bare thigh touched his under the table.

Jamie shuffled the cards for a new hand and tried to focus—he thought Freddie's concentration lessons should be of some practical use—but then he felt Lauren's lips brush his ear. He thought of Abby in the ocean, telling him it was okay. He thought of Margot in the white convertible with Mr. Tucker. He thought that men were hound dogs, and he was no exception. But how could they not be? Girls were—girls. Lauren's breath was warm on his neck.

"You're letting me win," she whispered.

Jamie shook his head.

"I don't like it," she said.

He turned to look at her; her face was close and smelled sweetly of beer, like Abby's had of champagne. "I'd never do that."

Lauren smiled wickedly at him. "Good," she said, and she

plunked herself back on her own side of the bench, round breasts in the white dress bouncing.

Freddie was losing the game, but he didn't seem to mind. He seemed happy. Jamie felt something cold and sloshy in his stomach, and he wondered if this was Freddie's plan, to install his newfound son with his beloved Lauren. Freddie had said a hundred times that reality was perception, to be arranged at will. Jamie went back to his hand, shielding his cards from Lauren. She won the game fair and square, threw her tanned arms over her head in victory, dropped them over Jamie's shoulders and kissed the side of his mouth.

Then she stood to give a speech, clutching an empty beer bottle as if it were a trophy. Feigning happy tears, she said, "I'd like to thank my dear grandfather Frederick Tucker for all his support. And my darling uncle Jamie—I couldn't have done it without your discards."

They clapped, and Jamie felt as drunk as she, and Lauren took a bow, lowering the scooped yoke of the dress. Jamie thought about Abby's son—his son—asleep in the back.

Freddie yawned and stretched. "You stay up if you want, Lauren," he said. "I'm going to bed."

"I think we should all turn in," Jamie said, too quickly.

As he was herding them out of the Airstream, Lauren stopped, as if remembering something, and lifted her face to Jamie to be kissed. Jamie kissed her warm cheek, then turned her around by the shoulders, sending her down the metal steps to the ground.

In the morning he knocked on Freddie's door and said it was time for him to move on.

31

YVETTE HAD JUST walked in from visiting a woman who was too ill to go to church, when the phone rang. Dozens of bee stings had been applied to the woman's paralyzed right arm, to treat the paralysis, and today she could lift the arm and move her fingers. Yvette was thinking about bees, and how strange are the ways of God. At first she mistook the ringing of the phone for the buzzing of a swarm. She came out of her reverie to find Jamie on the line.

"I want to exchange some information," Jamie said.

"Tell me where you are," Yvette said. "Tell me where you've been."

"What was Father Jack's last name?"

Yvette tried to think back through the Anthonys and Josephs and Johns to find a priest named Jack.

"The one who taught me guitar," Jamie prompted.

Then she remembered him, young and handsome, drying

dishes and telling her that celibacy twisted the mind. "I don't think I knew his full name," Yvette said.

"You wrote him checks for the lessons," Jamie said.

Yvette thought how hurt Teddy would be to know that Jamie had asked for the priest Teddy had so distrusted, instead of asking for him.

"It was so long ago," she said.

"I'm running out of quarters for the phone."

"Tell me where you are!" she cried.

"Tell me what his name was."

"Don't hang up," she said, and she ran to her bedroom, to the address book that was falling apart at the spine. She never erased a name, because she never felt she had really lost anyone, even when they died or dropped out of touch. Priests went by first name, and she found him in the *J*'s: Father Jack Caffrey. She had the address of the diocese he'd gone to, and an old phone number. She read it out to Jamie.

"Thanks, Ma," Jamie said. "I'm at a pay phone in Tucson. T.J. is four. He's so cool. He likes beauty contests and older women— I mean older for him. His hands aren't big enough for guitar yet, but he's great at lyrics."

"Where will he go to school?" Yvette asked. There was a click on the phone.

"That's my last quarter," Jamie said. "I'm taking good care of him. I'll write, okay? Say hi to everyone."

A long tone came on, to indicate that the call was over, and Yvette put down the phone. She wished she had told him that she understood, that she had seen that T.J. was his the moment he was born, having seen Jamie also the moment he was born. She could have told him that she understood his pain and his shame, and he didn't need to run away. No one would challenge his right to T.J., and no one would blame him.

When Teddy came home from visiting his own shut-ins, he brought an old man's broken electric razor and studied it in the light over the kitchen sink. She watched him unscrew the top of the mechanism and frown at the underside, and then she told him that Jamie had sent his love. Teddy looked up, amazed. It wasn't exactly true, but it lifted Teddy's spirits for the rest of the evening. They both waited for Jamie's promised letter, but it didn't come.

32

THE COLLEGE OF St. Francis Xavier was built on a hill that sometimes—when there was no fog from the Bay—had a view of the Pacific. It was staffed by aging Jesuits, and had a small theater for the college plays. Jamie sat in the audience, with T.J. beside him, and waited for the stage lights to come up.

Romeo was a thin, contemplative Chinese boy. Juliet was a small-featured girl with a clear voice. Jamie thought they'd been right not to cast the prettiest actress, whoever she was. The ordinariness of this Juliet was somehow moving; she could have been any girl. Friar Lawrence, when he appeared, was Father Jack, the guitar-playing priest: twenty-six years older, in a friar's robes, but unmistakable. His hair had gone gray around his ears.

T.J. became interested in the play, and stood up in his seat to see over the heads in front. He gasped when Mercutio died. Father Jack gave Juliet her potion, and fooled everyone, and delivered his message too slowly. Romeo stopped on the road to buy poison from a hooded apothecary who had also played Tybalt. The lovers died in the tomb, one by one, and Jamie found himself with tears on his face. The parents wanted to kill each other, so the children, wanting to do the opposite and love each other, killed each other.

T.J. was urgently concerned about Juliet and the knife, whispering questions in Jamie's ear. He clapped with joy and relief when she came to life for the curtain call.

"*There* she is," he said.

The audience cheered Father Jack as a favorite, and the priest grinned as he bowed. The old Jesuit on the phone, who had told Jamie about the play, had sounded disapproving about Father Jack being in it.

When the houselights came on, the students and parents began to file out of the theater.

"I guess we go backstage," Jamie said.

"Will the girl be there?" T.J. wanted to know.

The dressing rooms were attached to the scenery shop; there were paint splatters on the floor, and stage flats stacked against the wall. Jamie thought of kissing Gail in high school, in the surrey with the fringe on top. There were three girls waiting for Mercutio, and a tall boy who found Juliet and hugged her tight, while T.J. watched her every move. Finally Father Jack came out to wash his face in the deep sink. He had eyeliner smeared under his eyes when Jamie approached him, feeling awkward.

"You were great," Jamie said.

The priest looked at him over the paper towel he held to his cheek. "Thank you," he said.

"It's great that your order lets you do it."

"Yes, it is."

"My little boy—he's four—he loved it. He was completely transfixed." Jamie wondered if he had ever used that word before, *transfixed,* and why he couldn't be casual and direct. The eyeliner was unsettling him.

"That's very kind," the priest said.

"You taught me guitar," Jamie blurted finally. "In Hermosa Beach when I was twelve. It changed my life."

Father Jack looked at him, then said, "Can you wait? I'll just be a minute." He disappeared into the dressing room.

Juliet left in jeans with the tall boy, and T.J. looked longingly after her. Then Father Jack came from the dressing room, in jeans himself.

"So you're Jamie, all grown up," he said. "Where shall we have this reunion?"

The café was small and bright, unclaimed by students. There was one couple in the back, sharing a piece of cake. A waitress brought T.J. paper and crayons, and set him up in a booth while Jamie and Father Jack took a table.

"Tell me everything," Father Jack said. "You can skip the 'Bless me, Father.'"

So Jamie began, and told how he got home from Hawaii and Louisiana that summer, feeling like he didn't fit in with his sisters, to find that the guitar lessons, the one thing that made him feel good, were gone. He told how his mother had found the magazines and Gail had moved away, and how he had some bad years after that. He checked to be sure T.J. wasn't listening, and he explained in a low voice how he'd taken care of Abby when Clarissa got divorced, and how he had loved Abby, and had made the mistake of sleeping with her when she grew up. He had felt, then, like he couldn't stop himself, though he knew now that he should have. He told about Abby dying and leaving him the baby, and how it seemed impossible to go on. He told about Margot being his real mother, and her staying in her room when he went to see her, and about finding Freddie Tucker. Finally he talked about Lauren, and how she wasn't like Abby but she *was*, kind of, and how he had felt, that night playing cards, like everything was repeating itself in a weird, dreamlike way, in this girl who was sort of his niece, with Mr. Tucker the dance teacher looking on.

"So you want advice from a celibate," Father Jack said when Jamie finished.

Jamie blushed and shrugged.

"I mean, isn't that an absurd idea?" the priest asked. "It's always struck me as one. I guess we're supposed to be objective." He sighed and rubbed his forehead. "Your mother," he said, "Yvette, I mean, was a fascinating woman. She was very devout, but she radiated sex. You would've thought she was having an illicit affair with God."

The description made Jamie uncomfortable. "Okay," he said.

"I thought she might have an illicit affair with me that summer, but it didn't happen."

"You're a priest."

Father Jack gave him a tired look.

"The thing with Lauren would have been a mistake," the priest said. "Tragedy repeating itself as farce. You were right to leave."

"I don't know where to go now."

"What do you want?"

"I want—I don't know," Jamie said. "A normal life. Maybe a house. I want T.J. to go to school somewhere. Living in an RV with no mother is going to get weird for him."

"That ship has sailed," Father Jack said. "The kid is four."

"He's happy," Jamie said.

"Of course he's happy. It's a great life."

It was Jamie's turn to sigh. In the booth, T.J. flirted with the waitress who brought him the crayons.

"You want my advice?" the priest asked.

"I don't know," Jamie said, trying to joke. "I saw what happened to those kids in the play."

Father Jack smiled. "But they didn't follow my instructions," he said. "You will."

33

GAIL WAS LIVING on Vashon Island in the middle of Puget Sound, perfectly happy with her imperfect life, when a dusty silver RV pulled up outside her house. She was weeding the window planters, and she didn't recognize Jamie at first. He got out of the Airstream with a little boy in a tiara, and she thought they must be friends of the gay couple next door. But there was something about the way he looked at her—this scruffy, lanky guy in cowboy boots who needed a haircut and a shave—that set off a disturbance inside her rib cage, something about to be remembered.

"Hi," she said, in a helpful-neighbor way. "Are you looking for Bill and Bill?"

But Jamie wasn't, of course. He kept looking at her, too shy to say anything, until she recognized the boy he'd been, beneath the half-beard and the years. She didn't know who moved first, although it must have been she who covered ground, because suddenly they were standing at the bottom of the steps. Jamie had his arms around her and his face in her hair, and he lifted her off the ground. He smelled a little funky, like he'd been on the road. She told herself she should be careful, that people shouldn't just show up out of the blue, but she was used to telling herself things she didn't quite hear.

Her aunt had left her the house when she died. It was a two-story wood-frame that rattled in the wind, and Gail sometimes felt her aunt was still in it, moving around overhead. Gail's sculptures were everywhere, abstract figures on the bookshelves and the coffee table and the floor. One of her first tries at casting in bronze had become a bench stacked with newspapers. Jamie walked the living room, looking at the sculptures.

"Would you like some coffee?" she asked. "Or a beer?"

"What are these?" he asked.

Gail was explaining that she was working with lighter materials now, and that she'd found bronze kind of restricting, when she trailed off. She was thirty-eight years old. She had a career; she had commissions and galleries; she had known many men and had thought none of them could unsettle her now—so why was she finding it so difficult to speak?

"They're beautiful," Jamie said.

Embarrassed, she escaped to make coffee, and asked if Jamie's little boy wanted carrot cake. She gave him a seat at the kitchen table and a square of cake, and he promptly got cream-cheese frosting on his chin.

"I like your crown," she said.

"It's a tiara," T.J. said. "Lauren won it."

"Who's Lauren?"

The boy's white-frosted chin dropped, as if it were impossible for anyone not to know Lauren.

"Lauren is," Jamie said, "my biological father's adopted grand-daughter. Not legally adopted. They just call each other that."

"Teddy's granddaughter?"

"Freddie's granddaughter."

Gail shook her head, trying to clear it. "You'll have to start at the beginning," she said.

So Jamie stayed, with T.J., and started at the beginning.

He started at the beginning with Gail, too. It was as if by doing everything they could think of in high school, they had come to a place, twenty-one years later, where the ordinary was enough—where holding hands seemed extraordinary, and kissing Jamie's forehead in the kitchen was enough to make her dizzy with desire. In the upstairs corner room, on the bed she had been sleeping in alone, with the trees leafed out in the windows and a cross-breeze coming through, they did the simplest things, as if they were carrying a very full glass that might spill over. Often the thought that pushed her over the edge was only: This is Jamie. This is Jamie here with me, doing this with me. He's back.

She gave T.J. the bedroom down the hall: her bedroom when she had lived with her aunt at eighteen, and again in her aunt's last years. The room seemed full of her own sadness when she opened it up, so she hung strips of bright gauzy fabric from the ceiling. The strips drifted in the air from the window, and T.J. laughed and caught them in his hands, then let them go. He crossed the room with his arms out wide, to let the cloth drape over his arms, then looked back to see it fall again as he passed.

The neighbors, Bill and Bill, were charmed by Jamie and T.J. and the Airstream. They had sometimes yelled and thrown bottles at each other in their kitchen at night, then brought muffins over in the morning to apologize. Now they were on their best behavior. They baby-sat, and baked muffins for no reason, and they gave Jamie a job as soon as Gail mentioned it. The older Bill had a design business, and Jamie went to work for him, painting and laying carpet in Seattle. The women whose houses he painted recommended a preschool, and he took T.J. there on the ferry each morning, and worked on the mainland until it was time to pick him up each afternoon.

Gail started cooking again, instead of eating tuna and mayo from a can with a fork, and she bought early vegetables from the Mung farmers who set up a stand in an empty lot. Weekdays, she worked in her studio in the morning and ran errands in the afternoon before dinner. Jamie started making up songs again, but now they were real songs, made up from start to finish, with lyrics that went all the way through. He was shy about them, and played them for her in the bedroom at night.

T.J. was a quiet, watchful little boy, intense about pretty girls. At preschool he fell in love with his young teacher, Mrs. Sims. The next year he started kindergarten with the equally spellbinding Miss Leon, and Jamie didn't leave, and Gail didn't want him to. Sometimes, walking with T.J. through the grocery store, or alone on the path through the woods, she was startled by her own good fortune. She offered thanks to the world in general, to God and fate and karma and Father Jack, and then she would go home to offer thanks to Jamie, too.

34

T.J.'S GREAT-GRANDMOTHER was a Catholic. His great-grandfather was a war hero. His grandfather was a head case and a healer. His grandmother lived with a woman. His mother was dead.

He knew all these things because he asked. For a while he hadn't asked, because he didn't know that other kids knew their whole families and lived in houses instead of Airstreams. But when he started preschool, the other kids talked about how old their brothers and sisters were, and what their parents did. T.J. didn't have any brothers or sisters; he only knew that his father worked for the Bills and his mother was dead. That gave him a kind of status at school, but it made him nervous.

"I don't want you to die," he told his father as they drove home one day.

"I won't," his father said.

"Ever."

"Well," his father said, "it won't be until after you're grown up."

T.J. thought about that, all through playing baseball with his father in the backyard, and through dinner, and that night in bed as he squinted his eyes to make the line of light from the hallway go blurry like he was crying, though he wasn't. That night he had terrible dreams that the skin of the earth opened up under his feet and he had to run to keep from falling into a black hole in the ground, with a new hole opening up every step. He didn't know what was below, but he knew it was bad, and he ran.

In the morning Gail drove him to school because she had an errand. They stood on the open deck of the ferryboat, looking down at the blue water until they got dizzy, and then the boat stopped at the dock. They got back in the car and waited for the other cars to go.

"I don't want to grow up," he confided.

"I don't think you have a choice, babe," she said.

T.J. had his lunch in a paper bag that crinkled in his lap, and he touched it, to feel the food inside. If he didn't eat the food, and he didn't sleep at night, then he couldn't grow up.

He tried this theory out on Gail as they drove into the city.

"I think you'll still grow up, just tired and hungry," Gail said. "Why don't you want to?"

"I just don't," he said.

Gail didn't say anything, and they went through a green light, then a yellow one. Then she said, "Is it because of what your dad said? About how he wouldn't die until then?"

T.J. was surprised. "How do you know what he said?"

"He told me," she said.

T.J. wasn't sure how he felt about that.

"Here's how it will happen," Gail said, and T.J. waited. "First you'll grow up, and be grown up a long time. When you've been grown up for many, many years, he will be very old and then he'll die."

T.J. let the breath he was holding go, and thought about it. "Does he know that?" he asked.

"Yes," she said.

"I don't think he does."

"He knows."

"Will you tell him?"

"Yes."

"Don't forget?"

"I promise," she said.

Then they were in the drop-off lane at school, and he had to go to Mrs. Sims's class. When it was time to eat his lunch—a bologna sandwich on Roman Meal, an apple, a bag of Fritos, and a grape juice box—he was hungry and he ate it all.

In kindergarten, the kids in his class talked about where their grandparents lived and whether they were rich, so T.J. asked if his grandparents (besides Freddie) were rich. Jamie said no, they were just regular, but they didn't care about being rich. When T.J. asked why they didn't care, his father said they believed in the camel and the kingdom of heaven, and told him the story.

T.J. thought about that, too, the way he thought about every-thing. People said he was spacy sometimes, but he was just trying to think everything through. He wanted to be happy and play all the time like the kids at school, but he couldn't always stop him-self from thinking. Miss Leon said he asked so many questions, so T.J. tried not to ask everything he wanted to know. The kids at school—except Gurpreet, who was Hindu, and Leyla, whose father was Muslim, and Allen, whose mother had been a Rajneeshee in Oregon and didn't like to talk about it—said that Jesus was the son of God. They agreed that you went to heaven when you died, and that Santa was real, but the Easter Bunny and the Tooth Fairy were parents. There were a few dissenters about Santa, but they had been mostly silenced. T.J.'s father, when T.J. asked which one was right, and who was real, said that different people believed different things, and that he could choose to believe whatever he wanted. This was not a satisfying answer at all. So he tricked his father. He waited a day or two, then said, "If I asked you a question, would you promise to tell me the truth?"

His father said yes.

"If you didn't tell me the truth it would be a lie."

His father said he would tell the truth.

"Is God real?"

His father sighed. "I don't know, Teej," he said. "I don't think so." He explained about evolution, and how everything on earth was the way it was from trying to survive.

It wasn't a yes-or-no answer, so T.J. thought he deserved another question. "Do you promise to tell the truth again?" he asked.

"If I know the truth."

"What about Santa?"

"Santa is parents," his father said. "But you shouldn't tell that to kids at school."

"They might make me promise."

"Then I guess you'll have to decide," his father said.

T.J. went to school the next day nervous and excited, but the kids were talking about baseball and a new video game, and it didn't come up.

That spring, a man with a knife made a fifth-grade girl get into his truck. T.J. didn't know what it meant, exactly, but when the girl finally came back to school someone told him who it was.

He saw her on the playground sometimes; she was quiet and wore braids. He thought about that knife a lot, and what it might have looked like, and what he would do if someone with a knife told him to get in a truck. The kids at school said it would only happen to girls, but he wasn't convinced. He thought he would run away, very fast, but he couldn't be sure he would escape.

Miss Leon said all the animals and plants had a purpose in the world, and they lived in balance in nature, and that was why we had to keep the oceans clean and save paper. T.J. asked what people's purpose was, and someone said it was to dump things in the water and cut down trees, and the class laughed. T.J. said he really wanted to know. Miss Leon gave him an agonized look and went into the coatroom to have a minute for herself. It was after the girl had been taken in the truck, and Miss Leon had gone into the coatroom a lot in those days.

T.J. understood that people didn't have a purpose, but that Miss Leon was too sad to say it. At school, he kept this information to himself. But one night at a picnic in the Bills' backyard, there were yellow jackets buzzing around his dinner plate. Gail waved them away so he wouldn't get stung.

"Do yellow jackets have a purpose?" he asked. He thought maybe he had found something else that didn't.

"They must pollinate something," Gail said.

"They do," the gray-haired Bill said, scooping a burger off the grill. "They eat flower nectar. They only go after meat to take it back to the larvae."

"So they help flowers reproduce themselves," Gail said. "And maybe they help dead animals decompose. God, they love these burgers." She waved the bees away from T.J.'s plate again.

"So," T.J. said, "are people the only things that don't have a purpose?"

The brown-haired Bill laughed. "Yes!" he said.

Gail hugged T.J. sideways on the picnic bench. "Our purpose is to love each other," she said.

T.J. looked to his father, who was sitting quietly in a lawn chair, drinking a beer. "Is that it?" he asked.

"I guess so," his father said.

"Tell that to the Serbs," the gray-haired Bill said.

"Bill, please, he's six," Gail said.

"Going on sixty-three."

T.J. knew about Serbs, because there were boys at school who played it as a game. The Serbians were the bad guys, he thought, but it was just like all the other games: you had teams and you shot each other and no one was really sure who was bad. He didn't say anything about the game, because he didn't how the grown-ups would respond. They might think it was bad, or they might laugh, and he didn't want them to do either. Gail said people's purpose was to love each other. But if there were no people on earth, then they wouldn't need other people to love them. So did it count as a purpose? He couldn't be sure.

35

WITH HIS SON LIVING in a house, starting first grade, learning social skills beyond the ability to get Jamie's jokes, Jamie felt like he could tell his family where he was. He was sure that when he called his parents, Yvette would insist on coming to visit. But instead she said that she and Teddy were going to Rome. She said it was wonderful to hear from Jamie, and she would call him when they got back. They were going with a group from the church. She said, in a thrilled voice, that there were many, many requests because of the approaching millennium, but that she might have an audience with the pope.

"She'll come back with magic powers," Jamie told Gail, lying in bed in the dark. He had been waiting to talk to her since the phone call—all through dinner, and a long game of Go Fish, and T.J.'s bedtime story, which wound up being about a bear on a journey to the special cave where the lord high mucky-muck of the bears lived. "She'll get herself beatified," he said, staring at the ceiling. "She already talks to God the way I talk to you."

"Would we have to call her Blessed Yvette?"

"It's like she's never heard about science."

"Maybe science doesn't change what she believes."

"What would it take?"

"Mm," Gail said. He could tell she was smiling in the dark. "Maybe Jesus, explaining."

Jamie rolled toward her. "Yes!" he said. "He'd say that he was sorry about the misunderstanding, but he was just a man with some enthusiastic friends."

"Coming back after two thousand years would hurt his argument."

"We'll work that out," Jamie said. "He'd have to be very clear about being human, no ambiguous parables. He'd have to say, 'I'm going to take a dump, people of the world, and then I'll have to wipe my ass. Now, if I had magic powers, wouldn't I have skipped that part?'"

Gail laughed; he loved making her laugh. "That was his sacrifice, becoming flesh," she said.

"'For those of you who are unconvinced,'" he went on in his Jesus voice, "'I will next whack off. You will notice that no one does it for me. At no point is this a hands-free operation.'"

"No one would believe it was him," she said. "It's not what Jesus would do. It's what-would-Jamie-do."

"You're saying they're different?"

"Thank God."

"Blasphemer."

"*I'm* the blasphemer?" she said.

The trees outside whipped in the wind, casting shadows from the streetlights on the ceiling. It was going to rain. Gail had gone quiet, and he could tell she was thinking.

"I still feel like someone is controlling things," she said, "like someone knows what we do. It's very hard not to."

That was what Abby had said. But it was still hard to talk about Abby, even with Gail, who understood it was hard.

"Whatever gets you through the night," Jamie said.

"I'm serious."

"So am I," he said. But he felt sadness looming, so he said, "Half my genes come from a man who can walk through walls. I'm a natural believer."

"You don't believe in the walking through walls."

"It's very hard not to."

She laughed. "You're quoting me out of context."

"Me?"

"You," she said.

He kissed her. "Say that again."

"You."

"Who do you love?"

"You," she said.

"More than anyone?"

"You."

Then it was just the two of them there in the dark, with the rain coming down outside the windows, and his family wasn't there, no matter what Freud said. She made him feel, briefly, as if everything had come together and no one had ever been as loved as he.

But then she fell asleep beside him, and the world came back into the room, back into his head, and he felt bad for making jokes about God, and he lay awake in the rain wondering why, when he didn't really want his mother to visit, her not visiting made him so sad.

36

YVETTE REALIZED AFTER Jamie hung up the phone that she would have to go and see him. She had been so concentrated on the pilgrimage that it hadn't occurred to her right away. So she spoke to Father Carrington, who was in charge of the group, and told him she would miss some of the preparations if she went to see Jamie. They had been praying and studying for weeks, but there was still much more to do. But Father Carrington said it was important to see her son, and it would be part of her own personal preparation.

Teddy was still angry with Jamie for disappearing for so long, and he wouldn't go with her. When Yvette brought up the prodigal son, Teddy said, "The father didn't have to fly to Seattle to see the prodigal son."

So Yvette arrived alone, on a Saturday when Jamie was working, and Gail brought her into the kitchen where T.J. sat drawing at the table. Gail was much prettier now that she'd grown up. She pulled her hair back simply, and wore what looked like Jamie's flannel shirt with jeans, but lots of girls dressed like that now.

T.J., at six, looked a little like Abby, but Jamie might have budded like a pear tree and produced him on his own. The same dark, serious eyes, the same face. She couldn't believe there was anyone who didn't see it. She knew Gail must know, and she almost said something to her. But Yvette had already had that conversation with God. She didn't need to have it with anyone else.

"I'm your grandma Yvette," she told T.J. "You've gotten so handsome."

T.J. held his pencil in both fists on the table, and looked to Gail, unsure.

"It's okay, sweetheart," Gail said. "She's come to see you, remember?"

"Why did she come?" T.J. asked.

"Because she loves you."

T.J. studied Yvette with frank curiosity. "Does she know me?"

Gail smiled at Yvette, offering the question to her.

"I know all about you," Yvette said. "I've seen pictures since you were a baby. And I knew your mother, she was my grand-daughter." She felt a quick rush of sadness for Abby.

"She's dead," T.J. whispered.

"I know, honey," Yvette said. "But she loved you so much, and she still does. She's watching you from heaven."

Something passed over Gail's face, but Yvette couldn't tell what it was.

"That's what Brandon says, at school," T.J. said. "But we aren't sure."

"Oh, it's true," Yvette said.

Jamie came in the door then, and Yvette was unprepared for how happy she was to see him. She kissed him over and over, and held his face in her hands. "I'm so sorry Teddy didn't come," she said.

"He couldn't take the cohabitation, right?"

"Oh, Jamie," she said, though that was part of it.

"He has two months to catch up with the twentieth century before it's over."

"He believes certain things," Yvette began.

"Clarissa told me he flipped about her having a girlfriend."

"I'm so glad you've talked to Clarissa."

"You said you were off to the Vatican," he said, "so I went down the list. Now, where should we eat? I guess you don't want spaghetti."

Yvette didn't care that he teased her. He was the same boy as he'd always been, except he seemed happier now, and didn't have that dark, troubled look on his face. They went out for Mexican food, which she loved, and Jamie made her laugh so hard she cried.

At home, T.J. said it would be all right if she tucked him in, and she did, every evening that week. She taught him to say his Our Father before bed, and he learned it easily. She told him how his mother had found God because of him, which made him so special and cherished by Jesus, and she explained that God had wanted Abby very badly, to take her so young. But when they prayed together for his mother in heaven, he said, "How do we *know* she's there?"

"That's what faith is," Yvette said. "God wants us to believe even if we don't know, because we trust Him."

"Do people have a purpose?"

"Of course," she said. "Our purpose is to love Him."

"Does he love the people with knives, and the Serbians?"

"Yes," she said. "He hopes they will find Him, and be forgiven."

"What if they do something so bad he can't forgive them?"

"There's nothing that bad," Yvette said. "If they truly are sorry."

"Did you ever do anything terrible?"

"Of course," Yvette said.

"Like what?"

"I've told God all of the things," she said, "so they aren't terrible anymore."

"Will he take me to heaven because he wants me?"

"No, sweetheart," she said. "Not yet. He wants you to grow up first."

By the end of the week, she felt she had won him over, if not for God, at least for herself, and that was a step. He'd inherited Jamie's resistance, but he had the temperament for God. He was such a thoughtful, contemplative boy. He liked women too much to be a priest, but he had that kind of mind. The young teachers at his school adored him, too.

"I'm not like the other kids," he confided, when she had tucked him into bed on her last night there. "Sometimes I have to think harder."

"That's fine," she said. "It's good to think hard."

"They all have grandmothers," he said. "I've never had a grandmother before."

"But you have," she said. "And you always will."

He looked unsure. "How old are you?" he asked.

She laughed. "Seventy-six," she said. "But I feel wonderful."

"What if you die?"

"Then I'll be watching you from heaven."

His brow furrowed for a second, but he didn't ask how she knew. "Why didn't you come before?" he asked.

"I didn't know where you lived," she said. "Your father thought it was important for you two to live alone."

"Do you have to go to Rome?"

"I'll be back so soon," she said.

She told him how little Teddy Kennedy, whose brother had become the president, had gone to Rome when he was T.J.'s age, and had received his First Communion from the pope. She had read about it in the Catholic newspapers when she was still a girl in high school. T.J. wanted to know if that was the president who was killed, and she said it was. Then he wanted to know if Yvette had been pretty when she was a girl in high school, and she laughed and said she didn't know. Then finally he wanted to know about First Communion, and she told him about the Eucharist and how wonderful it was.

The next day was a Sunday, her last day with them, and Yvette asked if she could take T.J. to morning Mass. Gail told Jamie she was curious and wanted to go, and Jamie rolled his eyes but came along, too. Yvette was thrilled. She led them into the pew, putting T.J. on her right and Jamie and Gail beside him. Gail wore a beautiful green scarf. It would have been nice if she had a wedding ring, but even that Yvette didn't mind.

The priest was stout beneath his robes and ruddy-faced, with white hair and small, round glasses. "It's good to see some new faces here today," his sermon began, and Yvette was proud.

"I have been thinking about the nature of faith," he went on. "Academics like to tell us that terrible crimes have been committed in the name of the Catholic Church. They remind us of the abuses of the Crusades, of the Inquisition. It is true those were terrible times."

T.J. wriggled in his seat, and Yvette hoped he would stay still. When Abby was three, Yvette had taken her, with Clarissa and Henry, to hear Handel's *Messiah*, and Abby had thrown a fit in the church. Henry had to carry her straight down the nave, while she screamed over the music, "Daddy's hurting me!"

"But what I've been thinking," the priest went on, "as this troubled century ends, is that those people of the Inquisition had faith. Here were men and women," he said, gathering momentum, "who believed so fiercely and so strongly in the Lord that they felt other people should *die* for not believing as they did. Now, that's *faith*."

"Oh, Jesus," Jamie said under his breath.

Yvette checked her program for the priest's name—Father Stephen—and wished every priest could be like Father Carrington. She had made such progress with T.J. all week. T.J. had found the pencil for collection in the pew, and he drew a house on the collection envelope.

"Those same academics like to tell us we can't know what happened in Bethlehem two thousand years ago," the priest said. "But by that argument, they don't know either. *They* weren't there. We know because we have *God's word*. So how can they tell us we're wrong?"

"I can't believe this," Jamie said.

"Where do we find the kind of passionate faith, nowadays, that people once had?" Father Stephen demanded. "In our churches? In our parochial schools? In our hearts?" He chuckled warmly. "I'm not advocating killing anyone over the catechism," he said. "But I ask you, do *we* have that kind of unyielding faith in our hearts?"

T.J. was studying the priest now, and frowning. Then he looked back at his lap. Yvette said an Our Father in her head, to remind herself why she was there. She had just finished *now and at the hour of our death*, when T.J. stabbed Jamie through the hand with the sharp collection pencil. Jamie yelped, and the priest looked up, surprised. Yvette did, too.

"T.J., what the fuck?" Jamie said, and Yvette looked to see who had heard. A few people had turned in their seats.

"I didn't mean to," T.J. cried.

The sermon began again, the priest watching them, distracted, as he spoke. Gail took off her green scarf and wrapped it around Jamie's hand, which had a hole punched in it and was bleeding in the soft fold between the first finger and the thumb.

"It's okay, T.J.," Gail whispered. "We'll talk about this later. Yvette, would you bring him home?"

Yvette nodded, and Gail led Jamie out of the pew.

T.J. was silent, staring at the pencil in his lap. Yvette put her arm around him, though she was suddenly afraid. "Why did you do that, sweetheart?" she whispered in his ear.

T.J. just shook his head and wouldn't answer. The priest went on talking, but Yvette didn't hear what he said. After Communion, she walked T.J. back to the ferry. He responded to questions as if he were under siege: head down, he answered nothing. "Was it because Jamie doesn't believe?" she asked finally, in desperation. "Was it because of what the priest said?" T.J. still didn't answer, but he broke his step as he walked, and glanced at her before looking back at the ground.

Yvette left on the evening flight, to go with Father Carrington's group to Rome. Jamie had three stitches in his hand, and T.J. maintained his silence. When she had planned her pilgrimage, it had been only for herself, for her relationship with God, because she wanted to go. Now she had a mission, to pray for T.J. and Jamie, and not just in the general way she always prayed for her family. She would pray for them in that holy city, that they might find Him, and find their way.

37

Y VETTE SPENT THE whole transatlantic flight talking to
Father Carrington about T.J., leaving Teddy next to a widowed
lady from the church to whom he had nothing to say. He
looked out the Plexiglas window at the white clouds below. The
boy had been raised godless and motherless in a recreational
vehicle, and now in a house where two people lived in sin.
What did anyone expect?

They arrived in Rome in the morning, and Teddy wanted to
sleep, but Yvette wanted to go straight to St. Peter's. She said she
wasn't ready for the Colosseum; the deaths of all those brave
Christians would upset her too much. So they walked the streets
around the hotel until they were in the Piazza of St. Peter's, inside
the vast Colonnade, with its arms of columns reaching toward
them from the mother Church. Teddy had read about St. Peter's,
and seen pictures of the columned front and the great dome, but
that was no preparation for seeing it loom up ahead, the white

stone blazing in the sun. Inside, he was so tired he got dizzy looking at the ceilings, so they walked back to the hotel. Their room was very small, and Teddy was aware of the closeness of the walls as he fell asleep.

In Teddy's dream, T.J. was in a cage in St. Peter's. The walls inside were not their true gold and stone but dark red, and the boy shook his bars with rage. Yvette was leaning over the cage, trying to soothe him. But then Father Carrington came and took her arm, and led her gently away. They walked like lovers, pressing closer together, until Father Carrington stopped and kissed Yvette. Teddy was powerless to stop them, because they didn't know he was there. When they began to walk again, he followed, and Father Carrington led Yvette into a golden room where the pope sat waiting. She knelt at the pope's feet, and the great man took her hand and brought it to his lips. Teddy knew that the Holy Father intended to keep her for his own, and he rushed at them, but Swiss guards caught him and held him back. Yvette looked over her shoulder sadly, as if Teddy didn't understand how important this was for her. Then he was at his grandfather's funeral again, with his grandmother crying, *"Il est mort! Il est mort!"* and throwing herself into the grave. And then it was Teddy who was in the grave, clutching the smooth sides of the coffin, and dirt was being shoveled onto his back. He thought he must be dead, and he looked up to see the mourners standing over the grave, but Yvette wasn't with them, and suddenly he knew *she* was in the coffin beneath him. In his dream, he was screaming, and he woke up in a sweat.

He was in bed, in a strange, small room. He grabbed at the space beside him, expecting to find it empty, and found Yvette's bare shoulder. She made a questioning sound in her sleep. The room was the hotel, in Rome. Yvette was alive beside him. They had gone to sleep in the afternoon and now it was dark. He lay awake listening to the cars in the street until his pounding heart had slowed to normal.

That night they went to a restaurant with Father Carrington and the other people from the church. The priest was talking to a cheerful young couple whose wedding he had performed; the pilgrimage was their honeymoon, which struck Teddy as unseemly. There was also a quiet, devout man who had come without his wife, and the church choral director with her sullen teenage daughter. The girl and her mother were having some silent quarrel. Teddy took a seat next to Yvette; he was disturbed by his dream, and didn't want to let her out of his sight. Father Carrington ordered for everyone and joked with the young waiter in Italian.

Yvette was drinking red wine, and she wore polished silver earrings and a dark red blouse. Her eyes shone in the candlelight from the table, and he wished she would look only at him. She was talking to the people across the table, another couple, telling them her grandson's questions about God, and they were laughing, charmed.

"It was like a catechism," she said. "But he'd never heard a catechism before. But it was the same questions, so many questions."

She didn't tell about the pencil through the hand, of course. Teddy shifted his napkin in his lap and thought about his dream. The dream had made him distrust Father Carrington, and he tried not to. The food the priest had ordered came, and Teddy was glad for the distraction, but when he had eaten, it felt heavy in his stomach. Yvette wanted to walk after dinner, and he was glad; he wasn't used to sleeping in the afternoon. They bought gelati from the street through a shop window, in English.

"*Mille grazie,*" Yvette said, taking her cone.

The ice cream man answered in a rush of Italian, as if Yvette had proven with her two words that she spoke the language. She laughed and said her two words again, and the man laughed, too, understanding that she understood nothing, and waved good-bye.

"I love it here," Yvette said as they walked down the street. "I feel like Thérèse of Lisieux coming here, I feel fourteen years old. I'm going to sneak away from the group and kiss all the relics, and lie down in Saint Cecilia's coffin."

Teddy stopped. "That was my dream," he said.

"I was Saint Thérèse?" she asked happily.

Teddy shook his head, and started walking again. He didn't want to tell her she had been in a coffin.

"I had a dream, too," she said after a little while. "I was in an airplane, but I could see out through windows all around me. Everything was bright blue, and I was just flying. It was so beautiful."

"Did you see any submarines?" he asked.

She laughed, the laugh that charmed people at dinner, but more intimate, only for him. "No submarines," she said. "It was very safe, and no one was at war. Oh, it was beautiful, Teddy. Teddy, I love being here with you. I want to come back with our whole family."

He frowned, perplexed. "Our whole family isn't Catholic," he said. It cost him something to say it, but it was true. And how would they all travel together? They barely spoke to one another.

"Of course they are!" Yvette said. "We'll tell them about it, and they'll want to come. We won't tell them how long the flight was. But once they're here—T.J. could take his First Communion, like little Teddy Kennedy."

"The Kennedys knew the pope."

"Oh, not from the pope," she said. "But just here, in this place. Wouldn't it be wonderful?" She took his hand. They followed the street into the Colonnade, into the Piazza, and came upon St. Peter's again. With the white dome lit up in the dark it looked magical, not quite real. Yvette gasped.

"Oh," she said.

They stood in silence, looking at the church that had been in his dream, but he wasn't afraid of it now. It was a holy place, magnificent, and his dream could have no damaging effect on it, even in his mind. Finally Yvette turned to him.

"Let's go home," she said. "I mean back to the hotel."

There was sex in her hurry. In the hotel room, with the walls close around them, and Yvette in his arms, Teddy knew that it had taken him a long time to realize it, but that no man was good enough to deserve the life he had been given.

In the morning when he woke, she wasn't in the bed. He checked his watch: it was six o'clock. Father Carrington hadn't scheduled a walk to Mass until seven-thirty. Teddy got up, and showered and dressed, and went downstairs in the hotel. No one was around except the staff, although the hotel had been full of pilgrims the night before. He went out into the street, where it was light and a café was open, with a few people drinking coffee. He stood a minute, thinking.

The road went around the hotel so that either direction led to St. Peter's. Teddy had once read that for people who read from left to right, left feels like the past, and right feels like the future. Yvette would have gone right, if she had gone walking; she had never been nostalgic. He struck out to the right, to find her.

38

YVETTE ROSE BEFORE dawn, as wide-awake as she had ever been in her life. Father Carrington had warned her about jet lag, and waking at strange hours, but she was in Rome! It was morning, and she couldn't stay in bed. She dressed and slipped out of the room, to not disturb Teddy's sleep, and went out into the half-light. She would go to St. Peter's and pray for Jamie and T.J.; that was the thing she had wanted to do first, but they had both been so tired the day before. She had stood amazed in the beautiful church, and prayed only in the way she always did, thanking God for every moment.

She turned right outside the entrance of the hotel, because that was the way she had gone with Teddy. A man outside a restaurant was washing fish, letting the water run into the gutter. She smiled at him, and he smiled back, stopping his washing for a moment and straightening his back. A gelato store was opening, and she wondered who would buy ice cream first thing in the morning—but then it sounded good. Teddy had all the Italian money safe in his wallet. She thought about going back for a few hundred lire, for an espresso gelato, but she was going to pray, and kept on.

In the passage beneath the Colonnade, a man spoke to her, and she turned. Then it all happened very quickly. He was thin but strong, and he pulled her into a dark place against the stone. He reached into all her pockets, with bony hands against her stomach and thighs, and she was so shocked she could hardly breathe. He demanded something in angry Italian, and she told him she had no money, no lire, *niente*—from somewhere came the word for nothing. His eyes were dark and sad, deep in his face, and he reminded her suddenly of Jesus. All these pilgrims coming to Rome for the Second Coming, and here he was, in the urine-smelling dark beneath the Colonnade. She said in English that she would help him, that her husband had money, that she was going to pray. Then she felt a strange warmth in her throat, and she could no longer breathe, and the man's dark eyes watched her as the blackness started to close in. His eyes were shiny, as if wet. He let her fall from his arms to the stone, but there was no pain. She understood that she was going to meet her Lord, and she remembered how wonderful that moment would be.

39

HENRY GOT THE CALL in the early morning, from his former father-in-law, phoning collect from Rome. The connection was so clear they could have been in the same room. Teddy wanted to know if Henry could speak to the embassy, if he knew the ambassador, if he could talk to the ambassador about getting Yvette home.

When he finally got Teddy to slow down, Henry understood that Yvette was dead. Teddy seemed ready to join her. The police had her body and wouldn't release her because they hadn't found her killer, and everyone Teddy talked to sent him to somebody else. There was a Father Carrington who was trying to help. There was something about Rome being overrun with pilgrims, and the millennium coming, and the crime rate being up, and something about Teddy's dream.

"I think she'd gone to pray for Jamie's boy," Teddy said.

"You mean Abby's boy?"

There was a silence on the other end, and then Henry knew what he must always have half suspected. He felt a strange relief that he hadn't known it before—back when Abby's loss was like a knife in his heart every time he thought of it. He might have killed Jamie with his own hands, back then, and orphaned the child, and spent his life in prison. He told himself he would not do that now. He managed to speak.

"Does the rest of the family know?" He meant about Yvette.

When Teddy spoke, his voice was hoarse with sorrow. "I can't tell them."

"They'll want to know."

"I can't," Teddy said.

So that was how Henry found himself going to Clarissa's house—his house once, in another life, with Abby—and sitting on a blue couch he didn't recognize, with Clarissa and Véra watching him, while he told them Clarissa's mother was dead. Clarissa went ashen. He told them what he knew: that there were no witnesses, and the Italian police had no leads. No DNA samples had been saved, and even if they could find some now, and get them analyzed, and get an Italian court to accept the evidence, they had nothing to match them to. They were unlikely to find her killer. If they pushed for an immediate return of the body, as Teddy wanted, they would effectively close the case.

Still the women said nothing, so Henry went on. He said that if it was any consolation, he'd seen murder trials drag on for years, and he thought they sometimes brought more sorrow than closure. Teddy was eighty-two, and in a foreign country, with Italian bureaucracy . . .

Clarissa stood up suddenly, and went into the room that had been Abby's, and shut the door.

Henry sat a moment in embarrassed silence with Véra, then told her how sorry he was. He asked if she had phone numbers for Jamie—he felt a new pang—and Margot. The embassy thought they could get Yvette home before Christmas, so there could be a funeral. They would want to cremate her first, and he was going to ask the rest of the family if that would be all right.

They heard an anguished cry from the back room, and then Clarissa's voice. "Why didn't my father tell me himself?" she cried.

"We'll tell Jamie and Margot," Véra said.

40

T.J. SQUINTED HIS eyes at the Christmas tree in Gail's living room, to make the lights blur red and green. There were only lights on it, because the phone had rung while they were stringing it the day before, and after that everyone was too sad to hang any decorations. T.J. wasn't tall enough to reach all the branches, and the box of stars and animals and silver balls seemed off-limits now. So he crouched in front of the tree and made it go blurry.

His grandmother Yvette had said there was nothing so bad it couldn't be forgiven. The priest had said how do we know it *isn't* true, about God and Jesus, but that was the same as his own question: How do we know? He had seen his father's hand beside him on the church bench, so much bigger and stronger than his, and the priest was saying maybe people should die if they don't believe. His father didn't believe. His father said he didn't know, or else he talked about science and evolution. He didn't want his father to die for that. Yvette said we know in our hearts. She said the human body was too wonderful to have been designed by luck. And the pencil was so sharp, and his father's hand was there, designed by something, and the priest was talking, and then he did that thing he couldn't think about now; it hurt to think about.

He blinked, and made the tree go dark and then come back bright red and green again. What he had done felt too bad to be forgiven, no matter what Yvette said. And now Yvette was dead. They didn't want him to know there was a knife, but he had heard them talking in the kitchen. He thought about the girl at school, who'd been taken with the knife, but then came back. Yvette had said his mother was watching him in heaven. And maybe Yvette was there now. And God would take him, too, someday. But he didn't want God to take him. And maybe his father was right and we turn into compost, and help the yellow jackets make the flowers grow, and that is our purpose. Maybe no one is watching. And if they're not watching, then no one is forgiven because no one is there to forgive. The last thing he remembered Yvette saying was "Why did you do that, sweetheart?"

He told God that if God was real, and could do anything, he should send Yvette back, to prove it. But nothing happened. He waited a little longer, watching the lights on the tree, and thought maybe it wasn't a time when God was listening to people in Puget Sound. He couldn't listen to everyone at once. T.J.'s father came from the kitchen then, and stood watching him. He knew it was his father, because he knew his father's sound when he walked. If he looked up, he would see that his father's hand still had stitches, and that his face was sad. He was embarrassed about asking God to send Yvette back, but he whispered, "Is she watching?" because he had to know.

His father came and scooped him up under the knees, and sat on the couch they had moved for the tree, and held him tight. "Does it feel like she is?" he asked.

"I don't know."

"Is she in your head? Do you hear her voice?"

"Yes," T.J. said.

"Then she's watching," his father said. "What does she say?"

He couldn't tell him she said *Why did you do that, sweetheart?* "I don't know," he said.

"She's in my head, too," his father said after a minute. "She asks me if the things I do are right, if I know it in my soul."

T.J. was startled. "Really?"

"All the time," his father said.

"Are the things right?"

"Not usually."

T.J. thought about that. "I'm sorry for what I did," he said.

"I know," his father said, and he squeezed him a little. But being forgiven by his father was not like being really forgiven. They were in it together too much. T.J. squinted his eyes at the tree again, and watched the lights swim.

"Do you pray for her?" he asked.

"I think about her," his father said.

"Did the man have a knife?"

His father didn't say anything right away. Then he said, "Yes."

"Did you pray for him?"

"No," his father said, thick-voiced. "But she would have."

With his father's arms still around him, T.J. closed his eyes and tried to pray. He tried to ask that the man with the knife would find God and be forgiven. But it didn't work. He didn't believe it would happen. So he tried to pray for Yvette, that she was happy in heaven and would forgive everyone. But that didn't work either. She was dead, like his mother, and he was shaking in his father's arms, and his face was wet, and the tree blurred without his trying, because he would never see her again, not even in heaven, because none of it was true.

41

CLARISSA HAD KNOWN before her parents left for Rome that she would be invited for Christmas. This was the year for rounding up the prodigals: Margot, whose secret was out; Clarissa, who'd betrayed her father by loving Véra; Jamie the vanishing act and Abby's out-of-wedlock boy. They would all be elaborately forgiven, and bathed in love, by an Yvette newly blessed by the man who told his millions of followers that pre-marital sex was a sin, and homosexuality an affront to God. There would be a kindly priest at Christmas breakfast, brought in to win them all over.

Clarissa had been ready to resist. She had been ready to say she wouldn't go. She would tell them she objected to the mythologizing of the Family, a family that had never been all that nurturing to her. Just because she had been born among them didn't mean they could determine her actions for the rest of her life. (Véra had raised her eyebrows. "They're doing it now," she said.) Clarissa had prepared a kind of speech. A line from a book had stuck in her head: *And Nature would not in her perplexingest mood have cast me as a family daughter.*

But with her mother murdered, all her principles dissolved. She wanted her mother back. She wanted to live again in her mother's house. She wanted Yvette to be in heaven with Jesus. Failing all that, she wanted to curl up in her father's lap and stay there for the rest of her life. When Véra suggested driving down for the funeral, just for the day, Clarissa said they should stay for Christmas.

"In your father's house?" Véra asked.

"We're invited."

"Are you sure he can take it?" Véra asked.

The wave of guilt broke over Clarissa again. "You're right," she said. "Let's not go at all."

"You have to go to the funeral."

"I can't go just for the day."

"So let's go have a family Christmas."

"*You're* my family," Clarissa said. "Oh, God, my mother is gone. My daughter is dead and my mother is gone." She went to bed and curled in a ball around the pain in her stomach.

Three days went by like that, and in the end neither of them knew which side she was arguing, so they agreed to decide when they got there.

They were the first to arrive, and Teddy opened the door. He looked older. For the first time in her life, he looked to Clarissa like an old man. He kissed her carefully and shook Véra's hand without meeting her eye. His eyes were watery, and he led them to the room that had been Clarissa's. It was a guest room now, with botanical prints on the walls. There were still the old twin beds, with green bedspreads, and towels and washcloths stacked on each.

"I think that's what your mother used to do, honey," he said. "I don't know how to do any of these things."

"That's perfect, Dad," Clarissa said. Margot and Owen would have a queen-sized bed to sleep in, but that was Margot's room. Clarissa had thought to push the twin beds together, but she decided suddenly to leave them apart. She put her arms around her father, and Véra looked out the bedroom window.

"This is very hard for me," her father said, holding her, and it felt as much like an acceptance as she was going to get. Then he went back to his room until Margot and Owen showed up in a rental car from the airport.

Margot seemed as calm and elegant as ever, a woman with a beautiful life, untroubled by children. Clarissa had a hard time remembering that it wasn't true, that there had been lust and deceit and longing. She felt like she was in a sad, stately movie with her sister. All she wanted was to blubber and cry, but you couldn't do that with Margot. She was relieved when Jamie's Airstream pulled up, and they all went outside again.

Jamie got out of the RV with Gail, and Clarissa thought her mother must have liked Gail; she was pretty in the way Yvette liked. Then T.J. climbed out of the Airstream and took Clarissa's breath away, he looked so much like Abby.

"This is Gail and T.J.," Jamie said to everyone standing on the lawn. "I guess you know that. Teej, this is my dad and Owen and my sisters . . ." But he couldn't finish, because his face was screwed up with pain. He went to their father first, and Teddy held his arms out awkwardly. Clarissa was suddenly afraid that she couldn't take three days of this without her heart breaking in two.

While everyone unloaded bags, Clarissa took Véra to meet Jamie, her darling, her brother, and then held him as tightly as she could.

*

At the crowded Midnight Mass on Christmas Eve in her child-hood church, Clarissa sat with Véra at the end of the pew. They had sat in the same pew the day before, for the Requiem Mass, with her mother's ashes in a small polished box on the altar, beneath a sheaf of white lilies. Clarissa had seen nothing but the box and the flowers and the faces of her family then, she had felt so desolate, but tonight she was able to look around. The church building and the altar, huge when she was small, had shrunk in the way schools do. The only thing bigger were the jacarandas outside on the lawn, where she had once kissed Henry and thought he was all she could ever want.

Next to Clarissa was Jamie, whose hand she held tight, as if he might disappear again, and T.J. and Gail. Next to Gail was Mr. Tucker, who had arrived that afternoon with a white ponytail and missing teeth, with his adopted granddaughter Lauren. Jamie had asked if he could invite Mr. Tucker for Christmas Eve, and Teddy had been too dazed by grief to object, and Margot had been too polite. Jamie said he wanted to have his whole family together, no secrets, no lies. He said it was tough on Margot but she would be all right. Margot, sitting on the back deck in sunglasses, had lost all color in her face and lips when Mr. Tucker arrived, but she had shaken his hand, surrounded by Yvette's flowers.

"I'm sorry about your mother," Mr. Tucker had said.

Margot had nodded her thanks.

"I guess you wish you hadn't known me," he said. "But Jamie's a fine boy."

Margot had nodded again and looked desperately uncom-fortable.

"I wish I could remember," Mr. Tucker said. "I hope Jamie's told you that my memory's like an old Swiss cheese."

Finally Jamie had taken the man inside the house, and let Margot be. Clarissa had been secretly grateful to Jamie, that he could be counted on to do absolutely the wrong thing, too.

Next to Mr. Tucker at Midnight Mass sat Lauren, wearing a red skirt and a tight green sweater, like *Playboy*'s idea of an elf. She had stayed in the background of Margot's meeting with Mr. Tucker, looking worried for everyone. She was in her last year of college, and she seemed so young. Clarissa couldn't look at her without thinking that Abby hadn't even made it that old. Beside Lauren sat Yvette's cousin Planchet, who had flown in for the funeral, then Margot and Owen, and finally Teddy.

Teddy was like a ghost without Yvette. He wasn't up to having the family back all at once. It wasn't that he refused to kill the fatted calf, but that there didn't seem to be one anymore. He had so little left of himself; it had all been wrapped up in Yvette. Clarissa could see his hands in his lap, if she leaned forward, and she guessed he was praying. Yvette had been scheduled to read Isaiah as a lector, and they had read it at the house before Mass:

> *For a child has been born to us, a son given to us;*
> *Authority rests upon his shoulders; and he is named*
> *Wonderful Counselor, Mighty God,*
> *Everlasting Father, Prince of Peace.*

Isaiah was Yvette's favorite. Teddy, reading, had broken down in tears.

Clarissa sat back among the warm bodies in new Christmas sweaters and the tired children, up hours past their bedtimes. She thought about the dark streets outside, and all the Protestants safely in their beds. The Methodist parents had stuffed all the stockings, and eaten the cookies the children left out for Santa, and poured out the milk in the sink. The Chinese families, Baptists and Buddhists, had kissed the children they loved without complications and fallen into dreams. The Unitarians did not upset their fathers with their choice of lovers, and their mothers were not mugged and killed trying to visit the pope. The Hungarian refugees, if they were like Véra, did not spend hours in therapy crying. The Jewish children must be happy, too, sated with days of presents and warmth and love.

Then Clarissa thought of what Véra would say—as she ran things past Véra in her mind all the time now—to her litany of happy families. Véra would laugh her brilliant laugh and shake her head and say, "Oh, man, you are joking." Véra had picked up "man" somewhere, to replace something in Hungarian, to intensify what she had to say.

Clarissa took Véra's hand, having let go of Jamie's, and laced her fingers with Véra's. Véra turned from watching the priest and smiled her slow-starting smile that lit up her whole face when it got to her eyes. Clarissa felt Véra's warm skin against her palm and the smooth wood of the old pews of her childhood against her knuckles. The priest kept up the Mass, swinging the incense, and Clarissa found herself wishing, suddenly, that it were all still in beautiful, half-conscious Latin—*Asperges me, Domine, hyssopo, et mundabor.* She thought she might even believe it then. Thou shalt sprinkle me, Lord, with hyssop, and I shall be cleansed.

42

TEDDY WOKE IN HIS own bed and surveyed the room to see where he was. He was not in Rome. The walls were covered with pictures of the three children growing up and getting older, and of Abby, who would always be twenty, and with snapshots of T.J. that Jamie had sent from different states, without a return address. The picture of Yvette and the children, taken in the house while Teddy was in Korea, hung there, too. For so many years he had hidden it away, pulling it from its envelope in secret, to acute pleasure and pain. It had lost some of its power over him, hanging on the wall, but this morning it gave him anguish again. The realization that she was gone came back as it did each morning, and he was sorry to be awake. She had been in a box on the altar. But she was in heaven with God. The pope had put his ringed hand on Teddy's head in sorrow and sympathy, and told him that this was so, that her soul had sped to the Lord.

Teddy showered and dressed, remembering the cool weight of the pope's hand on his head, and told himself he should be happy to have a house full of people, whatever people they were. There had been a family meeting to decide whether to have a normal Christmas so soon after the funeral. They had all looked to Teddy, the way they used to look to Yvette. Teddy didn't want Christmas; he wanted to lock himself in his room and not come out. But Yvette would want him to go on, and celebrate light in the face of darkness. She would want him to forgive her vanished killer, who had delivered her to God, and Teddy had struggled to do that. If he could forgive that man, he could welcome anyone.

So he left the bedroom, reluctantly, and placed himself in an armchair near the open kitchen. He was determined to love the crowd moving back and forth through his house, and he surveyed them in preparation.

The girls were making breakfast, and the house smelled like coffee. Margot separated strips of raw bacon, and Clarissa slid a casserole dish into the oven. The girl Lauren was in the kitchen, too, in what they used to call Capri pants, but she seemed to have no task beyond getting in the way. Margot ignored her, and Teddy knew it must be difficult for Margot to have the girl here with the dance teacher. He could have protected her from it, but he hadn't, he'd let Jamie have his way. The boy T.J., swooping through the house with a model fighter plane, stopped to hug the girl's lovely legs, then resumed his Corsair's flight. Jamie played Christmas carols on his guitar, quietly, as if to himself, but the sound was strange with Yvette gone.

T.J. flew his plane past the kitchen again and stopped at Teddy's chair. He grew solemn.

"Was this your plane?" he asked.

"A long time ago," Teddy said.

"Did you get shot at, flying?"

"Sure," Teddy said, and he thought of Korea, of fire from the dark hillside, and troops below.

"Did you shoot people?"

"We were aiming for buildings, usually, with bombs," he said. "Targets." It was not a conversation he liked to have. He kept in mind the brave and wounded men he had been working to save. "Sometimes it was hard to tell," he said.

"Did they die?"

"I suppose so, T.J. Some of them did."

T.J. stood there, resting the Corsair lightly on Teddy's knees. He had his unfathomable look on his face; he seemed to be thinking. Jamie picked out "Joy to the World" on the guitar.

"If they didn't die," T.J. said to Teddy's knees, "they would kill more people?"

"Probably," Teddy said.

"Did they go to heaven?"

"I don't know," Teddy said. "I don't think they believed in heaven, not our kind."

T.J. looked up at him sharply. "Do you have to believe in it to go?" he asked.

Teddy wished Yvette were there to field these questions. "I think it helps," he said finally.

He and the boy stared at each other, and he thought the sadness and perplexity on the boy's face must match his own. Then T.J. took the plane off his lap and flew it slowly away at elbow level, not bombing the living room carpet but patrolling, maybe: surveying the scene. Yvette's French cousin, Planchet, eyed the boy warily over the top of a newspaper. He must know about the pencil, Teddy thought.

Gail had gone jogging with Owen, and came from the shower with her wet hair tied up in a knot. She sat beside Teddy's armchair, smelling of shampoo, and put her hand on his. He remembered how she used to make him stammer. He took her hand and felt he was accomplishing, with Gail, his goal of accepting the crowd before him.

But then there was Clarissa's Véra on the living room couch, listening to the dance teacher beside her, and Teddy was not up to loving Mr. Tucker or Véra, not when sorrow had left him so exhausted. The thought was unchristian and made him sad, but he knew it was true. Tucker had robbed Margot of the life and the children she deserved; Véra was proof that Clarissa had lost her way.

Teddy would trade everyone in the house, he suddenly thought, for another day with Yvette—just like he would kill the man who had killed her, given half a chance.

43

WHILE THE JOHN WAYNE eggs were baking, Clarissa mixed tomato juice and Tabasco and Worcestershire, because her mother had written in her recipe book that gin Bloody Marys went with the eggs. There were notes on other pages, about which recipes came from Yvette's mother, and which came from Teddy's mother, but Yvette must have found John Wayne eggs on her own. Her mother's scrawled handwriting made Clarissa ache, but she was glad to have something to do with her hands.

She carried two full glasses to the living room couch just as Mr. Tucker was telling Véra, "I was adopted, too. Just like Jamie."

"Really," Véra said, taking one of the blood-red drinks. Mr. Tucker wouldn't take one.

"My biological father's family were Swiss Huguenots," he said. "They settled first in Savannah, Georgia. I've done a bit of research on it."

"You found your father?" Véra asked.

"I know who he is," he said. "It's kind of a secret. But I guess you should know, since Jamie and T.J. are descendants, too."

Clarissa waited, thinking that T.J. was not actually Mr. Tucker's descendant, because he wasn't Jamie's.

"It's Howard Hughes," he said with a shy smile. "My mother was Katharine Hepburn."

There was a pause. The drink was sweating in Clarissa's hand.

"You know this?" Véra asked, and Clarissa loved the way she sounded—wise and wary of untruth.

"I'm ninety-nine-point-nine-nine-nine-nine-nine-percent sure," Mr. Tucker said. "I look just like him. I'm an inventor just like him. A friend of mine was his limo driver, and he assures me that there was, you know, contact." He looked at them both to see if they understood, and Véra nodded, so he went on. "I went to see Katharine Hepburn once, for confirmation," he said. "We couldn't speak outright because her nurse was in the room, but she made it very clear to me that it was true."

Clarissa began to wonder if it *was* true, though she knew Véra would assure her later, in the twin beds, that it wasn't. So she accepted Véra's assurances in advance, and moved on. Véra could have the conversation and not believe it better than she could.

Jamie was still playing carols on the guitar—*O tidings of comfort and joy*—and Clarissa took him Mr. Tucker's drink. Jamie's hand had almost healed from where the pencil had gone through it. He had a pinkish scar.

"Mr. Tucker is telling Véra that your grandparents are Howard Hughes and Katharine Hepburn," she said.

"Has he gotten to the part about how T.J. looks like Hughes?" Jamie asked.

"T.J. looks like Abby," Clarissa said.

"And a little like me."

Clarissa frowned as T.J. ran past with his airplane. T.J. looked like Abby.

"It's a good story," Jamie said. "I want to keep it going. Take T.J. to see the Spruce Goose, say it should have been his birthright."

"But he's not really your son."

Jamie looked at her. "Clar," he began.

"He's Abby's son."

"And mine."

"Not really," she said. "The father was a one-night stand."

He didn't say anything for a second. "That was me," he said. "I'm sorry, Clar."

Margot touched Clarissa's shoulder from behind. "Breakfast," she said. She moved on, rounding everyone up.

The pit of Clarissa's stomach felt suddenly cold, and she found it hard to speak.

"Why did I never know this?" she said. "Why do I never know anything?"

Jamie set his guitar aside. "Because you believe what everyone tells you," he said. "Nothing wrong with that. It's what they want." He wrapped his arms around her, and they walked into the dining room like a two-headed beast.

44

AT THE TABLE, Jamie took the seat next to Margot so she wouldn't have to sit by Mr. Tucker, and she was grateful at least for that. M. Planchet moved in to flank her on the left. Mr. Tucker went to the other side of the table. Margot felt a little faint. When he had arrived at the house, Margot had not wanted him to shake her hand or come near her. She had held her breath while he did, then kept perfectly still on the back deck until he and Jamie and Clarissa and Lauren had all gone inside. Then she got up to weed her mother's untended garden. She was there on her knees, furiously pulling weeds, when her husband found her. Owen had been through it all, and knew without her saying a word. He knelt on the grass beside her and she curled into his chest, held tight.

Afterward, she slipped inside to wash her hands and press a cold cloth to her eyes. Old M. Planchet, when he arrived from the airport, had eyed her carefully and said, without any French bluster, "Oh, *ma petite.*"

The old Frenchman took her hand now, and squeezed it once, and she felt stronger. Mr. Tucker, when she was able to look at him across the table, seemed frail and small, with his missing teeth, and she found with surprise that she felt sorry for him. Owen sat at the far end between Clarissa, who was frowning again, and Gail. Next to Gail was Father Carrington, her mother's favorite priest, who had been such a help to her father in Rome. The priest began the grace.

"Dear Lord, bless this food You have given us," he said. "We all wish Yvette were here to share it, but we know she is with You, whom she loved so much. We are grateful to have her family here to remember her. Everyone at this table was truly included in her love."

Margot reflected that her mother had never met Mr. Tucker, or Lauren, and she glanced at her father. He seemed to be holding up.

"We also remember Abby," the priest went on, "who went to You so young. We are grateful for the presence of her irrepressible son."

"Is that me?" T.J. whispered to Jamie.

There was a ripple of subdued laughter down the table. When the priest prayed for peace and said "Amen," there was a chorus in reply and a clinking of silverware. They were going on, as they had agreed to, as her mother would have wanted. Having children and priests and strangers there made it possible. Margot had considered T.J. carefully, since the pencil incident. She was not a good judge of children, but she thought he might be on the pensive side of normal.

With a spatula she had given her mother, she served M. Planchet a square of steaming cheddar and tomato and green chili and egg. He looked at it, suspicious.

"Try it," Margot said. "You used to feed me offal and brains."

"That was good for you."

"I was pregnant," she said. Having said it, she felt a strange relief, though it ached, too: she had been pregnant, and she had had a child. She scooped a square of egg onto Jamie's plate.

"Thanks, Margot," he said.

"And what a fine boy you had, this boy!" M. Planchet said. "If you had stayed in America, to eat cornflakes and candy, he would not be so fine."

"Kids do all right on a vegetarian diet," Mr. Tucker said.

"I have seen these children," M. Planchet said. "They have the gray skin, and the skinny arms, and the bad teeth. Children need meat."

"Lauren is a vegetarian," Mr. Tucker said, and they all looked over to see Lauren bite a strip of bacon.

Lauren shrugged. "It's really good," she said.

"You see?" said M. Planchet.

Clarissa frowned absently and poked at her eggs. "I put in too much cheese," she said.

"No such thing," Jamie said. "It's just like Mom's."

Margot looked to her father, who was quiet, staring at his plate. He must be thinking that Yvette would never cook anything for them again.

"Is there more of this thing?" M. Planchet asked, raising his drained Bloody Mary glass.

"Oh, there's champagne!" Clarissa said, jumping up from the table.

Margot watched her sister go, then pushed her chair back and followed. "The champagne glasses," she said to excuse herself, but no one noticed.

In the kitchen, Clarissa stood by the sink with her head bowed, one hand on the wire cage of a champagne cork, the other hand over her eyes. Margot stood next to her sister. She didn't touch her, and she didn't know what to say. Finally Clarissa looked up, red-eyed.

"Does it hurt, sometimes, to be here?" Clarissa whispered. "Does it hurt? Not just from missing her?"

Margot held out for a moment, then nodded.

"But it would hurt to be anywhere else," Clarissa said.

Margot nodded again.

"Oh," Clarissa breathed, as if she were in pain. "Did you know about T.J.?" she asked suddenly. "About Jamie?"

Margot was going to hedge, and pretend the question was about the pencil through the hand, but then she heard herself say, "I know."

Their father came into the kitchen and stood watching them.

"Hi, Dad," Clarissa said in a cracked voice with a sheepish smile. "I'm coming back."

Then T.J. came around the corner, and peered at them from behind Teddy. Margot thought how much he looked like them all. Her father's namesake, Abby's baby, Jamie's son: people wanted their families to be carried on, but Margot wasn't sure they should be quite so distilled, in one child.

In the other room, Jamie proposed a toast, but the words were muffled.

"Wait for the champagne," Clarissa called to him.

"Where is it?" Jamie called back, and then he came into the kitchen, too. He stopped when he saw the rest of them standing there, his sisters and his father and his son.

In the dining room, they didn't wait. There were clinks and warm voices as the rest of them lifted their coffee cups and toasted—what had Jamie meant to toast? Yvette, or the family, or the century about to begin. Or the cooks, or the patriarch, or the boy scion who would carry the family on—who were all standing in the kitchen in silence, almost ready to go back in.

I am deeply grateful to Nick Halpern, to Michelle Latiolais, and to Geoffrey Wolff.